Published by **Black Lion Media**.

WITHOUT MEASURE

A JACK WIDOW THRILLER

SCOTT BLADE

Black Lion Media

CHAPTER 1

His nametape read: "Turik."

He looked like a lone gunman. The kind who walks into a school or airport or, in this case, a military base, shoots five people, turns the gun on himself, and pulls the trigger.

Lone gunmen stick out like sore thumbs. The very definition of a lone gunman is a lone man with a gun. Easy enough to spot.

Turik looked as much like one as any other lone gunman that I had seen before. And I had seen them before. Plenty. These guys have two dead giveaways. They're alone—thus, the lone part. And they've got guns.

I was staring at a guy who fit the bill, but there was also another element to consider—targets. What were the intended tactical targets for a lone gunman? I was near one of the traditional targets for a lone gunman. I was near a military base, not a stone's throw away, but close. Arrow's Peak Marine Base was only ten miles away, by my guess, in a north and uphill direction. I had never seen it before, but I knew it was an old Marine installation, concealed behind thick, snowy woodland areas and built in the valley of long, rolling hills—white in the winter and green in the summer.

Arrow's Peak took its name from one of the region's most notable natural sculptures. The tallest mountain in the county had a crude, rugged arrowhead-shaped peak. It was especially easy to spot in the cold of winter when the peak was painted white with snow. I'd seen it when walking in above the tree lines.

The mountain didn't stand alone, but it stood out. It didn't appear to be reachable by road. The terrain surrounding it comprised thick, high trees, also heavily sprinkled in snow.

The Marine base wasn't in the mountains, but north of town.

I had seen many road signs for it on my way along the highway.

The guy I was staring at had a gun strapped to his side. It was a military-issued M45 MEU (SOC), originally based on the M1911 handgun designed by the famous gunmaker Browning, from way back in the day in Utah. The MEU (SOC) was a heavily modified version of that firearm.

His was well cared for. It looked well-worn too, like a firearm that had been fired many times in its career. This wasn't a feature that most men noticed, but I did. I had been trained to notice things like that until it became second nature. The M45 is a tactical gun issued to Marine Special Forces. This gun is used by MARSOC, which stands for Marine Forces Special Operations Command. The Corps loved long titles that made for bad acronyms. Unlike the Navy, which was better at it. Like SEAL, which means Sea, Air, and Land teams and is a much better acronym.

The Critical Skills Operators are also called Marine Raiders. The Raiders have gained credibility in the last several years. In many circles, they are considered as deadly as the SEALs, not a claim that I agreed with. Then again, I was a little biased because I'd spent most of my career with the SEALs.

I sat in a worn vinyl booth next to the window at a dive called the Wagon Hash Diner, an old but well-kept diner built on a wagon trail off a small two-lane highway, the 96. Green, lush landscape towered around it; only I couldn't see much of it because it was half-covered in snow. I was in a small mountain town called Hamber, which the locals believed to be the first gold rush settlement in the forty-niners' era. The locals believed this, but no one else did. At least, I had never heard of it, but then again, my history recall on California gold mining wasn't just dusty; it was practically nonexistent. The only thing that I could recall about the forty-niners was that I lost a hundred bucks on the football team's game about twelve years ago to an old CO, when we were at sea for six weeks.

I never cared for them again.

All the historical information that I knew about Hamber was what I had read on the back of the Wagon Hash menu.

When I was done reading the menu, I leaned across the booth and picked up a newspaper left behind by another patron. I liked newspapers, liked to hold a physical copy of something that, long ago, was the coveted way to get the news. Once upon a time, the newspaper was the only form of media besides word of mouth.

The newspaper used to be the first and last line of defense. But one day, capitalism came along and did what capitalism always does. It squeezed the life out of newspapers and smothered the pages with ad revenue, exploiting newspapers until they were bled dry. Then capitalism moved on to the internet, which is where most people get their news these days. Smartphones have allowed instant news coverage and unlimited ad buy revenue.

The *New York Times* is still considered today's paper of record, but most of their income comes from online ads. Ironic, I guess.

I didn't have a smartphone or a tablet or a PC. I owned little of anything. All my possessions were provisional. I was a minimalist in the truest sense. For me to keep up with current events, I had to read newspapers.

I opened the paper. It was a day-old copy of the *LA Times*, far from home, but the pride of the entire state. Therefore, it was read here.

There was a lot going on in the news today. A new president had come into office. A new Congress was holding cabinet confirmations, and the DOD was upsetting people because they had blown their budget last year and were up for a hearing on a bigger one. Washington business as usual.

I didn't vote for this president, and I didn't vote for the other guy either. The Washington shuffle bore little weight on my life. I didn't care either way. One political party argued this, and the other argued that. One party won and one didn't. Life went on.

In my mind, it was a bad choice versus a bad choice, like choosing between getting shot in the head by a total stranger or being shot in the head by a loved one. In the end, what difference does it make?

I flipped to the sports page, checked the games, checked the scores. Nothing of interest except a university basketball game. It was the LSU Tigers, which wasn't particularly interesting to anyone else, but I was born in Mississippi. It raised my eyebrow; that was all. They had lost.

I flipped back to the front page, ignoring the local politics until I found a story of interest. Another terrorist attack in Berlin. It was a story about a hijacked truck that rammed through a busy square and killed dozens of people. Witnesses said that the driver drove the truck in an erratic and dangerous way. The cops were still searching for the driver. He'd escaped. A massive manhunt was underway. The Germans had good cops. I'd been stationed there more times than I could remember. The German police back then didn't mess around. I had faith that they'd catch the guy.

ISIS claimed the attack.

I presumed Interpol would find a dead body if they hadn't already. The body would belong to the truck's owner, not the hijacker. The hijacker drove erratically because he probably didn't know how to drive the complicated sticks and gears of a commercial truck.

Lately, ISIS terrorists have used trucks in Europe to kill innocent civilians. In America and Turkey, they have used gunmen to shoot up public places, which was part of the reason I was more than concerned about Turik.

A waitress came over and ignored the lone gunman, who was seated two booths in front of me.

He stared straight on, not looking at me, not making eye contact. The waitress hadn't noticed his gun. I figured because she had her back turned to the door when he walked in and sat down. The M45, holstered at his right side, was now out of sight under the tabletop.

No one else seemed to have noticed it either.

The waitress asked, "Sir, would you like a refill of coffee?"

I looked at her name tag. A quick glance. Her name was Karen.

I didn't want to cause alarm, so I said nothing about the lone gunman. I answered, "Yeah. And let me get a fresh mug as well."

The one I was drinking out of just didn't quite look so clean once I had drained it to the bottom.

She paused and stared at me. She stared at my lower sleeve tattoos, two American flag gauntlets, one covering each forearm, masked with multiple other designs that meant nothing to anyone but people in my line of work, and me. Tattoos are usually either an occupational hazard or a spiritual totem—or both—depends on who is making the assessment.

Because I had been an undercover cop of sorts, to me, they were both. I had once been an NCIS agent—a Navy cop—assigned to Unit Ten, which was a highly secret black ops unit. We investigated the things that no one else would investigate, or even knew or cared about. Often, we were used as a surgical instrument for the military to uncover things that no one wanted uncovered. We investigated crimes involving the SEALs and Black Ops teams within the Navy and Marine Corps.

As far as I knew, there were only a handful of us. I'd only known a few agents from Unit Ten, which I had minimal contact with.

Because most NCIS people were civilians, they needed military agents who could penetrate military units undercover and hold credibility all at the same time with the unit personnel. I was the only agent ever to penetrate the SEALs. Which meant that I had to live, eat, and breathe like a SEAL. There was no margin for error. For years, I lived a double life, sixteen years. But a double life was never the right description of who I had been, because a double life implied that I had two lives.

In fact, I had no life. I had only double identities, one real and one fabricated. I didn't have a real life, not until I stopped living how they told me to live, how I had been expected to live. Now, I lived nowhere, a man without a home. I was a drifter—homeless but not in poverty, although I looked it from time to time.

I considered myself to be wealthy enough. I always had food, clothes, shelter, and had enough money to get by, continuing my chosen lifestyle. If I ever was hard-pressed for money, there were ways of making it. I had a passport. I could get transient work if I had to. Pay-by-cash work was always available.

Karen was still inspecting the coffee mug like I had said that there was something wrong with it. I saw her expression as she searched for a defect on it.

I coughed involuntarily, a kind of under-my-breath cough because I had caught it right at the beginning, and I attempted to stanch it out right before the end, like catching yourself saying something inappropriate halfway through the words. I failed.

The cough that would've counted for nothing suddenly turned into a big deal. Everyone in the diner looked my way, like I was choking. But then, after a long few seconds, the cough subsided.

Karen stopped looking over the coffee mug and asked, "You okay, sir?"

"Ye-Yeah," I said, covering my mouth. I got too caught up in the cough just to flat-out answer her straight.

She stayed quiet and stayed where she was, like she'd been at attention in front of a commanding officer. She had good posture.

"I got a little cold," I said. And I wasn't lying. I was fighting a cold, nothing bad, not yet. It was still the beginning stages. I felt a soft, irritating tickle in the back of my throat and a headache that felt three days old, but I knew it would only get worse and last at least three more days.

"Okay. I'll get you a new mug. Do you want some soup? Today, we got chicken noodle."

I shook my head. I hadn't eaten since the day before. Not much appetite. It wasn't like I was sad or depressed or something; I just had no desire to eat, maybe because I wanted to sleep more.

I had been up most of the night before.

Even though I had come in here originally intending to order breakfast, I changed my mind as soon as I sat down. I just wasn't hungry.

I watched Karen walk across the square tile floor and over a long, black rug, back behind a long countertop with one of those old-fashioned cash registers perched on it. They had no computer system in sight. All business was done with hand-writing and paper.

Over the food window, between the kitchen and the front of the house, I saw one of those old tin spinning wheels, where the wait staff stuck in a paper order, called out that they had a new order, and then spun the contraption toward the kitchen. Once the meal was completed, the ticket spinner was spun to the front again. No tickets were on it. I doubted that they even used it. They probably bought it at a flea market.

I turned and looked again at the guy who fit the gunman profile, trying not to stare. I pretended to look over every-thing in the diner casually.

The rest of the diner was relatively empty. Two other tables had patrons. One was a pair of truckers who were here when I walked in the door. They sat far off, near a unisex bathroom entrance. They laughed and kidded each other in hearty tones, like they were old friends who stopped on this route every six months and reunited in the Wagon Hash diner.

The other table was a young married couple; the wife was somewhere between seven months pregnant and on the brink of delivering a child. I wasn't sure. I wasn't an expert on the subject. Never had I ever been a parent, or had a wife or girl-friend—hard in my line of work—or even known a woman who was pregnant.

I looked back at the guy who fit the lone gunman profile. Two other things jumped out at me about him. First, he looked

Arabic, which meant nothing, not necessarily. But being that this wasn't the Middle East or even near a major city, and this was basically the backwoods mountains of California, it was safe to assume that the overwhelming majority of townspeople were white, mid- to lower-class Americans. Not that they weren't welcoming of strangers, just that it was unusual for a Muslim to stop for gas here, much less live here. I'd spent a lot of time overseas, and some of that was on tours in Iraq, Afghanistan, Qatar, and even a couple of unrecorded missions in Iran. Over there, I was the one who stuck out.

I'd seen so many Middle Easterners that I was good at spotting their localizations. This guy, minus a beard and Islamic attire, looked like he had gotten straight off a plane from Tehran, or possibly Istanbul. He was clean-shaven and somewhere in the neighborhood of his late thirties, not much older than me, if I had to guess. He had thick, dark hair in a jarhead cut.

On the table in front of him was a bunched-up Marine cap with woodland camo patterns. It looked like it had been folded and pinched and thrown around for years. It was a part of the second thing about him, the most obvious thing.

This guy was in the United States Marine Corps. No doubt about it. He wore a woodland-pattern combat uniform.

CHAPTER 2

The second hand on the wall clock, which was exactly forty-five degrees to my right and above the countertop, showed the time as being 6:45 a.m. The dayshift at Arrow's Peak Marine Base would be starting soon, and this Marine was still seated in front of me. He stared blankly at the empty wall behind me—nothing there to look at but wallpaper.

He had the somber expression of a man waiting on death row, like the day had come. No backing out now. No escape. He looked about as desperate as anyone I'd ever seen before.

The waitress had brought him a coffee. I didn't hear him order it, but I saw his lips move. He shot her a brief smile—an expected courtesy and nothing else.

Turik had bushy eyebrows, well trimmed but bushy. He wasn't a gym rat, that was for sure, but he was far from being above his fighting weight. He had a small belly, broad shoulders, and big arms that looked like they hadn't lifted a dumbbell in years but still had the muscle memory.

He wasn't enlisted. I was damn sure of that. The Marine woodland camo uniform doesn't provide information of rank, only name, but I knew I was looking at an officer in the United States Marine Corps. He had that worn and weary look in his eyes, like he'd seen real battle time. An American Muslim was something of value to the USMC because, most likely, he spoke a foreign language, which has been thought of as a strong attribute for about the last ten years. I knew he spoke a foreign language. Kurdish. Had to be. This wasn't a shot in the dark, but an accurate estimation, because the base that was close by wasn't an ordinary base. Four hundred miles to the south and east was the Marine Training Base in Bridgeport, California. This was where the Marines sent their best to train for mountain warfare. However, Arrow's Peak was a lesser-known military training base. It served as a mountain combat and warfare training facility. The difference was that Arrow's Peak was strictly for training the Raiders. These were dangerous guys, the Marine Corps' elite.

They ran Special Ops training up in the mountains. I had no doubt about the kinds of simulations they ran. They probably did extreme survival, combat mockups, and recon exercises. These were the guys who were combat-ready. Meaning that they were probably running Afghanistan Special Ops missions out of there. It all depended on what was needed.

Turik's work uniform and weapon told me all of that, because the M45 is assigned to MARSOC units. Therefore, he must've been a part of that unit.

A uniformed Marine carrying a sidearm wasn't alarming, not in itself. That's not what raised my suspicion about him. I knew that ever since 2013 commissioned officers were able to carry concealed and non-concealed service weapons when off duty, off base, or on leave. But the price for this is to be approved by law enforcement or working with law enforcement. They had argued for that privilege for years, claiming it could've prevented mass base shootings. And finally, it had been granted to approved soldiers back in 2013 because of a string of military base shootings, like the 2009 shooting at Fort Hood, Texas.

It wasn't that he was Arabic, either. I'd known plenty of Muslims and Arab Americans who fought in the military. There was something else about him.

The thing that worried me about Turik was that he was wearing his camo uniform and carrying his weapon. The uniform was his operating combat uniform. The US Army could wear theirs in public, but not the Marines. It was a major no-no, a major violation of military law and off-base operating conduct.

That was the first thing that worried me about him. The second was the look in his eyes. He looked like a soldier distraught, like he'd just seen his buddy blown to bits on the road outside of Bagdad, which was a look I'd also seen before.

A new man walked into the diner. The bell at the top right corner of the door chimed as he bent his head under the door-frame and stepped in. The guy was a giant, much larger than me, and I'm tall. He wore dark jeans, a black peacoat, and silver sunglasses. He removed the glasses and stared around the room, not in a lingering way, just quick enough to note the layout and casual enough not to draw suspicion. It was impossible not to notice him because of his height. He must've been six eight at least. Maybe he was even seven feet.

He looked at me first and then everyone else. He walked by the officer and looked around the room. He walked to the counter and plopped down on one of the stools welded down low on a long bar and bolted into the counter. He was massive. The whole structure wobbled under his weight like someone dropped a wrecking ball on the seat.

Karen offered him a menu, but he waved it off with a goliath hand, like a sandblaster attached to his forearm. He said only one word: "Coffee."

She gave him a cup and poured black coffee in it. I grinned because she had used the older coffee pot. I had noticed the pot when I walked in. Since I'd been there, she'd made fresh coffee in the other pot, the one that she served me with. The burner for the old one wasn't even switched on when I ordered mine. I watched her switch it on after she made the fresh pot.

I glanced over at the giant one more time and then back to the rest of the room. I watched the married couple get up and put on their coats, the husband helping the wife slip hers on, and they left. I let my eyes look around the room, recounted the patrons and staff. Nothing else had changed. There was still the pair of truckers laughing and talking. Karen stood back behind the counter until the couple left and then took a tray over to their table and started to clear it of the remaining dishes.

I guessed that there was probably at least one employee in the back. Certainly there was a cook on staff, and possibly a manager.

I grabbed my coffee, which was still warm, and I slid out of my booth. I carried it over to Turik's booth. I stopped and asked, "Hi, friend. Mind if I join you?"

He stared up at me slowly, like I'd interrupted him out of holy prayer.

He said nothing, but his face had a big question mark on it.

I said, "I served once. I notice you're wearing your uniform."

He broke out of his stare. He glanced at the counter, at the giant. Then he looked back at me and said, "Yeah." His voice broke and cracked like he hadn't used it in days. That was a feeling that was no stranger to me. Sometimes I'd go days saying very little.

I didn't wait any longer for a response. I just set my coffee mug down and slid into the spot across from him. The vinyl crinkled and crunched as it scraped across my black jeans. I'd worn a pair of day-old black jeans, a gray T-shirt, and a navy blue denim jacket. It was a comfortable jacket, but not very warm. The winter months were rolling to a stop, but the higher altitude of Northern California made up for it with shadows of the cold wind and low temperatures.

I got comfortable and looked at him with a big smile on my face. I said, "My name is Widow. I was an O-5 at my last rank."

Turik looked at me; his eyes finally looked focused on the present moment. He asked, "Colonel?"

I shook my head and said, "Commander."

"Not Marines?"

"No. Navy. I'm not from here. Just passing through."

He nodded.

I said, "You're in the Marines, obviously. I like Marines. Always did. My Marine friends used to joke and say they had a great love for the Navy. They'd say we'd always give them a ride so they could go fight real battles."

Turik didn't smile but didn't frown either.

I asked, "You an officer?" I took a sip of my coffee.

"Yeah," he said but didn't divulge rank.

Silence fell between us. His coffee was still full.

"You teach out there? At Arrow's Peak?"

He nodded.

"You got a specialty?"

"I teach Arabic," he said, and he paused a long beat. Then he said, "And Middle Eastern studies."

I nodded and said, "I see. You help our guys blend in?"

"That's part of it."

Another long pause filled the space between us. We both looked out the window.

The highway was about forty yards away across a basically empty parking lot. I saw the truckers' trucks—both generic, big-rig trucks. Both had big trailers on the back, hauling God knows what.

I had had a stranger experience the night before. I started to think about it. I decided to share it to make small talk. I said, "I had a different night last night. Not bad but different."

He looked at me, possibly interested, possibly not. So I didn't talk about my night. Keeping it light was key. Instead, I asked, "How long you been in?"

Must've been at least a decade for him to reach his current rank. He said, "I joined after 9/11."

I nodded. There was a huge influx of hiring after 9/11. Especially then, the armed forces sought out Arab Americans. We needed everything from translators to Special Forces operators who could speak and understand the local cultures.

He didn't elaborate and I didn't ask.

I said, "I was in sixteen years. More or less."

He stayed quiet.

I said, "I'm from Mississippi. Originally. You?"

He made eye contact with me, nothing sinister in his eyes, but I saw a lost man in there. I hadn't made any presumptions that he'd had intentions of using that gun. I hadn't ruled it out either. He said, "You don't have an accent?"

I smiled and said, "That's a myth, like Hollywood shit. I know people who talk like that, but it's not rampant. In some places, there are people who talk slower, but it's far from all of us."

He nodded slowly. He said, "Like being Muslim. I get that."

I asked, "You Muslim? From Istanbul?"

He made a half smile like he had been recognized by an old friend. He said, "How'd you know? You been there?"

"Nah. I been in the Middle East enough to guess, but it's your name. Turik is from Western Turkey."

He nodded.

"How long you been in the States?"

He said nothing.

I waited, took another sip of coffee, and stared out the window. I saw a big-rig truck blast by. It looked like it was going at the top speed limit, which was high—nothing really out here but highway and trees.

Finally, he said, "I was born here. Only been to Turkey once. My parents moved here before I was born."

I nodded and asked, "Got any brothers and sisters?"

He stayed quiet.

I asked, "You married?"

Silence. He took a long breath and a sip of his coffee and stared back out of the window.

I looked past him but was looking at his shoulders. A seated man with a gun strapped to his side usually had a hard time brandishing his weapon. The shoulders would move long before the weapon was out. The elbow would have to fight to pull back a weapon. Booths were tight spaces, and this one was no different.

He didn't move his shoulders or elbow. He didn't go for his weapon.

I said, "My name is Widow, by the way." I held my left hand out for a handshake. He was right-handed. I could have grabbed his hand tight and jerked him forward. I could've disarmed him fast, but he didn't give me his hand.

He said, "I know. You told me."

I nodded and let my hand fall to the tabletop. I left it there, out and obvious. I said, "Right. I did."

He stared down at my tattoos, said nothing about them. He looked at my stature like he was seeing it for the first time. He asked, "You a SEAL?"

"I used to be. Among other things."

He was quiet again, and then he said, "Look. I better go."

Before he got up, I said, "I was a cop once too."

He looked at my face.

"I was a cop with the SEALs."

"MP?" he asked.

"Not MP."

"NCIS?"

I nodded and said, "I can help you."

He paused. Hope seemed to peer through the darkness in his eyes. He asked, "Why do you say that?"

"I can see something's off with you. Something that appears to be serious."

He stayed quiet.

I said, "You're not supposed to wear your woodland camo in public."

He looked off in the distance and then at me again. He nodded like he got that I had noticed he was breaking military law.

He said, "Good luck, Widow." And he stood up, took up his camo hat, and put it on. He walked out like a ghost, like he'd never been there in the first place.

CHAPTER 3

The night before, I had ridden into town with a nice enough trucker who had a lot of opinions. Opinions are fine to have—I certainly have them—but some are dangerous to talk about with complete strangers. So I listened and nodded in agreement. On most topics, I can agree and talk about them, and on others, I have no clue. The trucker I rode in with had everything on his mind, and nothing was going to stop him from pouring it all into my ear, which meant that nothing was going to stop me from listening.

I hadn't slept right the night before, and I wanted nothing more than to sleep, but I had been hours from the nearest town and I wasn't going to sleep on the freezing ground. So I ended up riding with the guy for around five hours. He was a good guy, a normal trucker—nothing unusual about him except for one small thing. He was hauling bullets.

He had told me that he worked for a major ammunition and gun manufacturer. They, in turn, dealt with a large distributor chain called Lexigun, a twist of letters from *Lexicon*. Not sure the reason why they picked this name, but that's what they were called.

Lexigun stored and sold ammunition for all sorts of weapons. It was a major employer in the area. Hamber had two industries going for it: Arrow's Peak Marine Base and Lexigun, which employed many of the locals.

I had spent the night listening to the trucker go on and on about an entire range of topics. Politics. Crime. Religion. And many more. I was exhausted.

I came into the Wagon Hash Diner around sunup and got a couple of cups of coffee. Now, my intention was to find a motel and sleep the day away.

I stayed in the diner for another thirty minutes.

The waitress came back over and asked, "Want anything else, sir?"

"Just the check."

She nodded and walked back to the old cash register. She jotted down something on a notepad and returned to give me a handwritten check. The coffee was a dollar fifty. I left a five on the table—a generous tip, but I had more than my fair share of refills.

She came back over to pick it up, and I asked, "Where's the nearest motel?"

She stopped and paused and looked out the window at the highway. Another truck came barreling down it, didn't slow.

"If you go out on the highway and head in that direction, there's one about a half mile up the road near downtown."

"Anything special about this town? Seems small."

"It's special. It's small, but it ain't dead. Then again, it ain't much either. You'll see some official buildings and some historical sites. They protect the old gold mines. Not sure why. No one really comes up here anymore to look at the gold mines."

"How many do you have?"

"We got one big one. Out of town about five miles. Then there's dozens scattered all over the valleys."

I nodded and thanked her. I got up and grabbed my coat. Put it on and headed to the street. As I walked out of the diner, I saw the giant get up from his seat as well. He tossed a five-dollar bill on the countertop to cover the coffee, and he followed me out to the lot.

I walked out to the center of the lot. There was a thin layer of snow on the ground, and gravel beneath. I waited, looking down the highway in both directions.

The giant stepped out behind me and stopped. I could feel him staring in my direction. I turned and glanced back over my shoulder. He was looking up at the sky in a blatantly obvious fashion. I'd seen bad surveillance before, and this wasn't that. He was doing it on purpose. He was letting me know, *Hey, I see you. Keep on moving.*

I waited.

He didn't linger long enough to make it a standoff. He walked over to a parked white pickup, opened the door, and got in. He fired up the engine and drove past me, slowly. I walked to the highway and stared off in both directions again. He stopped at the edge of the lot. He also looked both ways and then at me. He smiled and drove off toward town. I followed, memorized his plate.

CHAPTER 4

The walk to the downtown part of Hamber was a hell of a lot longer than the half mile that the waitress had told me, but I didn't give up. Walk long enough on a road, and you're bound to come across something, right?

I made it to downtown and wasn't disappointed. It was small, maybe one of the smallest downtowns I'd ever seen, at least for a town that was actually on the map. I passed a small church, fenced off and tucked back away from the road. There was a cemetery to its south side and a garden to its west. On the cemetery side, there was a long drive that came out to the street. I imagined there was a hearse parked somewhere on the property. Probably out of sight.

However, I was wrong about the hearse being parked in the back out of sight. After passing the church, I saw an enormous line of cars. They moved along at a snail's pace. At the front of the long line of cars was a local police escort—one police car at the front and one way in the back. There were several police motorcycles along the sides and following the leading car. All the cars had their headlights turned on. The police escorts had their blue light bars flashing, no sirens.

There was a black motorcade near the front, which was where the bulk of the police escorts were concentrated. Little American flags attached to the front corners of the main vehicle waved in the wind. They were designed to fly at half-mast, which was neat. I'd never seen that before.

This was a funeral procession. I saw the hearse near the middle of the procession. It was a plain, old black thing with dark curtains hanging in the windows along the sides and the back. The driver was visible.

I stepped on the side of the road and put my hand over my heart as I had done many, many times in the past.

One of the police motorcyclists pulled over to the side. He slowed his approach and stopped twenty feet from me. He waved me over. I lowered my hand and walked closer.

He said, "You local?"

"No, sir," I said.

He looked me up and down. He had a visor on his helmet, but it was retracted up. He wore aviator shades like I'd seen a thousand bike cops wear in the past.

"You got relatives here?"

"I'm just passing through."

He nodded and again looked me from top to bottom, bottom to top, with a natural suspicion that I'd also seen a thousand times before. He asked, "When are you leaving?"

I waited before answering. I looked past him and watched more cars from the funeral procession crawl by.

I said, "I don't know."

He was silent a long, long beat, then he looked at the line of cars and back at me. He said, "You make sure to keep on going wherever it is that you're going. This isn't the time to be sightseeing."

I could've talked back, but what would that have accomplished? I nodded, and then I asked, "Who died?"

"Why?"

"Looks important. You got a government car and about the longest funeral procession that I've ever seen."

He nodded and said, "It's Mike Danner." He paused at the end of the name and then added, "Senior. Mike Danner, Senior."

"Was he like the mayor or something?"

"Nah. Just an important man to this community. The motorcade is the governor's car. Mr. Danner was a big campaign contributor."

As he spoke, I looked at the end of the funeral procession and saw several vehicles: pickups, sedans, and a couple of panel vans. They were company cars. On the side of each of them were a logo and a name. They read Lexigun, the local small arms manufacturer.

I asked, "Is Danner the CEO of Lexigun?"

"No, he's the founder. The CEO is technically his son."

"I see."

The cop looked back at the procession one more time and then at me. He said, "You have a good day, sir."

I nodded, and he rode off, rejoining his fellow cops.

Every car that I had seen was packed with people. Danner must've been a well-liked man.

I waited until the last car passed, and I continued.

I passed a small public building with the fire and police departments. It was the only two-story building in sight. The parking lots were nearly empty. I suspected that every available cop was at the funeral, as it seemed most of the town was. The downtown was basically a ghost town.

I walked on and passed another restaurant, a long stretch of outlet stores, and strip malls. I passed several office buildings, cluttered with various local companies and brands that I'd never heard of.

I turned onto the main street, and kept walking, looking for the motel.

Even though it was the early morning hours and the sun should've been beating down on the streets by now, it wasn't. There was enough cloud cover overhead, and tall trees lining the streets, to block out what little sunlight there was.

I passed a post office, a bank, and a farmers' market, where skeleton crews were setting up shop. One of the banks was closed. The digital sign out front, the kind that displayed the temperature and time, was set to read, "Today we're sad to be closed. In memory of Michael Danner, Sr."

Which told me two things. This Danner guy was prominent in this small town, just as the cop had said. It also told me that the son must've been equally respected for the businesses to list the father as "Senior" instead of just by his name.

A car passed me on the road. The driver stopped for a moment and stared at me like he knew that I wasn't from there, but then he kept on going.

Finally, I found the motel on a corner. I rented a room without any fuss and found it far down by the end, which was good because it was away from the street. I couldn't wait to lay my head down and sleep.

The room was tight, overpacked with furniture. Blue high-backed chairs were situated against the far wall, matching the comforter on the bed. A stack of pillows topped the head of the bed. The carpet was off-white, corresponding to the color of the walls. The baseboards were clean, which was generally a sign of a well-kept room.

A flat-screen TV hung off a steel arm on the wall. The remote was Velcroed to the corner of a nightstand on one side of the bed.

I walked in and stepped into the bathroom. A light flickered on automatically, a motion sensor setup. It flickered and brightened and then dimmed. I saw the dark shadow of my reflection in a large mirror above the sink that went up to the ceiling. No trim or border around it. The mirror was all glass with the edges smoothed out into a safe dullness. Neatly laid out on the sink was a small toothbrush about the size of a lighter. It was wrapped in plastic. Next to it was a travel-size tube of toothpaste. And two thin bars of soap also wrapped up, but in paper. The shower didn't have a door on it, but a cheap-looking, clear plastic curtain on cheap plastic shower rings that weren't all the way snapped into place.

I looked at my face in the mirror, compared it to the image of myself in my brain. I'd looked better. I had bags under my eyes, and early signs of crow's feet had started setting in. Not sure if that was permanent or not. My vision wasn't spot-on either. Not because I was losing my sight, just because I was so tired. The light was slower to take in. The neural patterns were a bit harder to focus on. My reaction time was slowed because signals from my body down my nervous system and to my brain would be a little slower than optimal. Either that or I was so tired that I was simply overthinking.

I needed to sleep.

I went back to the bedroom, closed the curtains, not that there was much light to begin with. Hamber was shrouded in shadows from the constant overcast, the tall, thick redwoods, or the mountains surrounding the town, or all three. It was strange that such a beautiful wilderness was so gray and gloomy.

I turned down the bed and kicked my shoes off, removed my coat and shirt, and tossed them onto one of the chairs near the window. I dumped myself down into the bed, not like a high cliff diver but more like a man free-falling off the Golden Gate Bridge, ending it all.

My eyes slammed shut like vault doors, and my consciousness fell into darkness.

CHAPTER 5

Power naps are a valuable thing to a SEAL. Out in the field, on long operations, we hardly ever slept. In longer than usual ops, sleep became a necessity. Power naps could mean the difference in being at full operating capacity or not.

Unfortunately, the little sleep that I got wasn't equal to the kind of nap that I needed.

A loud banging echoed through my room, and my eyes shot open. I stared up at the ceiling. At first, I wasn't sure what was making that noise. Then someone banged again. It was a loud pounding on my door.

I sat up and pinched my forehead and stared at the door.

The person on the other side pounded on it again, and a loud voice said something that wasn't audible. Probably because I was still half in my dream, all I heard was a muffled voice. It sounded male.

I got up out of bed and moved slowly. I walked barefoot to the door, skimmed my hand along the wall. I leaned into the door and looked through the peephole. I saw, with a fishbowl view, two people—a man and a woman. They stood close together, center of the hallway. They were dressed in full camo uniforms. They were Marines.

I backed away from the door and said, "Yeah?"

The man said, "Open the door, sir!"

"What's this about?"

"Sir, we are military police. Open up!"

I frowned. What the hell did they want?

I unlocked the dead bolt and cracked the door open enough for them to see my face and for me to see them.

My eyes were still a little unfocused, and the light from the hallway beamed into my room and right in my face. I squinted. I said, "What's this about?"

The man said, "Sir, are you alone?"

I tried to focus, looked at his insignia and name. The guy wore his woodland-pattern BDUs, armored vest. No head-gear. His nametape read Kelly.

Kelly was about four inches shorter than me, not a small guy, just shorter than me. He had a slender frame with plenty of muscle definition. He wore thin, black-framed eyeglasses. He was graying around the temples and thinning in the part in his hair, but only slightly—a battle that was at a standstill at the moment, but in future years, things might be different.

He pushed against the door with his hand like he was going to push his way in, but I didn't budge. He stopped, said, "Sir, stand back from the door, please."

I focused as best I could. It's always sobering to have someone cross that invisible line where politeness and civility meet intrusiveness—a line in the sand. Kelly had crossed it when he pushed against the door, as far as I was concerned. It didn't matter if he was a military cop or not. I wasn't under his jurisdiction.

I said, "What's this about?"

Kelly stared at me, a cold, hard cop stare. No doubt one that he had used a thousand times, and no doubt it had been effective a thousand times. Batting a thousand didn't mean that he'd make it to one thousand and one. And he didn't. I wasn't intimidated.

He started to speak, probably to repeat himself, but the woman put her hand on his shoulder, and he stopped.

She stepped forward to his right side and said, "Sir, please let us in."

I tried to focus on her, but the light was still too bright on my retinas. I asked, "What's going on?"

"Sir, this isn't for the hallway."

I shrugged, stepped back, and let go of the door. I turned my back on them, which was out of character for me, but I didn't realize it until I had already done it.

I walked back into the room to the center. I spun and plopped down on the bed.

The woman said, "Sir, I'm going to flip on the light."

"Go ahead."

The light flipped on, and I squinted for a couple of seconds. Not too long since my eyes had already started to adjust to the light in the hall.

The man said, "What's your name?"

I stayed quiet.

The woman said, "Sir, we are military police. We'd like to ask you some questions."

I said, "Shoot. But I'm not in the military."

The man said, "Sir, that's irrelevant."

I stared at him and said, "It's completely relevant. This conversation is irrelevant since I'm out of your jurisdiction, so get on with it and be on your way, Lieutenant."

Not sure if my knowing his rank had impressed him or not. He had a black insignia pinned into his collar, signaling an officer's rank. The Lieutenant part was a guess.

He said, "You are in our jurisdiction."

I repeated, "What's this about?"

The woman stood at the center of the room ahead of Kelly. She was short, a whole foot shorter than me, and eight inches shorter than Kelly. She had solid blonde hair tied back in a bun. The color looked like the cover of a hair dye box, only unrealistic to get, which told me it was probably completely natural. Her skin was sun-beaten, like she was no stranger to the desert. She wasn't all that tall but built like a rock. She didn't have many curves but was rock-solid, like even Kelly would have a hard time knocking her down. Her face wasn't soft but wasn't uninviting either. She had flawless eyes, a blue-green mix, blended together in whorls. She was stunning and fierce-looking all at the same time.

Her nametape read Romey, like the empire, but with a Y on the end.

She said, "Sir, what's your name?"

"Widow."

Kelly asked, "Widow, what?"

"Jack Widow."

Kelly circled in a slow arc around to my right. He wore a standard-issue M9 Beretta in a holster on his right side. He made sure that I saw it by resting his hand on the butt. The safety snap was still closed.

Romey said, "Mr. Widow, what's your business in Hamber?"

I looked at her. She looked straight at my face in a way that seemed deliberate, like she was avoiding looking at my chest. I had my shirt off, which wasn't what she was trying to avoid. I figured she was trying not to stare at my tattoos, which took up a lot of the canvas of my body.

"What's this about?"

I noticed that Romey looked to be about my age, but she appeared to outrank Kelly. *What the hell were two officer Marine cops doing in my motel room?* I thought.

"Answer the question, Mr. Widow," Kelly said.

I didn't look at him. I shrugged and said, "I'm here on vacation."

Kelly asked, "Vacation? Vacation from what?"

"I'm passing through."

"Which is it, sir? Holiday or passing through?" Romey asked.

"Both."

"What's that supposed to mean? Exactly?"

"It means that I'm a tourist. That's all. It doesn't mean anything else."

"You're a tourist? Here? What kind of tourist comes through here?" Kelly asked.

"You disrespect your town, Lieutenant. Hamber is quaint. You got mountains. You got gold mines. Why wouldn't I tourist here?"

They said nothing to that.

Romey asked, "What do you do?"

"Do?"

"For work? What do you do for work?"

"I don't do anything."

Romey asked, "Nothing?"

"I worked for sixteen years. It didn't agree with me. Now I just go."

"Go?"

"I just go. You know? I go here. I go there. I do whatever pleases me."

Romey asked, "Whatever pleases you?"

"Whatever pleases me that's legal."

Kelly said, "You're a drifter."

"Some people might say that. I go from place to place. But I prefer to think of myself as just a traveler."

Kelly looked at Romey. She said, "Sir, we need to ask you some questions."

I said "Shoot. Go ahead."

"Sir, we need to ask you questions somewhere else."

"Where?"

"Would you come with us please?"

Romey was calm, calmer than her counterpart, but she was also straight to the point, in a by-the-book sort of way like she was trying to be all official, like this whole thing was going to be under heavy scrutiny later in some military conference room with superior officers and witnesses. I had a bad feeling.

"Where do you want me to go?"

She said, "We need you to come back to base with us."

Kelly said, "Just put your clothes on and come along, please."

"Sorry, but like I said. I'm not under your jurisdiction. I'm not going to a base until I know what this is about."

"Sir, you *are* under our jurisdiction," Romey said.

"How's that?"

Kelly said, "Widow, you can come quietly. Or in cuffs." Just then, he unsnapped the leather safety button on his weapon. Romey unfolded her arms and lowered her hand near her weapon.

This was serious. I said, "Look. I'm not military. I haven't committed a crime."

"Sir, were you meeting with a Marine officer this morning?" Romey asked.

"What?"

"You were seen, Widow. We got more than one witness," Kelly said. He drew his weapon, which was a violation against SOP—that I knew. But it was a gray area at this point. Plus, my word against theirs, and they already knew that I was a drifter, a nobody. And they were two decorated military officers in the military police. So I doubted that anyone would take my word over theirs.

I stayed quiet and where I was. I didn't want to agitate Kelly any more than I already had.

Kelly said, "Just come with us. No reason to make this into a scene."

"I don't know what the hell you are talking about," I said. Then I remembered Turik, the officer from the diner. I asked, "Wait. Is this about Turik?"

Kelly stepped back, pointed his gun in my direction, but not straight at me. Still, the muzzle was a flick of the wrist away from aiming at my center mass. Romey followed suit and pulled her weapon out.

"Okay. At ease, guys. I'm not a threat. I'm just asking what the hell is going on."

Romey said, "Jack Widow. By military code, we have the right to arrest you for suspicion. Please stand up. Keep your hands clearly visible. Turn around and face away."

"At ease," I repeated. "Tell me what the hell this is about."

"Jack Widow. By military code, we have the right to arrest you for suspicion. Please stand up. Keep your hands clearly visible. Turn around and face away," Romey repeated.

The two of them stared and waited. I wasn't sure what the hell was going on or how I'd managed to escalate this situation into one of national security, but that's what it felt like.

I said, "Okay. Okay. Can I put my clothes on?"

Kelly said, "Widow, don't make her ask again. Turn around."

Kelly continued to use a stern cop voice and expression, but he never yelled. His voice never went above a professional octave. They were good.

I rose up off the bed, slowly. I kept my hands visible. I didn't want to turn, but by the look in Kelly's eyes, he'd shoot first and ask questions later. No doubt about it. Between getting shot and arrested, I had a clear choice.

I turned and placed my hands on my head, which I assumed was the next command. Romey stepped forward and circled around behind me. She grabbed my right hand and pulled it back behind me. Then I heard the second-worst sound that I hated to hear when someone was behind me, the metal clanging of handcuffs. The first-worst sound I hated to hear was the crunch of a shotgun. This was better. At least that's what I thought at the time.

CHAPTER 6

Romey and Kelly sat me down on the bed and holstered their M9 Berettas. Romey stood about four feet from me, leaned to one side, rested her hand on her gun. Up close and even in her uniform, she looked like she spent eight hours a day working in the field and two hours in the fitness center on base after. I doubt she had much social life with that kind of dedication.

Kelly looked like he stayed in shape but rarely visited the gym for more than thirty minutes. In my experience, guys in the gym are there to pack on muscle as much as to get stronger. He didn't have much meat on his bones to make a lot of muscle. I guessed his weekly regimen probably consisted of just enough to get stronger, with little effort in aesthetics. Nothing wrong with that. But Romey was spending extra time on her fitness. I wondered if she competed professionally. If she didn't, then she should've.

"What the hell is going on?" I asked again. I was starting to feel like a broken record.

They didn't answer me.

Kelly said, "I'm gonna put your shoes on for you. Don't fight back, or we'll have to make this less comfortable. Got it?"

I just nodded. This wasn't how to get on my good side.

Kelly grabbed my boots and ignored my socks. He pulled them over and kneeled in front of me. He lifted my foot and shoved the boot on like a guy putting a shoe on a horse; only the guy hated the horse. First, he did the right and then the left. He stood up and said, "Come on."

He grabbed under my right arm and pulled me up to my feet. I said, "I gotta say, guys, this feels a lot like a violation of my civil rights. Not to mention wrongful arrest."

Kelly said, "It's not wrongful."

"How you figure that?"

"We came here. I asked you to cooperate. You resisted."

"I didn't resist. I invited you in."

Romey said, "You refused to come with us and kept pushing for answers."

"So?"

Kelly said, "So it's our job to ask you questions."

I stayed quiet.

"You got a shirt?"

I nodded and said, "How you expect me to put it on in cuffs?"

"I didn't ask you to put it on. I asked you if you got one."

I pointed my head in the direction of the chair and said, "It's under the jacket."

Kelly nodded, let go of my arm, and walked over to the chair. He scooped up the jacket and T-shirt. He sifted through it and separated my shirt from my jacket. He went into the pockets and came out with my passport and debit card. He said, "You really are nobody."

Romey said, "What?"

"He's only got a passport and debit card. Nothing else."

I nodded.

Romey said, "Take it all."

Kelly put everything back into my jacket pocket and tossed the jacket around me like he was doing me a favor.

I said, "Don't you think you should put my shirt on as well? It's cold outside. I could catch a cold. You could get involved in a lawsuit."

Romey said, "There's heat in the car."

Kelly jerked me and led me out of the room and into the hall.

We left the motel and entered the parking lot. It was still early in the morning. I was guessing it was around nine but wasn't sure. I saw no sun in the sky, just the overcast—gray and dreary.

They had come in a new Dodge Charger, a black police car with "Military Police" scrawled on the side in big white block letters. It came with a top-of-the-line police tactical package. It was all steel where it counted.

They took me around to the back and shoved me in, nothing gentle about Kelly's treatment, but not quite unprofessional either. I hadn't broken any laws or given them any reason to use force, not that I was aware of. I could've kicked up dirt and made a fuss with lawyers and complaints, but what good would that do me now or in the future? I went along.

CHAPTER 7

We drove in silence. They took me out of downtown, no sirens or lights. We drove the speed limit back to the highway and then headed north out of downtown. Once we were a good few miles away from the locals, Romey accelerated, and we hit about five miles over the speed limit. I stared out the window.

I wanted to sleep.

The terrain was thick and green. It contrasted heavily with the gray sky overhead. The road was smooth. I saw a sign that said we were headed exactly where I suspected, Arrow's Peak Marine Base. The sign said it was another five miles ahead, for a grand total of about ten miles from downtown Hamber.

We drove on in more silence, except for ambient chatter from their police radio.

Finally, I leaned forward and said, "Please tell me what this is about."

Kelly said, "You said it already. It's about your friend."

"I don't have a friend here. I told you. I'm just passing through. Don't know anyone."

"Then how do you know Turik?"

Romey said, "Wait till we're there."

"I don't know Turik."

Kelly obeyed Romey's orders and didn't respond.

We turned off the highway; overhung trees and high grass covered both sides of the road. The blacktop turned into a two-lane, and the shoulders vanished. I saw another sign saying: Arrow's Peak Marine Base.

There was a huge opening where trees had been cut down and plowed away. I saw the base. The road parted into two directions. One went off to the east and looked abandoned. The blacktop didn't follow it. The second branch of the road headed onto the base.

There was a guard shack, small but made of brick. There was one way in and one way out. The guard shack stood under a large brick shelter with overhangs protecting the area underneath from rain.

Inside the shack, I saw two MPs, one for exiting traffic and one for incoming traffic. Not unheard of to have a guard posted on the exit side, but not customary for them to be there either. They normally aren't stopping cars that are leaving.

There was also a huge barrier set up that incoming cars had to slow and zigzag around. All of that was normal about the entrance, but this base did have something completely unusual except during times of heightened alertness, like wartime or terrorist attacks. That was the four armed guards that stood on opposite sides of the road. Four MPs in full body armor and helmets, and armed to the teeth. They had M16s down and ready. They looked like good sentries, like they should be guarding Marine One and not some obscure Marine training base in the California mountains.

We drove slowly around the barriers. Romey decelerated and came to a full stop at the guard shack. The MP stepped out. He was also in full body armor and helmet, and armed with an M16, which he kept pointed at the ground. He saluted our vehicle.

The MP had a distinctive face. It was rugged with a boxer's nose that was closer to a snout. He was bigger than your average MP. He was bigger than me. I was six four but pretty lean. I didn't know my weight, not precisely. I guessed it was somewhere between two hundred and two hundred thirty pounds. I'd given up days in the gym and long SEAL training sessions. I was lean because I walked every day, and I walked a lot. The extra weight I carried was solid muscle.

Romey rolled down the window, flashed a badge, and stared up at the MP. She saluted and said, "Let us in."

The MP recognized her immediately and hopped to it. He said, "Yes, ma'am."

He stepped back into the shack, hit a button, and a white, metal arm ascended. Romey said, "Thanks."

The MP gave me a look like he knew me. He stared at me with contempt on his face. I'd seen it before. It was like he was blaming me for something, but I had no idea what.

Romey accelerated, and we were through the gate.

The base was spread out. There were buildings neatly scattered around. Multiple streets snaked in different directions. Military bases were often like little cities. This one wasn't anything special. Average size. Average setup. I was surprised about it being as big as it was, but not shocked. The military liked small, out-of-the-way towns. Easier to keep bases away from public interference when they were stationed in the middle of nowhere.

We turned right and, two minutes later, stopped at a four-way stop and then took a left. Romey followed the speed limits and made full stops at the stop signs.

I looked around, studied the buildings. Some were clearly marked, and others weren't. The highest were the four-story buildings, which I gathered were dorms for the enlisted. Most of them were grouped together in a square shape with a large, grassy field between them. At the center was a huge flagpole holding an American flag. It had a large rounded cement area at the bottom with benches around the pole.

The flag was at half-mast, which told me that my visit here was more serious than I had thought. I had mentioned Turik, the guy from the diner. I didn't know him. But they thought I did. *What the hell did he do?* I thought, even though I had a suspicion.

After we entered the base, there was something obvious and disturbing that I couldn't stop noticing.

Instead of speculating, I just asked them. I said, "Where the hell is everyone?"

CHAPTER 8

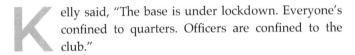elly said, "The base is under lockdown. Everyone's confined to quarters. Officers are confined to the club."

I nodded. Something had happened here.

We drove one last street, and Romey turned the car into the parking lot of the MP station. The lot was full of the same Dodge Chargers. All military police cars. All with the same tactical police package—PIT bumpers, blue light bars, and probably reinforced steel, not that fiberglass crap.

Romey parked the car at the space that was nearest to the entrance ramp. There was a white sign that designated it her spot. It read, "MAJ Romey." She said, "Let's go."

They got out and opened my door. Kelly pulled me out. He was less aggressive this time around. I supposed because he saw that I was cooperating, not that I had much choice.

"Go up the ramp. Follow Romey in," Kelly said. He shoved me gently, like he was herding me in the direction that he wanted me to go.

I complied and stepped out in front of him.

They hauled me into the MP station. We entered through the front entrance, which was a good sign to me. They didn't pull me through the rear entrance, which was normally designated for customers, which is the terminology for people going to booking and then to jail. At least, it was the terminology used in my circles. Even though I was in handcuffs, they were considering me as either a witness or a person of interest. Either way, I was going to disappoint them. Maybe I could be out of this mess in a few hours and then back in my room—back to sleep.

The entrance to the station thrust us into a long hall with several glass doors that went to different departments. But before we could enter, there was a metal detector station and two armed guards. They didn't wear helmets, but every other stitch of gear was just like the sentries outside the guard shack—armored vests and M16s, which were more for show of force than for practicality, because the hall was too narrow to make use of an assault rifle efficiently in guarding the station against attack. I assumed that the MPs were completely aware of this, and their first choice of weapon was going to be the M9s holstered at their sides.

The walls were generic gray with white tile floors. Everything was clean and tidy.

Romey nodded at the MPs, who saluted and ushered us through. Romey grabbed my arm for the first time and tugged me behind her. Her hands were cold but soft. Probably the only soft part on her. I followed her through the metal detector. It beeped twice as we passed through.

She released my arm, and I followed her down the hall. She stopped and stared through a glass partition at a desk corporal, a black woman, who was maybe six months pregnant, the second pregnant woman I had seen that day. She had quite the baby bump. So far, she'd been the only Marine that I had seen who didn't have a look of death on their face. She wasn't smiling, but she had a natural glow about her, like how some people are more engaging than others. She avoided eye contact with me but smiled at Romey. She buzzed us in through a metal door.

I was still carrying my jacket draped over my back.

On the other side of the door was a series of areas in an open floor plan. It appeared that the first area was a record-keeping department or something to do with computers. It was full of uniformed personnel, all busy at their desks.

We walked past them and through the second area, which was more conventional to police work. I saw what looked like special investigators combing over their cases or over the same case. They were prying through internet pages and files.

Romey led me into a third area with a set of two doors, an interrogation area.

We went in. The room was small but classic. In the center was a table with two chairs on either side. A thick file lay on the center of the table. It was closed. The north wall even had a medium-sized mirror, which I guessed was a one-way, like in the movies.

"Stop," Kelly said. He spun me around and pulled out his keys. He undid my cuffs and said, "Don't cause any problems. Got it?"

I stayed quiet, didn't respond, didn't nod in agreement.

Kelly took the cuffs back and handed me my T-shirt, which I slipped on, and then put my jacket on over it.

I dumped myself down on the chair that I expected was meant for me, the hot seat. I said, "Better offer me some coffee."

Kelly said, "We're not offering you shit!"

Romey said, "Joe, get him some coffee." And then she swiveled her head and looked at me. She asked, "How do you take it?"

"Black. No sugar. No milk."

Kelly looked at Romey and nodded, and then she said, "Bring two."

He nodded back and left the room, leaving us alone. He didn't even bat an eye at leaving her alone with me. Which I suspected was either because he was reckless, or we weren't really alone.

I looked at the one-way mirror and said, "How many guys back there?"

She looked at me in the glass, made eye contact, and asked, "What makes you think they're men?"

I nodded, said, "So, this is good cop, bad cop?"

She shook her head, said, "No, Widow. Nothing like that. We just wanna ask you some questions. Kelly's always like that. He's an on-edge type of guy."

"What about you?"

"I'm more level-headed."

I nodded and got a little annoyed, which I hadn't meant to, but I spoke anyway. I said, "Let's get something straight. I don't know you. You don't know me. I don't even know why I'm here. And I'm tired. So get on with it."

"Okay, Widow. Tell me about Turik," Romey said. She pulled out the chair across from me and sat down. She didn't sit in the way that most women did. She didn't sit with her back straight in a good posture like I'd seen most women in high-ranking positions do before. She sat more like she was lounging as a guy does. It was different. It was not disre-spectful or insolent, just noteworthy.

I paused.

She said, "Go on."

"There's nothing to tell. I don't know him."

"You mentioned him."

"Sorry, I don't know him."

Silence fell between us for a long moment. I don't think she was lost for words. I think she was waiting for Kelly to return, which she had been. The doorknob turned, and the door opened slowly, like Kelly was making sure that no one was on the other side of it. And then the door was kicked open gently with the toes of Kelly's boot. He had his hands full with two piping hot cups of coffee. He didn't have paper cups as I expected. He had two coffee mugs from their breakroom. Both were white with no markings.

He set mine down in front of me. I stared at it. I wasn't sure if I should take it or not. Not because I suspected there was a hidden agenda behind the coffee, like they were going to take it and test it for my DNA or anything like that. I had nothing to hide. I simply didn't trust it, like second nature to be distrusting of two uniformed MPs who haul you in when you have no idea what it's about.

After a moment, I took a sip from the coffee. It was okay—not good, not bad, but serviceable.

Kelly walked over to the opposite wall next to the mirror and leaned against it to one side. This was a move I'd seen before. He was leaning near the mirror so that when he asked me questions, I'd stare in that direction. It was so the camera and the suits on the other side of the mirror could get a clear view of my face. Everything is about tactics—a Marine's life.

Finally, I repeated, "I don't know Turik."

Romey cleared her throat and opened the file. She said, "Captain James Muhammad Turik was a decorated officer in the

United States Marine Corps. He was a lifer. Nearly twenty years of flawless service with only one citation in his record for misconduct, and that was over five years ago."

She paused and looked up at me like I was supposed to add something more to her story.

She continued, "Captain Turik was born in Houston, Texas, in 1971 to Ali and Medina Turik, who were a pair of refugees from Turkey but originally from Iran. They migrated to the US when they were children. Turik had three sisters, no brothers. Two sisters are married and living in Texas. The youngest changed her name but is unmarried. She is a teacher and, ironically, a well-known advocate against Islam. She works at UC Berkeley. We looked her up because the changing of her name was interesting. She's got quite the story.

"She's got five hundred thirteen thousand hits on Google. She's even got a detailed Wikipedia page. But not as her real name, which is Ayaan Turik. She changed it to Maya Harris; we don't know why.

"Turik's parents are old now, but the father is still the patriarch of the family, and we spoke to him on the phone already. They were cooperative but didn't deny anything that happened."

I said, "What happened?"

Kelly said, "No, they didn't. In fact, they seemed damn proud of what he did."

Romey stared at Kelly and said, "I wouldn't go that far."

"What? They're hardcore Muslims."

Romey said, "So?"

"They didn't seem surprised. That's all I'm saying."

I repeated, "What happened?"

Romey ignored me and said, "By all accounts, Turik was a good soldier and a good officer too."

Kelly said, "On all accounts, but the two asterisks against him."

I stayed quiet.

Kelly said, "Do you want to know what the two asterisks are?"

I didn't respond.

Romey read from the file. Turning the page, she said, "The first was the citation. A black mark against him."

"Six years ago, he had an affair," Kelly interrupted. He paused a beat, looked at me. Waiting for my reaction, I guess.

Romey said nothing.

I took another swig of the coffee, swallowed, and asked, "How did he die?"

Kelly asked, "How do you know he's dead?"

"Simple. An E-1 could see that. You referred to him in the past tense multiple times. You said, 'He was' or 'Turik was.' You dragged me out of my hotel. He must've been killed. And you told me he had an affair—just blurted it out. Turik was an officer. You can't share his records freely unless it doesn't matter. Therefore, he's dead. Simple observation."

She stayed quiet. I said, "Yeah, I saw him this morning at a diner. I saw him for a whole thirty minutes. If that. He was alive and well. He must've died afterward. And I can tell you I have an alibi for where I was. The hotel clerk will vouch for that. And you can check the keycard reader on the door, which probably records the time I entered and will show that I didn't leave."

Romey said, "You think that we hauled you in here because we suspect that you murdered him?"

"Why else would I be in here?"

Romey took my passport out from her pocket and handed it over to Kelly. He took it. She said, "Go check it out."

Kelly nodded, left us again, and took my passport with him.

Romey said, "Widow, Turik is dead, but we didn't bring you here because we suspect you killed him."

"Then why the hell am I here?"

"You're here because three hours ago, you were seen talking to Turik by several witnesses in that diner."

"So what?"

"So a decorated officer with a purple heart and a silver star walked into a diner in Hamber, as he does three mornings a week, and a total stranger, a guy that no one has ever seen before, sits with him. You guys are seen talking. Then Captain Turik exits the premises, and fifteen minutes later, he enters the base as usual. He parks in his designated space. He enters the CO's office. He draws his service weapon and discharges it, killing three officers and two enlisted Marines."

CHAPTER 9

Romey said, "Captain Turik shot and murdered five Marines for no apparent reason. Then he walked out of the command office and shot himself in the head, right in the yard."

I stayed quiet.

"I've got questions for you."

I nodded and said, "I doubt I'll have answers. I told you I'm nobody. Just a guy passing through."

She ignored me and took out a department-issued smartphone. She swiped through it with her fingers and must've found a voice recording app, because she turned it on and faced the phone toward me. She also had a legal pad out in front of her.

She said, "State your name, please."

"Don't I get a lawyer?"

"Name, please?"

I stayed quiet. I felt at odds because I was a big believer in civil rights and civil liberties, but at the same time, I'm not involved with Turik. I've got nothing to hide. I shrugged again and said, "Jack Widow. You want me to list my life history, pedigree, and all that?"

"Just the basics. We can pull up all of your records ourselves. If you've got records."

"My name's Jack Widow. I was born in Mississippi. I'm six four. White. Scorpio. And I like long walks on the beach."

Even though she was recording, she wrote the first parts down on the legal pad, and then she stopped, looked at me, and said, "This isn't a joke. Six people are dead."

I nodded and said, "Sorry. But you got the wrong guy. Wrong idea. I don't know anything about Turik."

Then I thought, *Except I thought he was suspicious earlier. Maybe I should've done something. A man who plays neutral is just as guilty. Right?*

"Okay, Mr. Widow. Tell me what you talked about. How do you know Captain Turik?"

"I told you. I didn't. I came into town with a trucker. I wanted to grab breakfast, coffee, and sleep. I saw Turik sitting at a table alone. I joined him. We talked about nothing. He barely said anything."

"Why did you join him if you didn't know him?"

I stared at her. I had a problem answering this question because I didn't want to be involved, but if I told her the truth, then certainly they'd involve me. I'd look suspicious. Then again, lying in these proceedings was like lying under oath. And I tried not to lie to people—general policy.

She looked me up and down, then she added, "Were you begging for money?"

I said, "No. I joined him because he looked suspicious."

"Suspicious?"

"Yeah, he looked like something was off. Wrong. You know? Like peculiar."

"Explain?"

"Look. I came into the diner. I had coffee. Turik came in. He looked suspicious. I sat with him. Tried to feel him out. See if I could figure out what was wrong about him. He barely spoke. He left. I got a hotel room. And then I was fast asleep for a couple of hours until you knocked on my door. That's all I know."

I thought about that giant guy that came in after him. I wasn't sure if I should mention him just yet.

"You said he looked suspicious. What made you pick up on that?"

"Old cop habits."

"You a cop? Where?"

I shook my head and said, "Past life."

She didn't press me on that issue. Maybe she was putting a pin in it to return to it at a later time. She said, "Okay. Tell me specifically what about him was suspicious?"

"He was quiet. Stared into space. His eyes looked wrong. But ultimately, it was his uniform."

"His uniform?"

"Yeah. He wore his BDUs in public. That's a big illegal taboo for Marines. And an officer wouldn't dare break that rule."

She nodded and asked, "How'd you know that? You ex-military too?"

I nodded and said, "Former military. Long ago."

"Where? Which branch?"

"I was a sailor."

Romey nodded and said, "Navy."

"I've been all over."

"That's vague."

I stayed silent.

She said, "If you were Navy, why did you know about his uniform? He's a Marine."

"I know a thing or two about the Corps."

"Okay. What else happened?"

I shrugged and said, "Like I said. I noticed he was acting strange. I tried to be nice. He didn't want to talk, and he left the diner. I never saw him before that, and I'll never see him again. That's it."

She sat back, put her pen down.

Just then, the door opened, and Kelly walked in. He carried a tablet with him, like an iPad, only it wasn't an iPad. I didn't know what it was. Instead of a name or recognizable symbol, it had an unrecognizable symbol on the back, and I couldn't see the front. I did notice that Kelly wasn't carrying my passport, which was a bad sign. That meant that he had secured it somewhere, and that somewhere was most likely where they put things for safekeeping, which had the word *keep* in it, which led me to believe that they weren't planning on letting me go anytime soon.

Kelly said, "Look at this." Only he had a sardonic tone with emphasis on *this*, like he'd found something interesting and was also patting himself on the back like he knew it all along. It was a vocal *I told you so*, only without the words.

Romey took the tablet and stared at the screen. She swiped right and read the information that was there. Then she tried to swipe right again. Only nothing was happening, I presume, because she was swiping right again and again.

Then she set the tablet down on the tabletop and began typing on it. A short phrase. Six letters and two numbers.

She typed it and then reacted with a stunned look, like she was typing in a password, and whatever she was looking at was denying her.

She said, "What the hell?"

Kelly said, "How is that possible?"

They were quiet and stared at the screen, and then they stared directly at me.

I said, "I would've never guessed that you were from Massachusetts."

Romey looked at me. She asked, "What?"

"You don't have an accent. I never met someone from Boston who didn't have one. At least, I never knew that I had met one. If I had."

"How the hell do you know where I'm from?"

I said, "Your password. It's Boston81. I suspect that means you are from Boston and probably about thirty-five years old."

She looked down at the tablet screen, then back at me. She asked, "You can't see the screen from there. How did you know the passcode?"

"I didn't. You just confirmed it. I only guessed."

Kelly said nothing, but I could see that he wanted to. What he wanted to say, I had no idea.

But Romey said, "Explain."

"It's not hard—the way you typed. I just watched your fingers. You're right-handed; I can see that from your gun. It's on your right side. And you drove the car earlier using your right hand. Low down in your lap. Therefore, you're right-handed."

"And?"

"No offense, but you're no millennial."

"What's that supposed to mean?"

"I just mean that you aren't a kid. You're in great shape. I noticed that immediately, like a normal guy would. But you hold the rank of major, which is higher than Kelly's. Therefore, it's doubtful that you are younger than thirty. It's a testament to your skills that you are at this rank now."

"Meaning?"

"Meaning that you take care of yourself. And that you're from a past generation, like me, which means that you use the old QWERTY keyboard. Where the letters are arranged a certain way, which was determined long ago, based on the original telegraphs; the keys were placed a certain way because it worked best for telegraph operators."

They both stared at me with a look like they were both thinking I was a freak, which I guess wasn't far from the truth.

Romey said, "That's stupid. That's a myth. Everyone uses QWERTY keys."

I shrugged and said, "It sounded good."

She eyeballed me in a way that told me she was warming to me. I don't think that Kelly appreciated it, but he didn't comment.

I said, "I watched your fingers. Right hand, not left to press the B key, which is near the middle bottom, above the space-bar, and then you returned to the typing position, moved your middle finger up. This was probably the I or the O key."

Romey interrupted me and said, "Okay. I get it. Now, how the hell did you know that?"

"I told you. I watched you. It's not rocket science."

Kelly slammed his hand down on the table, not too hard, just enough to still show that he was playing the part of bad cop. He said, "Where did you learn that?"

"Relax. I learned it for the same reason why you can't access my file. Which is what you are trying to do, right?"

Romey nodded.

"Your passcode won't work. Right?"

She shook her head and asked, "Why?"

I said, "'Cause my file's classified."

"I've got a security clearance."

"Not high enough."

Romey said, "I'm a senior ranking officer investigating a mass homicide and potential terrorist attack on a Marine base. On top of that, I've been granted top security clearance."

"By whom?"

"By the Office of the Marine Commandant, who's a member of the Joint Chiefs. Which means the Pentagon."

I shrugged and said, "It may not be high enough."

"What's that supposed to mean?"

"You won't get into my files because they aren't just military files. They're sealed by the Department of the Navy, the DOD, and probably a few other places with letters that stand for long titles."

Romey and Kelly looked at each other.

Romey said, "Who the hell *are* you?"

CHAPTER 10

"Look, I want to help," I said. "I'm not a part of some conspiracy. I don't know Turik, hand to God. And I never heard of him until today. You guys are barking up the wrong tree. And I can only guess it's because you're desperate, which is understandable. You got a mass shooting, and from a decorated officer who happens to be Muslim. It looks bad. But I'm really not involved."

Kelly said, "We need to confirm who you are."

"You just did. Why else would my military records be sealed above top-secret?"

Romey asked, "I thought you said that they weren't military records?"

"No, I said that they weren't only military."

No one spoke.

"You can't keep me. I'm a civilian. And I didn't do anything."

Romey looked at Kelly. She said, "Step into the hall with me."

They stood up and went into the hall. I waited there, staring at the tablet and the back of Turik's file. I looked over at the mirror. If Turik shot and killed the CO for the base, I wondered who was in charge now. I wondered if, whoever he was, he was standing back there now, staring back at me. I wondered if it was Romey. It might've been. She might've woken up today third or fourth in command, and Turik shot the other two or three above her.

Turik had shot and killed five people, they had said. It must've been a couple of hours now since then. The shooting explained the heightened alert at the gate. It explained all the body armor and the guns and the sense of urgency. It explained how they got to me so quickly. They identified Turik easily enough as the shooter. Then they retraced his steps. The waitress told them about me. She knew where I was going. Hamber is a small place. Only one motel in town that I could've been at. Plus, she'd given me directions.

They were being thorough, which I understood, but finding out that they were unable to access my records would've been enough to tell them I was a guy with a past, which was what they were counting on. Only my past was classified by the military and the government, and it was classified at a higher degree than they were used to. Which meant that my past wasn't the past they were hoping for. It meant that I had once been one of the good guys and important. It didn't quite get me off the hook, but it was a major roadblock.

They were hoping to pin this on me, maybe dish out some swift justice. That's the problem with a lone gunman: they often commit suicide, and then there's no one left to arrest. These guys wanted someone else to blame, an accomplice. Unfortunately for them, it wasn't me.

They came back into the room. Romey asked, "Is there someone we can call to confirm your service record? What-ever it may be?"

I said, "There's not."

"Don't you have a former CO? A friend or something?" Kelly asked.

"My former position doesn't exist. I can't hand over contact information. That would be acknowledging the existence of something that doesn't exist. Understand?"

Romey thought for a moment, and then she said, "If you were a cop, maybe you can help us."

"How? You want me to work your case for you?"

"I don't know what kind of cop you were, but all this top-secret stuff tells me it was a good one. We could use the extra help."

"What is it you're not telling me?"

"You think we aren't telling you everything?"

"A Muslim Marine kills five people and then shoots himself. It's happened before. It'll probably happen again. It looks open and shut. What's with the witch hunt?"

Kelly looked at Romey, and she looked back at him. She nodded. Then she said, "Turik was a trainer here, but he wasn't always just a teacher. He used to be a Raider. He was quite good too."

"What else?"

"Turik has a purple heart. He's got a silver star."

I stayed quiet.

"The thing is the CO that he shot, a man named John Carl …" Romey said, and then she paused a beat.

I said, "Yes?"

"Turik saved Carl's life. Back in Iraq. That's how he got the purple heart. He took a bullet for him."

CHAPTER 11

"Turik murdered the guy he rescued in Iraq?" I asked.

Romey said, "Right. You see? It's more than strange that suddenly this decorated soldier went on a killing spree this morning. It's damn insane that he would murder a guy that he was willing to take a bullet for five years ago."

"That *is* different."

Kelly said, "That's it? That's all you can say?"

"What else you want me to say?"

"Turik was a good Marine. He killed his friend in cold blood. It doesn't make sense."

Romey said, "It's even more complicated than that."

I asked, "How so?"

"Turik double-tapped Carl. Like he was the specific target."

I paused a long beat and sat back in the chair. I stared up at the ceiling. They seemed to be waiting for me to speak.

Finally, I said, "I have to admit that it's unusual. Mass shootings are common, however. This one falls under the same premises. Basically."

"Widow, the Fort Hood shooting, the Dallas thing, and the Orlando thing all have something in common. The shooters all had a past of mental instability."

"Not all of them."

Kelly said, "Yes, all of them."

"Not true. Some were religious-based shootings. And you forgot to mention Fort Hood had more than one shooting. Some shootings have been over jealousy. People will do all kinds of things."

They didn't respond to that. Romey just said, "I guess we're going to let you go, Widow."

I nodded.

Without another word, they motioned for me to stand up. Kelly opened the door, and Romey picked up her phone, switched off the recorder, and scooped up the tablet.

She said, "Follow me."

I followed her back down the hallway, past the three rooms to the front. I wasn't going to a cell, which was a new one for me.

Romey took me to the front and stood with me while we waited for Kelly, who disappeared down one of the offset rooms. He came back with my passport and handed it to me.

Romey said, "Widow, this is an unusual set of circumstances. I'd like for you to stay in town for another day or so. Just in case I need to speak with you again."

I nodded.

"Of course, I can't make you. You're a civilian now. But I'd like for you to. I'm sorry we dragged you into this."

I said, "Why's there no media?"

"What?"

"This is like Fort Hood, right? But there's no media outside the gate? This seems like national news to me."

"The story hasn't broken yet. We're hoping to close this case fast before that happens."

I nodded. It was amazing that the story hadn't broken yet. Guess that's one of the perks of having a half-forgotten military base in the middle of California wilderness.

I said, "Turik killed five people. Killed himself. Nothing more to it than that. I'd say it's done. It sounds that simple." I said it, but I felt like she was holding back information. It was her case, not my business.

She nodded and said, "We don't want to end up like Orlando."

I looked down at the floor for a second, just noticed that her shoes were a little mud-covered. She must've been walking the yard around Turik's body. Then I remembered numerous occasions where I had been in her shoes. Not exactly the same, but close. I'd scoured around crime scenes and dead bodies, too many to recall, which was a good thing in a way, because the faces were blurred in my memory. When I was new to NCIS, I'd investigated some murders and I remembered them all back then. Now, they faded away like it was all a bad dream.

Then I stopped, tilted my head, and asked, "Orlando? Don't you mean Fort Hood? That was the last military base shooting. And it was similar to this."

She shook her head and said, "No. Not Hood. That wasn't like this. I'm worried about mass panic. Like Orlando."

"I don't get your meaning?"

She looked up at my face and said, "Isn't it obvious?"

I shrugged.

"Widow, Captain Turik was a Muslim."

"So?"

"Orlando was done by a Muslim who claimed to be a part of ISIS," she said.

"Was there panic after that?"

She looked at me with big, stunned eyes. She said, "For a guy who can crack codes by watching my typing, you sure are dense."

I shrugged. I'd heard that before. I said, "No one's perfect."

"Of course, there was panic, but that'll be nothing compared to what will happen here."

"How so?"

"Turik was Muslim. If there's an ISIS connection, the people here and all across the country will panic."

"Wasn't the guy from Orlando not connected to ISIS? Not really?"

"He operated on his own, but that didn't matter. No one cares about that. He was an ISIS fighter, whether he ever set foot in the Middle East or not. You know that. No one will care."

"True. What kind of panic are we talking about here? Hamber is a small place."

She said, "It's not just Hamber. This'll be national news. Small towns everywhere will panic. The fact that he was a decorated soldier won't matter. People will only talk about an ISIS fighter sneaking his way into the top ranks of the military. At best, they'll be suspicious of all of our men and women in the service who are Arab. Worst case, they'll suspect every brown person, and I don't even want to think about what could happen then. This is unprecedented."

I nodded and said, "I get your point."

She replied, "Thank you. I'm sorry that I thought you were a part of a conspiracy to assassinate five Marines."

She smiled. She had a dark sense of humor, which was an asset among cops. Humor helps to fight off the horror that comes with the territory, keeps cops sane.

I smiled back, said, "I'll be at the hotel for at least one more day."

She nodded. We shook hands, and then she asked, "Am I supposed to salute you?"

"Not in the military anymore."

"Not going to tell me your rank?"

"Still classified."

She smiled and we shook hands. She had a good grip. Her hands were soft in places and a little rough all at the same time.

I asked, "Can I get a ride back?"

"Kelly'll take you."

I nodded, a little disappointed. I had hoped that she would take me. Maybe give us a chance to talk more.

I stopped and said, "Listen, there was something I didn't tell you."

She looked at me.

"There was another guy in the diner."

"We know. There were a few other people. You're the only suspicious one."

"No. I wasn't."

She stayed quiet.

"There was a giant. He came in after Turik and left after Turik left."

"No one mentioned him to us."

"I don't know. He was there. Ask Karen, the waitress. She served him. No way would she forget him. He was huge."

She looked at me and asked, "Bigger than you?"

"Oh yeah. At least six inches taller."

"Anything else unusual about him?"

"Nope. Just a big guy."

She asked, "Age?"

"I'd guess maybe forties."

Kelly shrugged and said, "I never saw anyone like that."

"That's all I saw."

Romey said, "Listen, you remember anything else or want to help us, give us a call."

She signaled the desk corporal to buzz me back through the security door. I went through, didn't look back, but I heard Romey say, "Just wait there for Kelly."

Which I did.

CHAPTER 12

Kelly came around the front of the building in the military police Charger and stopped at the sidewalk. He leaned out the window and said, "Come on."

I nodded, walked to the car. I wasn't sure if it was the same one that they had brought me in or not. They all looked the same, and I hadn't paid attention to the car number, which was clearly marked on each door in blue font.

I started to open the rear door, but he said, "Nah, get in the front." Apparently, the bad cop act was over now, and we were buddies.

I went around the trunk and opened the passenger door, dumped myself down on the seat. Kelly accelerated and reversed the course that we came in on, only instead of turning to the gate at the main intersection, he swung a right and then a left and stopped in front of the command building. Which was a two-story thing made of red brick with obtuse corners, like the Pentagon, only it wasn't five-sided. I wasn't sure how many sides it had from just looking at the front.

The street was packed with more armed military police. It looked like two units. One was a group of five Marines, each with the same armor and hardware. They were in a table guard position, which was a four-point position. Each armed Marine stood at one corner, with one guy who patrolled the perimeter.

The second unit was posted up on each end of the street, like a checkpoint. We drove through the southern checkpoint without having to stop and talk to the guards.

Kelly drove up next to the command building and stopped the car in the middle of the street. He looked across me and asked, "See that building?"

I nodded. My eyes felt heavier than ever. I only wanted to go back to the hotel and sleep for a lifetime.

"That's HQ. Two hours ago, Captain Turik walked in there, checked in with security. He signed himself in. He walked up the stairs, entered General Carl's office just as calm as could be. He took out his M45 service weapon, shot Carl in the head, and double-tapped him. The desk corporal, a nice woman, entered the room, and he shot her in the chest."

I kept staring at the building like I could see the inside, which I couldn't. But I closed my eyes and listened, imagined the scene.

Kelly said, "Turik entered the hall and shot the next two people he saw after that in the back. Both unarmed. Both completely innocent. Both friends of mine."

I opened my eyes and looked back at him, stayed quiet.

Kelly said, "Do you know what he did next?"

"He shot the security guy?"

He nodded and said, "He waited at the top of the stairs against the wall. He shot the security guard right in the back. Like a coward."

"Where did he shoot himself?"

Kelly pointed at the grass, center of the yard. A long line of police tape was staked in the ground at four corners. The whole area was about fifteen by fifteen feet, two hundred and twenty-five square feet. There was a puddle of dried-up blood in the snow and grass. I stared at it.

"We got here too late. Our guys pulled up and jumped out. He pulled the trigger right in front of them. Just blew his own brains out all over the place."

"Your guys moved his body fast."

"No reason to keep it there. They saw him do it. We moved all of the bodies already."

"Where?"

"Hell, they're in the morgue."

"Your hospital has a morgue?"

"Of course."

I said, "What about forensics?"

"We got a team in there now, but they aren't going to tell us nothing we don't already know."

I paused a beat and asked, "You got video?"

"We don't have any of him killing anyone, just entering and leaving the building."

I said, "Why no surveillance cameras inside?"

"It's a command building. Why would we?"

I nodded, said, "It still sounds clear-cut."

"Yeah, all but the why."

I paused again and looked back at the road ahead, wasn't sure if I should get involved. I had no reason. But I asked, "He got a wife? Kids?"

Kelly put his gloved hand on the steering wheel and started to accelerate slowly. He said, "No kids."

"Wife?" I asked again.

"Yeah, but …" he paused.

"But what?"

"We can't find her."

The car went forward, and we passed back through the checkpoint and headed out the gate. We had to stop, just like before, and the guard on the exit side came to the window, saw Kelly and saluted. With one hand on his rifle, he used his free one to wave us forward.

He turned to the other guards and called out, "Vehicle leaving." Which was weird to me. I wasn't used to being announced when I was leaving a place, and I had been on a lot of bases, more than I could remember.

I said, "That doesn't mean anything. Not necessarily."

Kelly was silent until we were past the gate and back on the drive back to town.

I asked, "You guys think she knew about it?"

"No. We think she's dead."

"You check his house?"

"Of course. We entered and searched every square inch of it. We can't find her."

"Still, that doesn't mean that's she's dead."

"Turik shot five people, and one of the five was double-tapped," he said and glanced over at me, turned back to the street. He said, "Then he killed himself. That's seven rounds spent."

I nodded.

"His weapon is seven plus one. One is missing. Unaccounted for. He shot it somewhere."

I stayed quiet.

CHAPTER 13

was back at my hotel, but not in my room. I stood outside it at the door. I tried the keycard and got a buzzing sound, like an angry buzzer on one of those game shows when the contestant says the wrong answer. I tried the keycard again and got the same sound, but this time I saw the light on the door turn red. I tried a third time and got the same.

I clenched my fist and began counting to ten. I was ready to break the door down just so I could get to sleep.

I turned and headed to the office.

The guy behind the desk saw me coming. He stayed seated with his hands out of view, which I noted.

I said, "My keycard isn't working."

"Yes. I know."

I stayed quiet and waited for him to go on, but he didn't. That was the end of the sentence. Full stop.

"Why the hell isn't it opening the door?"

"I turned it off," he said. He must've seen the rage boiling across my face because he started to tremble.

"Why?" I asked. I stayed standing, feet planted firmly. I stared down at him.

"Because we reserve the right to refuse service," he said. He showed one hand to me, pulled it out from behind the desk, and pointed at a sign on the wall. I glanced at it and then back at him. It said their policy in big block letters.

"You're refusing me service?"

His hand was back down behind the desk. I suspected that he was holding a weapon down on his lap, which was probably a gun.

"Those were Army cops that arrested you?"

I closed my eyes tight for a moment, opened them, and said, "No."

"No, they didn't arrest you? I saw you in handcuffs."

"No, they weren't Army cops. They were Marines. And they didn't arrest me."

"I saw you in handcuffs, sir."

I shook my head and said, "That was nothing. They didn't arrest me."

"I saw it. Right there in that window. I saw the whole thing. They took you to the parking lot in handcuffs."

"Yes, I was in handcuffs, but now I'm not."

"But you were. And I can refuse service to anyone for any reason."

"I paid for that room."

"Not my problem."

I stepped closer and put my hands on the desk, leaned forward. I said, "Look, I've been up all night. I paid for that room. I just want to sleep. I wasn't arrested. They got the wrong guy. I just had to answer some questions. Now, give me a new key. Don't make me get my own key."

"What's that supposed to mean?" he asked. He was trembling even more. He scooched back in his chair like he was trying to get farther from me.

"It means what it means."

Then I heard the cock of a hammer from what sounded like a thirty-eight. And it was. He pulled out a black snub-nosed thirty-eight, showed it to me. He didn't point it at me, not directly. He just pointed it in my general direction.

I stood up straight, removed my hands from the desk. I kept them calm and out in front of me like I was surrendering. He didn't say a word.

I said, "You sure you want to be doing that?"

He said, "I told—" And he didn't finish because halfway through his second word, I sidestepped right, fast. My left hand dashed left, hard, and in one movement, I swiped the revolver right out of his hand. I flipped it in a fast second movement back to my right hand. Now, it was pointed right at his face.

He wasn't trembling anymore; he was shaking—violently. He said, "Please. Please."

"Please, what?"

"Don't shoot me."

"I could. I could blow your head off right here. And take my money back. What do you think?"

He stayed quiet.

I dropped my hand and retracted the gun muzzle from his face. I turned it and flicked my wrist. The chamber opened. I shook out the bullets into my open palm. I clenched my fist closed and kept them in my hand. I said, "Relax. I told you.

I'm not a bad guy. Those cops just wanted to ask me questions. It's not a problem."

He stopped shaking but still looked terrified. He said, "I want you to go."

"Even after that? You're brave."

"I want you to go," he repeated.

"Fine. Give me my money back."

He stared at me, but his eyes seemed out of focus, like he was staring past me. I could see that he just wanted me gone. I could've threatened him, told him that he'd better let me in my room. And he would have, but that's not the kind of guy I am. He was in the wrong, but I figured he did have the right to refuse service. But he wasn't keeping my money. I paid sixty-five bucks for a room I had for two hours. No way was I going to leave without it. I'm not made of money. In fact, my bank account was getting thin. I'd have to start thinking about that. For now, I just wanted to sleep.

I watched him reach into a cash register and pull out three twenties and a five. He handed them to me. I asked, "So where the hell is another hotel?"

"South. But …" he said and paused.

"But what?"

"It's far."

"How far?"

"About fifteen miles or so. It's out on the highway, just south of town."

Great.

I sighed long and deep. I asked, "You got a bus station?"

Romey had asked me to stick around, but for what? I needed to sleep. I could just as well sleep on a bus out of this town, out of this county, and out of California.

"We got a stop."

"Where is it?"

"It's the same direction. About three miles, on the edge of town. Just head that way," he said and pointed.

"Why's there no station closer? It seems like there would be one in downtown?"

"No reason for one. No one comes here."

I nodded.

"The bus don't stop but twice a day, and you missed the first one. I think the second one is at eight p.m."

I nodded again, turned to walk out the door. I stopped in the doorway, looked across the parking lot, and looked back at him. I said, "Wait ten minutes after I leave. Go over to that dumpster on the corner. You'll find your gun and bullets underneath it."

He nodded.

I wasn't going to steal his gun. "Ten minutes. Not a second more. I'd hate for some kid to come along and steal it."

"I got it."

I walked away, left the empty gun, and the bullets as I said. Five minutes later, I was down the street and on my way to find a bench to sleep on, like a homeless man.

* * *

I HAD WALKED the better part of three miles and was passed by several vehicles going my way. Most American made. Most in the form of a pickup truck or an SUV. I'd say it was about eighty percent trucks.

The incoming traffic was a slightly different variation. I'd seen about sixty percent trucks, twenty percent SUVs, and the rest split between a few big-rig trucks and compact cars. Most of the big-rig trucks had out-of-state plates, mostly Oregon and Washington.

I started to come across signs that indicated I was nearing the end of town. There were some places to eat, a couple of small shopping malls, and a gas station. At the end of the strip, I found the bus stop that the clerk at the motel had told me about. It wasn't much. There were two benches with no cushions or covering, but at least they were empty, and they were long enough for me to lie down and stretch out on.

The benches were on a service drive off the highway, just in front of one of the strip malls. In between the benches, there was a telephone pole with a plastic plaque with the bus schedule printed on it. I glanced over it, and it was as the clerk had told me. The next bus was at night, at eight.

I picked the cleaner-looking of the two benches. I brushed off the snow, plopped myself down, and laid out straight. The ends of my feet hung off the bench. I stared up at the sky.

Good thing for me that it was overcast. It'd be easier to nap in the daylight when there was so little of it.

I closed my eyes.

CHAPTER 14

My eyes stayed closed for probably twenty minutes, although I wasn't sure exactly. I power-napped, until a voice came from a guy standing directly over me.

The voice said, "Get up!"

I opened my eyes and squinted. I saw four guys standing over me. I looked up, but I couldn't make out their faces. My cheeks felt colder than I remembered when I went to sleep.

Snow fell slowly and gently from the sky. I sat up, rubbed my face. I asked, "What is this?"

The voice said, "That's him."

I looked at the guy and immediately recognized him. He was big, with a huge nose like a snout. It was the MP from the gate at the base.

He said, "Get him up!"

The other three guys were smaller than him but just as brawny. Two of the three were bald, but they all had facial hair, and none of them kept it up neatly.

I said, "Fellas, what the hell is this?"

Two of them put their hands on me, each taking an arm, and they hauled me to my feet. Now I was awake.

I looked at them face by face. I said, "Guys, you don't want to be putting your hands on me." I was nicer than I had expected, more than I usually would've been. Maybe it was because I was tired. Maybe it was because I'd seen the big guy in uniform, not a sailor's but a Marine's. And that still meant something to me.

The MP said, "Shut up!" And he looked around the strip mall, stared at the parking lot.

It was moderately full of vehicles. He said, "Over there." He pointed at a space between a panel van and a couple of SUVs. Which I didn't like the look of.

They dragged me off in that direction. I pulled my arms out of their grip and said, "I can walk."

I walked over to the direction that they wanted me to. My first thought was that they were going to try to put me in their vehicle, but I crossed that off as a possibility because the MP had looked around for a certain type of place. He wasn't searching for where he had parked his car. The lot was too small to forget. They wanted me to go to that spot because it was cornered off from street view.

We made it between four big vehicles, including the panel van.

I turned and asked, "What is this about?"

The three other guys circled around me, taking a stance around me like I was the center of a clockface, and they were all the right angles that the hands would make. The MP was at the twelve o'clock position, while the others were at the three, six, and nine.

I kept my feet planted, swiveled around, and looked each in the eyes. My hands were down by my sides, relaxed and obvious.

The guy behind me, who was the heaviest of the four, asked, "This that boy?"

The MP nodded and asked, "You know why we're here?"

"If I knew that, I wouldn't have asked twice."

"Watch yer mouth, boy!" the fat one behind me said. I didn't look back at him. I hadn't seen that these guys were the local roughneck types. They were dressed normal for this area. Clean shirts. Clean jeans. Thick coats. But he had spoken with that less-than-educated English, which I'd heard before.

I said, "You planning to do something to me? 'Cause I'll tell you now, that's not going to work out. Not for you."

The MP said, "This is him."

The guy to my left said, "You're friends with that Islam." I wasn't sure if he said it as a statement or a question.

I said, "I don't know what an Islam is, not the way you mean it. I know it's a religion making up almost two billion people."

The MP asked, "You're friends with Turik?"

"So that's what this is about. I'm afraid I got bad news for you. I don't know him."

"You're that guy they drug in today. I saw you with my own two eyes," the MP said.

"Sorry. You are wrong."

"Then why they drag you in?"

"I told you. I don't know him. You want to know why they dragged me in; then I suggest you jump up several ranks. Maybe go to college. Become an officer."

He scoffed at me.

The MP wore a thick peacoat, brown and all buttoned up. I couldn't see if he had his uniform shirt on underneath. But he was still wearing his uniform pants and combat boots. He wore a Cleveland Indians ball cap. I liked that team, but I preferred the Cubs, not that I took sides. It was just that at the moment, I was more of a Chicago fan.

I said, "Say what you gotta say so I can go back to my bench."

The fat guy said, "We don't like American-hating Islamists here."

"That's good. But I'm none of those things."

The MP said, "They brought you in. I saw it."

"Yeah. We established that already."

"They brought you in, which means that you must be linked to that Muslim."

I stayed quiet.

The MP looked dead in my eyes. He said, "You see, that Muslim killed two of my friends."

I nodded.

The guy to my right finally spoke. He said, "Three of our friends."

The MP said, "They had families. Sons. Daughters. They had wives."

I pulled my hands up, just above my hips. I kept my palms open and hands flat. I said, "Look, guys. I get your anger. I'm sorry about your friends. But I'm telling you point-blank. I didn't know Turik. I don't have anything to do with the whole thing. I'm just a guy trying to sleep."

The MP said, "Kelly said you aren't a nobody. He said you are a prime suspect. The way I hear it. You are a huge question mark."

I shook my head and said, "I'm really not. I just want to be left alone."

I breathed in and breathed out. I felt the fatigue in my breaths. Every time I inhaled, I felt lightheaded, and I even fought off a yawn. Not good. It meant that I was so tired, not even adrenaline was waking me up.

In the SEALs, we had four important points in hand-to-hand combat. First, protect your face; second, stay standing and keep moving; third, hit hard; and last, haul ass. I added my own personal points to it, which means that I threw out three of theirs.

The first and the second points are second nature to a SEAL— no need to worry about protecting my face when I just protected everything. For the second one, I tried to dance around as much as possible. And the fourth one I always threw out. I didn't run. Not my style. Not when I was alone. Better to execute your opponents first. Take them out of commission, and there's no need to haul ass.

My personal favorite was the third point. Hit hard. So I did. There was no need to talk this out.

The MP said, "Kelly told you to stay in town. If you aren't with Turik, then why you running away?"

I didn't strike right off the bat. The MP was the biggest guy and military trained. And the other three had been drinking. That was apparent because I'd smelled the booze on them.

Therefore, the MP would be the toughest opponent. Best to take him out first. He spoke some more, but I ignored him, concentrated on my tactics. I looked over my left shoulder, clocked the other three guys with my eyes.

The MP said, "I asked you a question. I'm not gonna ask again."

At least that's what I thought he was going to say, because I palm-struck him straight in the big nose—fast, like a bolt pistol used to fire one quick bolt into the brain of cattle for the slaughter. The strike stunned him, which wasn't surprising because his nose had been a big target.

The guy to my left was my next target. I shifted, fast to the left. I fired a right cross, fist closed, and from my hip. The guy moved on his feet, dancing left, turning his head—instinctively. I busted a big fist into his left ear. It was hard, not as hard as the palm strike had been, but I knew it did major damage. Maybe busted his eardrum, or at least rang a loud bell in his head.

The quiet guy that had been to my right was a surprise; he was now behind me. He wasn't a big guy but wasn't small either. He was wiry and fast on his feet. He leaped on me from behind, locked his arm around my neck. He started a rear choke hold. He had strong arms and a powerful grip.

I struggled, weaved around, but he had me.

He spun me to the fat guy. The fat guy said, "You're gonna pay for that."

He fired a right jab at me. Jabs are the weakest punch. They come straight out and back in. There was not much shoulder or core thrown in. Therefore, there's little momentum.

I didn't wait for his jab. I rocked back on my feet and catapulted forward. The guy behind me was skilled but had no mass about him. He felt around one hundred seventy-five pounds at the most. I was lighter than I'd been in years, but I still had fifty pounds or more on him. I lifted him off his feet and wrenched him forward. The fat guy's fist skimmed by my face and caught the guy over my shoulder, right in his eye. Which stunned him, and he loosened his grip. I had pulled him far over my back enough so that when the fat guy jabbed him in the face, I jumped back from bent knees. I came up off my feet and used my weight plus gravity. We landed in a heap back on the hard, cold concrete. I tried to ball myself up so that he'd feel all my weight in his stomach.

The blow was bad. The guy let out a gasp and even spit up blood. My head had slammed back into his when we hit the ground, like dropping a cannonball onto a watermelon. It wasn't pretty. He spat out a couple of teeth.

I rolled as fast as I could and hopped back up to my feet.

The fat guy looked at me. The odds had shifted. And his expression changed drastically.

The guy who used to be at the nine o'clock position was getting back up. I waited for him to get on all fours, but I stared at the fat guy. I pretended not to notice the nine o'clock guy. I took a step toward the fat guy, and he backed away. The nine o'clock guy was back on his feet.

I turned quickly and kicked him right in the nuts. He screeched like a bird and toppled forward, hands grabbing his groin in a desperate attempt to save what was left.

I turned and looked at the fat guy. I said, "Now, it's just you and me."

I saw fear on his face, and then I felt the adrenaline. It was a little late, but it was there.

"Don't. Don't ya hurt me," he said.

"I warned you," I said.

"We were only tryin' to scare ya. We just wanted answers."

"I'd say you got an answer. Do you know what the lesson here is?"

He shook his head and backed up into the front of an SUV. I stopped a few feet from him. He said, "What? What's the lesson?"

"You assumed that you knew me. You assumed that you measured me up. You assumed that I had something to do with your friends getting killed. And you assumed that you four would be enough to take me on. You were wrong."

He nodded, stayed quiet.

"Get your facts straight next time."

He nodded frantically.

"You know what happens now?"

"You … You gonna hurt me?"

I faked him out like I was going to throw a right cross, but I stopped it.

He flinched, even raised his hands to defend his face.

"Relax, I'm not interested in you. Better avoid me from now on. You see me coming; you turn tail. Got it?"

He nodded and said, "I got it."

"That goes for your friends here too. Make sure they understand it."

I turned and walked away, didn't look back.

CHAPTER 15

could've waited back at the bus stop. I could've been on my way out of town, but I decided I didn't want to be in the area if someone had called the local police. I'd had enough of handcuffs and cops for one day. In case they were looking for me, I thought, *Where's the last place they'd expect to find me?*

I sat back in the same diner that I was in earlier. I sat at a different booth this time, but the same waitress was there. She came over to my table and said, "You?" like a question.

I nodded and said, "Coffee."

"Did the cops talk to you?"

I nodded again, said, "I already spoke with them. Don't worry. I'm not mad at you."

She nodded and asked, "You want something to eat?"

"Just the coffee."

She walked away. I wasn't sure what I was going to do. I could return to the motel and demand that the guy give me another room, but I didn't leave him with the best impression of me. I doubted he'd forgive me so quickly. I couldn't sleep on the bus stop bench anymore. My only option was to try and get a ride out of town or wait here all day and then walk back to the bus stop after dark.

Karen returned with the coffee. She said, "I'm real sorry for reporting you to the cops."

"Don't worry about it. I already told you I'm not mad. You're just doing your civic duty."

She nodded.

I started to look out the window. Then I turned back to her and asked, "Have you ever seen that guy before?"

"Oh yeah. I work five shifts a week. And he comes in here for the last three of them. Every week. Always sits at the same booth."

"Three times?"

"Yeah."

"Same times?"

"That's right. Early morning before he goes to the base. I guess."

"He ever come in here with anyone?"

"Oh, no way!"

"Why did you say it like that?"

"Like what?"

"You said it like it wasn't possible for him to come in here with someone."

"You know. 'Cause he's one of them."

"What?"

"He's a Muslim," she said and shifted her weight to one foot. She peered around the diner like she was looking to see if anyone heard her.

I nodded, stayed quiet.

"I don't mean nothing bad by it. No one here mistreats him or anything. We just don't have any of them around here. It's unusual."

"Hamber's a small town."

"Right. Most of the people been here their entire lives. People don't leave here. Not normally."

"What about the Marines?"

"Oh, they are all from out of town."

"Then, not everyone here is from here."

"Not everyone. I mean the locals."

"Turik was the only Muslim Marine that you saw in here?"

She nodded. It wasn't unusual to have a Muslim soldier, not in the sense of being a rarity. It wasn't typical, I supposed. But I had known a few in my time in the service.

I asked, "How do you know he was the only one?"

"You know. Because he was Iraqi or whatever."

"You mean he was Arab?"

She shrugged and said, "Whatever."

"Did he ever speak to you? Small talk or anything?"

"Oh, sure. He was a nice guy. Normally."

"You mean he acted differently this morning?"

She nodded.

"What about his uniform?"

"What about it?"

"Did he ever come in here wearing it before?"

"Oh, sure. He always went straight to work after here."

I asked, "He wore the BDUs?"

She had a blank look on her face.

"He wore his woodland-pattern uniform? The camouflage outfit that he was wearing this morning?"

She looked up at the ceiling for a quick moment, like she was pulling up files in her brain. Then she said, "You know. I don't think so. Normally, he wears a different uniform. I think. Like *An Officer and a Gentleman*."

"Solid color?"

"Yeah. Like an officer."

"He ever come in here with his gun belt on before?"

"No. I can't be sure, but I don't think I've seen him wearing that before either. He was totally weird this morning. I knew something was up."

I was quiet for a long moment, and she waited like she knew the conversation wasn't over.

I asked, "What about his friends? You know anything about that?"

She shook her head.

"What about his job?"

"What about it?"

"He ever talk about his duties?"

"Oh, sure. Nothing top-secret. Or anything like that. But he told me things. Actually, now that I think about it. I suppose I'm the closest thing he had to a friend here."

"What did he say about his job?"

She thought again and looked up again.

I said, "Try to remember."

She said, "He said once that he was a teacher. On the base. Which makes sense. It's a training base."

I stayed quiet.

"He taught language. You know, he taught the soldiers to speak Arabic."

I thought for a moment. That didn't sound right. She must've been wrong about what he taught. Or he lied to her. The Marine Corps wouldn't waste an Arabic language instructor at Arrow's Peak. No way. Why the hell would guys that were training in mountain warfare need to know Arabic? But I didn't press the issue. Then I thought about it again. And I realized why they'd have a native speaker here teaching the Arabic languages. They were training for missions in Afghanistan. They had mountains. They even had snow.

She said, "I told all of this to the cops."

"What about his wife?"

"His wife?"

"You know anything about her?"

"No. I didn't even know he was married."

I nodded. That didn't mean anything. But someone in town must've seen her.

"Thanks. You can bring the check. I'm only going to have the coffee."

She turned and walked away. I stared out the window. I watched the cars pass by. I saw a blue Nissan Maxima barrel down the road. Then it stopped and U-turned and went back in the other direction like the driver was lost. I ignored it and stared up at the gray sky.

CHAPTER 16

Karen said, "You want a refill?"

I opened my eyes, completely unaware of where the hell I was for a moment. I squinted, hard, and tried to focus. I was still in the diner, but I'd fallen asleep at the table. My eyes were very heavy, like being wakened up way back during my first week training to be a SEAL. Hell Week, we called it.

The instructors would wait until four a.m., and then they'd wake us all up at the same time by tossing flash-bangs into the barracks. They stormed our quarters with smoke grenades too. It wasn't a fun week. Hell Week was when most candidates dropped out of the training. It was just about the worst week of my life, which was the point.

I said, "Yeah. Sorry."

She started to walk away, and I said, "Wait. How long have I been asleep?"

She said, "It's afternoon. I'm not sure when you first closed your eyes, but I'd guess at least an hour. I didn't want to disturb you, but we don't allow patrons to sleep in here. You know."

I looked around, and the place had several tables full. I nodded.

"Maybe if it was late at night. I'd let you sleep."

"It's okay."

She turned to walk away, and I said, "Wait. Forget the refill."

She nodded.

I stared down at the table, saw that she had left the bill. I tossed some money on it and decided I'd better walk around.

I left the diner and headed back in the direction toward downtown.

CHAPTER 17

I had time to kill. I decided to keep moving. I didn't want to stay in Hamber any longer. Romey had asked me to stick around, but she was a military cop. Technically, I had the right to travel—no sense in getting any more involved than I already was.

I walked through the town, past the church again, and out toward the highway.

I started thinking about what Kelly had said. He'd told me that Turik fired eight rounds, and one bullet was unaccounted for. Eight? Not seven. Not six, but eight.

Six people were dead, not seven, which indicated that Turik had probably killed his wife.

I shrugged to myself. I came to a four-way stop and a light. Vehicles passed me on both sides, but there were more incoming than outgoing. I looked at one of them. It was a blue panel van with a news station's call sign plastered along the side.

Great, I thought. The local media was here, which meant that they must've picked up the story or were told that there was a story. A local probably called them—some local citizen looking to sell the story, I figured.

Keep moving, Widow, I told myself.

Turik had been a decorated officer, Romey had told me. They suspected somehow that he was involved with ISIS, which had been calling out to Muslims all over the world to commit acts of terrorism. And shooting innocent people for no reason was a part of their MO. No question. They'd committed acts of gun violence in Paris, blown up airports in Belgium and Turkey, and carried out the mass shooting in Orlando not long ago.

It made sense. A Muslim officer in the United States Marine Corps made the perfect target to recruit. I imagined the headlines once word got out. I imagined the national media. I imagined the talking heads on TV. Pundits commenting and fighting over topics of gun violence and then religion and immigration. People would be afraid. The fear-mongers would spread fear and do exactly what groups like ISIS had wanted.

I kept walking. I saw another big-rig truck hauling bullets or whatever. The side of the truck read *Lexigun*.

About twenty minutes later, I was a good way out of town, and my adrenaline was winding down. I started to feel fatigued again.

A blue Nissan Maxima drove by me heading west out of town. It was the same one that I'd seen earlier. I watched its brake lights flare on, and then it made a sloppy U-turn like before and headed back in my direction.

I stopped on the shoulder and watched the Nissan pass me and swivel around with another sloppy U-turn. The car came up beside me and stopped.

The passenger side window buzzed down. I half squatted down and looked in.

The driver was a dark-skinned woman with thick black hair, slick, straight back. She was about my age. She had huge brown eyes, glassy like she'd been crying all morning. She wore no makeup, which she didn't need. At first glance, she had a flawless face. I couldn't tell how tall she was because she was seated, but she had long arms. And her seat was pushed back farther than most female drivers, which made me think that either she was tall or she had big wooden blocks strapped to her pedals. Which was plausible, I supposed, but unlikely. She had a gangly body, which was genetics. I imagined her to be a runner.

I said, "Hello. You headed out of town?"

I thought she was stopping to offer me a ride. Then I noticed that she wasn't alone. In the back seat, a small boy looked up at me. He looked to be about five or six years old. He wore a patterned T-shirt with one of those new comic book movie characters on it underneath a tightly wound white scarf and a green winter coat that was at least one size too big for him. Maybe he was meant to grow into it.

He wore a little baseball cap with two orange letters and logo all on a black background—the San Francisco Giants. *Good team, once*, I thought. But like the 49ers, they had been a complete disappointment to me in the last decade or so.

The little boy looked up at me, with big brown eyes like the woman driver's. In fact, he was a little replica of her, except that he had curly, fair hair. She must've been his mother, and there must've been a fair-haired father somewhere.

The woman said, "Are you him?"

"Him? Who?"

She said, "Widow?"

I said, "Do I know you?"

"It is you?"

I nodded.

"Get in."

I stayed where I was and asked, "Who are you?"

She said, "I'm Maya Harris. Turik is my brother."

CHAPTER 18

Maya Harris looked like she was bundled up in two layers of clothes. A sweater under a short coat and a green scarf wrapped over twice, like a big green snake choking her to death. She had wire-rimmed glasses with thin lenses, almost like she was barely off the mark of twenty-twenty vision. She was a little underfed, a little too thin, but not in a sick way, just a little too lean. I could see it in her face and cheeks, but she was attractive.

She said, "I've been looking for you."

I paused a beat and then asked, "How'd you find me?"

"The waitress at the diner. She told me about you."

"She told you about me?"

Maya nodded.

That waitress sure did like to run her mouth about me. Small towns.

I looked back at the little boy. He stared at me with utter confusion in his eyes. He was clean and healthy-looking and well-behaved. He didn't ask questions. Maybe he was a little shy because there was a new face in his life, my long concrete-looking face. I could only imagine what I looked like to a kid his age.

Maya spoke again. "She said you were the last person to talk to my brother. I didn't tell her that he is my brother, of course. I just asked her if she knew a Marine who was Muslim. I figured he would stand out in a place like this."

I stayed quiet.

She said, "I've been looking for him."

"What made you stop at the diner? Why not go to his house?"

"I drove by his house, but there are police cars everywhere. And police tape. And soldiers."

"Marines," I said.

"What?"

"They're not soldiers. They're Marines."

"I don't know the difference."

"It doesn't matter."

"I saw the Marines, and I didn't know where to go. I drove around town. I stopped at the diner. Everything else seemed closed. I asked the waitress what was going on. I told her that I saw the Marines everywhere."

I nodded. Hamber wasn't the smallest town that I'd ever seen —far from it. But it was small enough for a coincidence like that to be believable. Plus, I had also noticed the local businesses were closed because of the Danner funeral.

"What can I do for you?"

"Can you get in?"

I stopped and looked both ways. She was headed out of town, which was where I wanted to go. Getting in the car meant that I was getting more involved, which was what I didn't want. I got in anyway, front seat. I turned back and smiled at the boy quickly.

I shut the door and felt the heat blasting me in the face. I looked around the front interior of the car. It was clean and new. There was a car rental sticker on the windshield. The carpets were vacuumed, and the seats were wiped and oiled.

I said, "I'm sorry about your brother, but like I told the MPs, I didn't know him."

"Can we go somewhere? I don't want to talk about it here in the car. In front of my son." Then she paused a beat and said, "Oh, sorry. This is my son, Christopher. Chris, say hello."

I looked back at Chris again, and he smiled and said, "Hi."

I put my hand out for him to shake, which he did. I said, "Nice to meet you, Chris."

"Nice to meet you, sir."

I let go of his hand, and he went back to just staring out the window. I turned to Maya Harris and said, "Sure. I guess so. We can go somewhere, but the only place I know of is the diner."

"What about your motel?"

"Don't have one."

She took a deep breath and said, "Let's get out of town. There's another roadside diner about twenty miles southwest. I saw it on my way in."

"Sure. Whatever you want," I said. Southwest was as good as any direction to me since it was out of Hamber.

We drove in silence, except for the occasional small talk for the better part of about thirty minutes. Occasionally, we slowed for vehicles turning across the highway, and there was one traffic light that seemed to be at the intersection of two highways, but there was no sign of civilization on either side.

We finally reached the roadside diner that she was talking about. It was set back off from the highway so far that I wouldn't have called it a roadside diner.

The structure was a one-story desert-colored building with a dark brown roof the color of coffee.

Harris pulled into the lot, which was all gravel and white shells. She drove up to the side of the diner and parked. She said nothing, just killed the engine and got out. I followed suit, and so did Chris.

We walked in together, and a young girl who looked like she should've been in high school greeted us. She said, "Hello. Are you guys looking for a table?"

Harris said, "Please."

The girl smiled and took two menus out of a wooden cubby and led us across a dining room and into an addition that seemed like it came much later after the main room, like an afterthought. The diner was about half full. Mostly truckers seated alone at their own tables. There was no countertop space like at the Wagon Hash.

The hostess took us into a less populated area of the diner and sat us at a booth near the back windows. Through the windows, we could see a great view of the mountains and tops of the forest.

We sat, and the waitress came. She took our orders, which for me was just coffee; for Harris, green tea; and for Chris, Maya ordered a soda and fries.

The waitress frowned at the simplicity of our order but brought the coffee, the tea, and the soda, and left us.

Maya reached in her purse for a moment, dug out a Game Boy or some portable gaming device, and gave it to her son. He slipped a pair of earbuds in and started playing.

I took a sip of the coffee. It wasn't bad. Better than the coffee at the diner back in Hamber and far better than the coffee at the Marine base. That was for damn sure.

Finally, Harris said, "Mr. Widow, I know that you don't know my brother."

I nodded.

"But you spoke to him last. Can I ask, why did you do that? The waitress didn't know."

I ignored the question and said, "Did you talk with the MPs?"

"They won't see me."

"That's not what they told me. When I spoke to them, they were very eager to talk with you."

"I went to the base. Of course, I did. That was the first place I drove to."

"And?"

"They wouldn't let me on the base."

"You told the guard at the gate?"

"Of course! I told him who I was. I told him that Turik was my baby brother. He dismissed me, asked if I was a reporter. I told him I wasn't. Then he said he didn't believe me."

I looked out the window for a moment. I shook my head. I said, "That doesn't sound right. The guard at the gate. What did he look like?"

She shrugged and said, "I don't know. He looked like a soldier. He was big."

"Did he have any features that stuck out to you? Think about his face."

She shook her head, said, "I can't remember."

"What about his nose?"

"Nose?"

"Yeah. Anything that you remember about it?"

She said, "I guess. The guy had a big nose."

I nodded.

She said, "Like really big."

I nodded, said, "About what time did you go there?"

"That was the first place I went after his house. I've been driving around looking for you all afternoon."

"How long since you were at the base?"

She thought for a moment and looked at her watch. She said, "It's two thirty now. I'd say I was there around noon."

"How long have you been in town?"

"I don't know. Since eleven. I rented a car and headed straight here."

"From San Francisco?"

"Yes."

"Your brother shot and killed five people around seven thirty this morning."

She nodded. Her eyes began to tear up.

"If you didn't know what he did, then why come?"

"I got a message from him."

"What message?"

"I was at home. I got a video message from Jimmy. I called him back—immediately. I called his cell, his house phone, and the phone he called me from. No answer. So I rented a car and rushed here. Only it was too late. The guard at the gate told me that he'd killed five people."

She paused a beat, and then she said, "I just can't believe it! I can't believe he'd do that!"

I noticed that she'd called him Jimmy. Not James. Not Muhammad, but Jimmy, which implied a kind of big sister feeling for him. I asked, "Maya, what video message?"

She didn't answer. She just looked away, out the window, and then back at her son.

I said, "The MPs there should be talking to you, not me. You should try to go back."

"I can't. They never gave me a business card or anything. I don't want to help them. I should be talking to Jimmy's lawyer. Don't they give him a JAG lawyer?"

"Technically, no. JAG isn't for Marines. They have JAD."

She looked at me.

"It's basically the same thing. JAG is for every other branch of the military. The Marine Corps has to be special. So they got their own thing."

"Whatever. But that's who he needs right now. He needs a lawyer. I want to talk to him."

I stared at her. Confusion must've been obvious on my face because she said, "What?"

"Why are you asking about his lawyer? That's not going to do him any good."

She said, "He has a right to a fair trial. Right? Just like we do as citizens."

I realized that she didn't know that he was dead. I leaned forward, slid my coffee mug out of the way, and took her hand. I said, "Maya, Turik is dead."

CHAPTER 19

"I knew it!" she said over and over. "I knew it! I knew it! I knew it!"

Chris quit the Game Boy and looked at her but didn't speak. He looked at me, eyes puzzled.

She started to cry, but not hard. She was tough. I'd seen sailors cry harder. She looked away and let the tears roll out of her eyes and down her cheek. She looked out the window, stared over the snowy, green landscape. Then she turned back to me and wiped her face.

My hand on top of hers dwarfed her tiny hand, like it had completely vanished underneath mine.

Chris looked at my hand and reached out and did the same. His pint-sized hand barely took up any landscape on the back of mine.

Maya stopped crying and smiled at me and then at her son. She calmed her breathing and said, "Thanks. I …"

But she stopped and was still a little choked up. We broke our hands apart, and she reached out to her son and hugged him.

I said, "Take your time. I'm sorry. I thought that you knew."

She didn't respond to that. Instead, she said, "I'm not close to my family. I haven't spoken to my sisters or parents in years. Turik and I kept in touch, but we had only recently become close. I heard from him about six months ago. Out of the blue. He wanted a relationship. He started to email me, and sometimes we FaceTimed."

I nodded, thought back to the years that I hadn't spoken to my own mother. That was something I regretted, a relationship that I'd never get to revive because she had been murdered.

She said, "Do you know how he died? Did they kill him? Did he suffer?"

I stared at her son. He seemed unaffected by the news. The only thing that affected him was that his mother was crying. He was at that age where death was still a misunderstood ambiguity, like the question of where babies came from. So I used a word that I hoped he didn't know. I said, "Suicide, Maya."

She was quiet again, looked away.

"You really should speak with the MPs."

"I tried. I told you."

"I know. But I think you should try again. I wouldn't worry about that one not letting you in. I doubt he'll be there."

She drank some of her tea and said, "The thing is, if he's dead, then I shouldn't meet with the MPs. At least not voluntarily. No, I should avoid that meeting."

"Why not?"

She paused a long, long beat.

"Why not?" I repeated.

"No. Meeting with them is a mistake. I have to think about myself now. I have a son. I have to think about him. I can't bring Jimmy back."

"What do you mean?"

"I've got a career to think about."

I stayed quiet.

She said, "Look. I changed my name many years ago to Maya Harris. It's not my birth name."

I nodded. Romey had told me that.

Harris wiped the remaining tears from her face and said, "Harris is my ex-husband's name, and Maya isn't my birth name."

I nodded and waited.

"The reason I changed it is because of my work. And because of my religion. Or rather lack thereof. I'm from a Muslim family."

I took a pull from my coffee and watched her eyes, a technique that I'd learned in the NCIS. Eye contact was a simple thing, but it was one of the most valuable weapons in a cop's arsenal. The eyes are the windows to the soul, after all. You do something that distracts and relaxes the other person, like drinking from a coffee mug. Make things seem routine, not a big deal. We're just friends talking. And they let their guard down. I wasn't doing it on purpose. I wasn't suspecting Maya of lying to me. It was more out of habit than anything.

She said, "I'm not a Muslim. I'm an atheist. A fact that troubled my parents. When Jimmy and I were little, I was in an arranged marriage situation. Can you imagine?"

She took another drink from her tea. Then she pulled her phone out of her pocket and checked the time on it. She must've forgotten about her watch. I'd seen a lot of people do this. I didn't have a cell phone or a watch.

She got a text message as if it was on cue. She tilted it and read the text to herself in one short glance. It was a quick, unimportant text, I guess. Maybe it was from her husband or ex-husband, a text asking where she was or if she was okay. She made no indication that it was important.

I said, "I can. I was in the service. I knew a lot of different types of people—all walks of life. The military is like that. I've met Muslims and Hindus; both had arranged marriages in their cultures."

She nodded and said, "I wasn't the family favorite growing up. I was constantly questioning everything: our religion, our father's control over us. After I graduated from high school, I was supposed to marry this guy my father picked out. And I bolted. I never looked back. Six months ago, my brother wrote to me. Of course, our father is so proud of him. Or at least he was. But my brother told me a secret."

I listened, stayed quiet.

She said, "He wasn't a Muslim. He was also an atheist. He'd been pretending for years. Just doing the right thing. I suppose."

"That must've been tough on him."

"It was."

I said, "Maya. I don't want to be insensitive, but why did he do it, then?"

"What do you mean?"

"The MPs are thinking this is ISIS. Like a terrorist thing. But if your brother wasn't Muslim, then he wouldn't have been involved with an Islamic terrorist group. Atheists don't tend to side with extremists."

She shook her head, and then she said, "He wasn't."

I asked, "Maya, what did he say in this video message that he sent you?"

She looked around the room like she was making sure that no one could hear. She said, "I got it this morning."

She had already said that, but I didn't interrupt her.

She paused a beat and then said, "First, he called me. Three times. Right in a row, but I didn't recognize the number, so I ignored it. It wasn't from his phone. I was in the shower. When I got out, I saw that he had left me a video message."

I stayed quiet.

She didn't explain. She just reached into her purse and pulled out her phone again. She unlocked it and swiped and pressed with her finger. Then she handed it to me. She also reached into her purse and pulled out a pair of earbuds. She handed them to me as well, and said, "Watch it with these."

I nodded, took them, and plugged them into the phone's headphone jack.

I looked down at the screen. The video file was paused. I saw Turik's face in the still. He looked just as he had hours ago. I hit play.

The timer said that the video was only forty-one seconds long.

Short.

I watched it. I turned the volume on the phone all the way up.

Turik looked the same, only completely different at the same time.

He said, "Maya … Maya. I'm so sorry."

He looked up and away from the phone like he was checking to make sure that he didn't get caught by someone. Then he said, "I'm so scared."

It was true. I could see it in his face, his eyes. He was terrified. He was even visibly shaking.

Then he said, "I'm innocent. Whatever they tell you. I'm innocent."

He paused and said, "There was this guy. Widow. Jack Widow. He was a cop. He can help. Find him for … *good measure*."

I stared at the video, a little thrown off that he had mentioned my name.

He said, "Maya, I love you."

That was it. The video was over. I touched the screen and scrolled the video back to the beginning and rewatched it. This time I looked all over the screen for clues. I tried to look for reflections, background images, or anything else that would tell me where he was, because he seemed to be in a confined space. The wall behind him was painted in generic, military green. And the room was dim, not dark, but not lit up either.

The waitress came by and dropped off Chris's fries, and Maya asked for the check. She kept her eyes looking down so that the waitress wouldn't see that she'd been crying.

I waited for the waitress to walk away again. Then I closed my eyes and played the video from the beginning, listened to the sounds in the background. I listened hard. I heard his words all over again and tried to concentrate between them.

I heard ambient echoes. Then I realized that he was practically whispering. Although it wasn't an actual whisper, more like he was speaking low enough not to be heard by anyone nearby, but loud enough for the phone's microphone to pick up his voice.

I continued to listen. I paused the video and replayed it one last time. I heard the same echoing room, ambient noises, and his low voice. Then I heard something else, right at the end, right before he shut the video off.

I replayed just the last few seconds.

I concentrated hard and listened. He said, "for ... *good measure.*" And then right at the last second, right as the video cut off, I heard what sounded like a gunshot.

CHAPTER 20

I n the video, I could see Turik's hands. The background of the video appeared to be the inside of a military building, but I couldn't be sure. If Maya was telling the truth and she received this video message right after the calls that she ignored, then it was probable that Turik had recorded it right after he tried to call her.

If that was the case and he made this video from inside the command building at Arrow's Peak, then it wasn't possible that he fired that gunshot that I heard. And that was a damn fact.

I wondered how hard it would be to prove that it was a gunshot. Proving the time and location wouldn't be hard.

We stayed quiet, both sitting in silence for a long time. I pulled out the earbuds and slid the phone back to her. She leaned forward and said, "I need your help."

I said, "We need to get this to the MPs back at Arrow's Peak."

She said, "No way! We can't trust them. They already wrote my brother off as a killer."

"Can you blame them? He looks guilty. They got him on base. Probably blood all over him."

She stayed quiet, just stared at me, pleading.

I said, "Why the hell did he kill himself if he's innocent?"

She shook her head and said, "I don't know. All I know is that my brother would never do what they're saying he did."

I nodded. I wasn't quite so convinced. If he was being set up, it was intricate.

I thought about Romey and Kelly. Kelly had argued that Turik was mentally unstable. He'd argued that all mass shooters were. And mostly, he was right. But not always.

Suicide bombers are often called whack jobs, crazy people, or insane, but are they? Certainly, that was an easy thing to say. But most suicide bombers are religious. They think that what they are doing is God's work. They think that what they are doing is right.

Beliefs are funny things. Ideas can destroy worlds.

She stared at me like she was trying to choose her words wisely. Then she said, "You were a cop, right?"

I shot her a vexed look that I didn't mean to. I said, "Yeah."

"Then you have to help. You can investigate. Or whatever you need to do. Prove my brother's innocence."

I said, "I really think that the MPs can handle this. You should give it to them."

"You heard my brother. He asked for you. They won't help. They'll just say that this is an example of how crazy he was. They'll say he's just another homegrown terrorist. A Muslim terrorist."

She reached out and spread her fingers in front of me like she was trying to grab my hand but didn't touch it. She said, "You know I'm right. They already think he's another Muslim terrorist. My brother's got a purple heart. He was no terrorist!"

I thought for a moment. I said, "Okay."

She said, "Oh, thank you! Thank you!"

I nodded and said, "I'll help, but we still have to get this video to the MPs. I met them. There's a good one. We can trust her. She'll follow where the evidence leads."

Maya nodded and asked, "What do we do next?"

"After we're done here, take me back to Hamber. Take me to the base."

She nodded.

We waited for the bill. She insisted on paying it and left cash on the table.

We left the restaurant and got back into the rented car. We drove in silence. Thirty minutes later, we were back in Hamber, and ten minutes after that, we were nearing the base.

I said, "I want you to go back to San Francisco and wait. Got it?"

"Don't you think that I should stay here?"

"No. There's no reason for you to be here. Besides, where would you go?"

"I can rent a room."

"No. That's not an option. Trust me. The hotel owner won't rent to you."

"Why not?"

"Just take my word for it. It's better if you go back home and go about your day."

"Give me your number. I'll text you the video."

I said, "I don't have a phone."

She said, "Take mine, then."

"No. Keep it. I might need to call you."

"How will you show them the video?"

I said, "Give me your number. I'll call you from the phone of an MP named Romey. You can send it to her."

"Okay."

We drove another minute, and then we had to stop. Maya slowed the car and pulled over as close to the ditch as she could. We stared out the windshield.

She said, "I guess the word's out."

I looked on at a long line of panel vans and cab trucks pulling trailers with logos on the sides. People in suits and ties and professional attire crowded the street ahead. I saw cameramen and news anchors.

The media was here.

I reached over and put a hand over Maya's hand on the wheel. Then I stepped out of the car. Maya made a U-turn, and I walked to the base.

CHAPTER 21

The only gate at Arrow's Peak was still under the same guard unit—minus the one with the big nose. I imagined that he was resting up somewhere from our last meeting.

Everything else seemed the same. Same armor. Same hardware. The only difference now was that the street was lined with news vans from both the local news channels and the major networks, the twenty-four-hour news stations. The word had gotten out, and the lid was off the story. This would make controlling the story no longer a concern for Romey, but it would also mean that navigating her investigation would be infinitely harder if she was still investigating.

I imagined dozens of hungry news chiefs all over the country waiting back at their respective headquarters, but not patiently. I imagined them hounding their reporters and other staff. The news business was a horse race for stories like this.

I walked through the tight crowd of camera crews and field correspondents and news producers, all waiting for their big break, all champing at the opportunity to get the scoop.

I guessed the time was around four o'clock. I used my hands to move shoulders and traverse through people. I tried my best to stay off camera, old habit, but not particularly necessary.

I found my way to the front. There were new, thick road barriers put up on the street, and new guards added to the gate. Everyone wore the same body armor and carried the same heavy hardware from earlier. I wasn't sure that would stop the bloodthirsty reporters.

At the front of the gate, there was an invisible cone of no-man's-land, where no one was supposed to step forward, but I did.

The guards all noticed at the same time. Even the guys who guarded the exit turned and faced me abruptly.

The main guard on duty at the entrance hut walked toward me at a steady pace. He stopped about five feet from me, hands on his rifle. He said, "Stop there, sir."

I stopped, kept my breath steady, and my hands by my sides.

He said, "We're closed off today, sir. I'm going to have to ask you to return to the road."

"I'm not a reporter."

"That doesn't matter, sir. Please go back the way you came. The base is locked down today."

"Marine, I'm here to see Major Romey."

The Marine paused, looked me up and down. He said, "State the purpose."

"Just tell her that Jack Widow is here. Tell her I have information."

"I need a little more than that, sir,"

"Marine, that's all you're going to get. I suggest you get her on the horn. I suggest you don't delay."

He looked at me, seemed to debate for a long moment on the right move to make. In the end, he knew that it wasn't up to him to decide. He looked back over his shoulder at the guard hut, kept checking back on me to make sure that I wasn't moving.

He called out to his partner and said, "Baker."

Another MP leaned out of the hut and said, "Yeah?"

"Call Major Romey down here."

"Sure," the MP named Baker said. He leaned back into the guard hut and got on the phone. I saw a landline, white receiver and long white cord. After a few moments, he leaned back out and said, "She wants to know what for?"

I didn't step any closer, but I squinted to take a look at the MP's nametape. His name was Berry, like Halle Berry, the actress, only she was much better looking, in my book.

Berry said, "Tell her that there's a guy at the gate. Tell her Jack Widow needs to see her."

Baker didn't respond; he just leaned back in and got on the phone again. He spoke and then he listened. I saw him hang up the line. He stepped out and walked over to us. He held his M16 one-handed with his left hand under the magazine and the barrel. The muzzle pointed at the gravel, a safe operating position. He stopped just feet from us and said, "She wants me to escort him onto the base."

Berry looked back at Baker with surprise on his face and then stepped aside like he was giving me permission to continue.

Baker said, "Follow me, Mr. Widow."

I nodded and said, "Lead the way."

I stepped past Berry and could feel his eyes on the back of my head as I moved on.

Baker led me past the guard shack. I turned and looked back at the gate. I saw the guards, the shack, the crowd of media and vans. I also saw something that I wasn't expecting. Several of the news crews were filming me. Huge, expensive cameras were videotaping me while a few regular cameras flashed pictures. Then I realized that they probably had tele-photo lenses or at least a decent zoom.

Baker said, "This way."

He led me down the street, and we turned onto the main street. There was still no one walking the base. I guessed that Romey was keeping these guys on lockdown for the whole night. A precaution to her, but for me, I was glad. If we found evidence that Turik was innocent, then it was best to keep everyone in check.

Baker took me out to the corner of one more street and said, "Walk down that way and stop in front of the flagpole."

I said, "You're not going to take me all the way?"

"No, sir. Major Romey will pick you up there."

I nodded and followed his instructions. I started to walk. The abandoned streets and space between the buildings meant that the breeze was doubled on my face.

I looked up at the sky as I walked. The gray overcast had changed to a grayer overcast. The tree line was jagged, like sharp spears ruggedly crafted centuries ago. Snow capped the tips of the trees, and below that, I could see the branches, with no signs of foliage left.

I also saw no signs of the sun, but I knew it must've still been on the other side of the clouds because it wasn't dark out.

I scanned the tops of the buildings. I looked for the command building. I couldn't see it, but I was pretty sure which direc-tion it was in. I looked off to the east and saw a small flight tower. I couldn't see a runway, but I was sure that there was at least one, probably a helipad as well. I hoped that there was, because it would be very hard to get off base if I had to go back through the reporters.

I could see the tops of the dorms to the north. I saw several blinds moved aside and saw dozens of Marines staring back at me. They were only dots, but I could see the shapes of heads and shoulders. I imagined they were staring down at me, wondering who the hell I was. What made me so special that I got to walk around free while they were cooped up under lockdown?

Being locked up like that was bad news for them but good news for me. It meant that Romey hadn't quite closed the book on this investigation, not yet.

I saw the flag, still at half-mast. I stared at it. The cold breeze washed over me and below the flag. It whipped and sputtered like clothes hanging on a line outside. It reminded me of being at sea. The sound of Old Glory whipping like that always reminded me of what America stood for. The American flag didn't need to speak. It always said the same thing, without words. I believed that it spoke the same words to me as it did every sailor, soldier, and Marine on the planet. I believed it said the same words to every American all over the world. I believed that it spoke the same words to everyone. It said words like *bravery, compassion, tolerance, democracy,* and *freedom*.

I doubted that the flag could even represent any other words. It spoke to me without measure.

I looked back down at the street and saw one of the black police Chargers headed my way.

It cruised the speed limit, even though there was no one else on the road and even though it was a police car. It had to be Romey. She was a by-the-book cop.

And it was Romey. She pulled up on the opposite side of the street and parked the car. I had expected her to buzz her window down and talk to me, but she didn't. Instead, she parked the car, left the engine running, and stepped out.

She put her hand over her eyes like a visor, which I thought must've been a habit, because there certainly was no sun in her eyes. She stared at me. She even looked both ways before she started to walk over to me.

I walked to her, and we met in the center of the street, right on the yellow line.

I said, "Romey."

"What are you doing here, Widow?"

"I wanted to see you again."

She smiled, lowered her hand, and reached it out to shake mine like we were meeting for the first time. I took her hand in mine. It was warm, and she had no gloves on.

She wore her camo uniform. She had an armband that said, "MP." She wasn't wearing body armor. Her hair was up in a bun, military regulation. She looked good.

I saw the veins in her wrist and felt the hard work that she put into her arms at the gym. It reflected in her handshake.

I said, "Really, we need to talk."

She said, "Shoot."

We stopped shaking hands, and I said, "Don't you want to talk back at the station?"

"Why? Is it serious?"

"I'd say so."

"I think it's better that we talk here."

I said, "Why?"

"It just is."

I stared at her eyes and said, "Who's at the station?"

She said, "Never mind that. What do you need to tell me?"

"Who is it?"

She was quiet for a beat. She looked right and then left like she was looking around for spies. Then she said, "There are some guys here."

"What guys?"

"I can't tell you."

"You already know that you can trust me."

She looked around again, thinking about it. Then she said, "They're from Secret Service and probably the State Department too."

"Secret Service? What the hell for? Why would the US Secret Service be here?"

She said, "It's not the US Secret Service."

I said, "I thought you said it was?"

"No. I said the Secret Service. I never said the United States Secret Service."

"I'm confused."

"It's another secret service."

"Another secret service?"

She nodded and said, "There are guys in my station. Some secret service and some State Department and some … Well, some with no credentials."

"What do you mean?" I asked. I stepped closer, not because I was afraid of someone listening in on our conversation. There was no one to listen. The streets were so empty that if a tumbleweed blew by, I wouldn't have been surprised.

"If you were the kinda cop that I think you were, then your guess is better than mine."

I looked above her head for a moment and stared at the building past her. Then I made eye contact with her and said, "DOD."

She nodded and said, "Probably."

"The secret service is foreign?"

"You got it."

"What do they want?"

She shrugged.

I said, "Come on. I know you know."

"I can't tell you. You know that."

"You already know that you can trust me, right?"

"No, I don't. All I know is you used to be somebody. Trust has got to be earned."

"I used to be somebody? You mean I'm nobody now?"

She said, "You said it yourself. You're just passing through. I asked you to help. You turned me down."

"That was because I knew you could handle it. No reason to get myself any more involved."

"Now you think I can't?"

"That's not it."

"What is it then?"

I said, "I got something."

"What?"

"I got something major."

"What could possibly be major now? Like you said, Turik killed five Marines and then himself, so the case is basically closed."

"I got a video."

She perked up and looked right into my eyes. She was a beautiful woman, rough around the edges, but I liked that sort of woman.

She asked, "You got the video confession?"

Normally, an ISIS operative is nothing more than a scared and confused teenager. Operatives are promised certain bonuses by ISIS after they commit martyrdom. They're promised that they will be remembered as heroes of Allah and that their wives and mothers will be given large sums of money.

Often, they make a confession video before their deaths. They confess on tape what they plan to do. They confess what targets they plan to blow up. And all of it is in the name of Allah.

This was the type of video that Romey was asking about.

I said, "No. It's not that kind of video. But it is from Turik."

"Where?"

"I'm guessing that he filmed it here."

"No. I mean, where is the video?"

"Bring me on as a consultant."

"What? No way. Not with all the people here."

I said, "Aren't you the ranking officer?"

She said, "Technically. But I have to answer to someone who answers to someone who outranks both of us, Commander."

"True, but you still can."

"How's that?"

"Don't tell him. No one on base will argue with you."

She didn't answer that. She said, "Why do you want to help now?"

"Maya Harris."

"You called her? We've tried to reach her."

"I didn't call her. I saw her. She was here in town. She's driving back to San Francisco now."

"Why? She should be here. Talking with me."

"I know. She came to the base earlier, but the guard wouldn't let her pass. And she wants to help, but she's got her career and her child to think of. Her brother's dead. Dragging her own name through the mud won't bring him back, and with the media here, they will connect the dots. Someone somewhere will find out she's his sister and implicate her. Her whole career is based on her views on religion. She's worried if word gets out that her brother was an ISIS terrorist, then no one will hire her. She'll be out in the cold."

Romey looked away and nodded. She said, "Okay, show me the video."

"Let me see your phone."

"For what?"

"She's got it on her phone. I'll have her text it to you."

Romey took her phone out of her pocket. It was a BlackBerry and not one of those new ones. It was an older model with a big keyboard. I held it in my hand and said, "Why do you still have this?"

"I don't like smartphones."

"Isn't this a smartphone?"

"You know what I mean. I'm talking about the iPhones everybody else has."

I said, "Don't forget about the Samsungs and LGs and Nokias."

"I don't like any of them."

I handed the phone back to her and said, "You call her. I can't use one of these."

"Why not? Are you more technologically illiterate than me? Weren't you a SEAL?"

"I can't use it because the keys are too small."

She nodded and said, "You mean your fingers are too big."

I said, "You flirting with me?"

"I don't think so."

"What do you call it then? Being mean?"

"What's the matter, sailor? Can't take a little flack?"

I stayed quiet.

She said, "Give me the number."

I gave her the number and she dialed. She waited and got an answer. She introduced herself and told Maya that I was here with her.

I couldn't hear Maya, but I imagined her professing that her brother was innocent. I saw Romey nod and listen for a few moments. And finally, Romey gave Maya some reassurances: "We'll do what we can," and so on. Then she hung up.

"She's sending it now. She sounds nice."

"She is."

Romey's phone vibrated, signaling her that she had an incoming message. I wasn't sure how this model of Black-

Berry would play a video file, but I'm sure Romey had some kind of app on there that would do it.

She watched the video, and forty-one seconds later, she said, "Oh my God!"

"He might be innocent."

"Not that. I know where he is."

"Where?"

"It's General Carl's private bathroom."

CHAPTER 22

"Get in the car," Romey ordered.

The one thing that I liked more than working with a strong woman like Romey was being ordered around by one. Some kind of ancient slave gene in me, I guess. Maybe long ago, my ancestors had been big guys, the kind who carried the queen on her mobile throne like in ancient Greece.

I jumped in the car and she gassed it. It was the first time that I'd seen her not be so uptight about procedure. She gassed hard, not super hard, just got us moving faster than she normally drove. I'd guess over the speed limit, but not break-neck speed or anything.

Neither of us wore a seat belt. She took the curves wildly and didn't stop at a single stop sign.

Within moments, we were on the street with the command building.

The guards were still in place. They recognized her and waved us through the checkpoint.

I said, "I need to see it too."

"You will."

We stopped in the street in front of the command building just as Kelly had done this morning.

Romey said, "Open the glove box."

I leaned forward and popped the box open.

"There's a visitor's badge in there. Grab it."

I reached in and sifted through some clipped-together papers until I found a visitor's pass on a lanyard. I looked at it. It read, "Police Visitor." Which I had never seen before but was self-explanatory.

Romey had hopped out of the car without saying another word. She scrambled back to the trunk. She must've pushed a button on her key ring because I heard the trunk lid pop open. I got out and shut the door, walked around to stand next to her over the open trunk.

She said, "Put these on when we get inside."

She handed me a pair of blue plastic gloves. She took some for herself and shut the trunk.

I said, "Did you guys already do forensics?"

"Just the basics. There was no need to do anything more."

"You guys just assumed he was guilty."

She stopped halfway in the grass up to the command building and looked at me. She said, "So did you."

I nodded and said, "You're right. He looked guilty."

"He still does."

I almost said the old cliché that you can't judge a book by its cover, but then I thought better of it. She already knew.

I followed her to the front door. We passed where Turik shot himself.

She looked at it and said, "That's where he died."

"I know. Kelly took me by here earlier."

"I know. I asked him to."

"Why?"

"Figured it would scare you into leaving town."

I said, "You wanted me to leave?"

She opened the glass door to the front entrance and motioned for me to go first. I didn't argue and I walked through.

She followed after me.

CHAPTER 23

The command building was only two stories, but it was long.

I was staring down a long hallway. It reminded me of breaking into a school during winter break, which I had done once with a friend. We didn't get caught, but years later, I found out that he was in prison for breaking and entering, whereas I'd been employed to do undercover work. And sometimes I had to break into places where I wasn't wanted.

My skillset had landed me a career. His had landed him in a cell with a prison sentence. Life is full of twists and turns.

I whispered, "I feel like I should have a gun."

"Why?"

"I don't know. Crime scene. It's quiet. Just a habit, I guess."

She asked, "Why are you whispering, Widow?"

I hadn't realized that I was doing it, but she was right. I didn't answer.

Romey took the lead and walked through a metal detector and security station. Of course, it was unmanned. The entire building was empty, like the streets.

She said, "Follow me."

The metal detector was off and didn't beep when she walked through it. I followed her, and she led me halfway down the long hall and stopped at a staircase that led up.

The lights were all on. No one had bothered to turn them off.

She led the way up the stairs, and I followed. I got a little too close, and she caught me looking at her in a nonprofessional manner, but an entirely natural one for any man. And I was, after all, only a man.

She said, "Hey."

"Sorry. Accident," I lied.

"Sure."

We continued on and went up to the top floor.

She stopped in the hallway and said, "Put on the gloves."

More orders. I still didn't complain.

I started to slip on the first glove. She watched and said, "Those are the biggest size I had."

I wasn't sure it would fit, but it did. I said, "It's snug, but it should work fine."

She nodded and said, "This way."

We walked slowly. The first murder scenes that we came to were in the hall. They were marked with chalk outlines and crime scene number markers. Two victims were shot in the hallway in front of the staircase.

He had shot them in the back, Kelly had said.

The top of the staircase didn't provide any cover for that. I turned and looked down at the other end of the hall. The hallway was brightly lit, like the first floor. Then I saw an office across the hall, about fifteen feet down on the opposite side. I walked over to it.

Romey said, "This way."

She walked with her back to me toward General Carl's office. But I kept going the other direction.

She stopped and watched me. She said, "Where are you going?"

"I'm looking."

I stepped carefully. There was broken glass from a door that used to separate the office across the hall. I looked through it. It was an automatic glass door that was still on. As soon as I stepped near it, the sensor kicked in, and the doors slid open. The rest of the hanging glass broke off as the door fought to swipe into its recoil position.

I looked down at the floor. The tile in the hallway was big square blocks colored white. The floor inside of the office was carpet.

I looked up at the wall outside the door. There was a plaque that read, "Colonel Jessop M. Warren."

I stepped through the door, past the glass. It was broken from the inside out. The office's first room was a receptionist's area with a couple of chairs set up against the wall as a place for visitors to wait.

There was no sign of a disturbance in this part of the office, only the broken glass.

Romey stepped in behind me and asked, "Widow, what are you doing? The general was shot in the office across the hall."

"Who is Colonel Warren?"

"He's nobody important."

"Aren't colonels usually in charge of Marine bases?"

"Normally, yes, but not this one."

I walked over to Warren's office door and turned the knob. It was locked.

She asked again, "Widow, what are you doing?"

I said, "Why's this door locked, but the office isn't?"

"You ask a lot of useless questions. The reception area doesn't lock."

"Who is Warren?"

"He's nobody. He's gone now."

"Where is he?"

"He got orders to ship out a week ago, I guess. I can't remember when exactly. He's probably in South Korea settling into his new assignment."

I said, "Who is he though?"

She said, "Warren is a pencil pusher, sort of a hack. He's not much of a leader. The training program here is General Carl's baby. So he insisted on overseeing it. The colonel was just window dressing."

"Did he have any responsibilities?"

"Sure. He handled the day-to-day ops. You know, the boring stuff. Carl passed off all of the admin ops that he felt were beneath him."

I stared at Warren's office.

"Come on. Let's get back to it."

I nodded and turned, followed her back out into the hall.

We passed the chalk outlines again.

I tried to imagine the way it all went down. There were two bodies in the hall. Shot in the back.

I said, "These two were shot in the back, right?"

"Right," she said, "Come on. We'll go over the whole thing."

I stayed quiet. In my experience, cops from other jurisdictions didn't like to have someone reimagine or question their assessment of a crime scene.

Romey led me into the general's office. It was the same as Colonel Warren's. Same carpet. Same reception area. The difference was that Carl's office had three chalk outlines.

Romey said, "Let's check out the bathroom. We can compare the video's background and see if they are the same location."

I nodded. We passed the first dead body outline. It was the receptionist's. Romey pushed open the general's office door. It wasn't shut all the way.

She stepped in, and I saw the second and third chalk outlines. The closest to the door was on the floor on the right side of the desk.

In front of the plain steel desk were two chairs for visitors. The first was upright, as it should be. And the second one was knocked over.

I stepped right past Romey and around the first chalk outline. Then I stood over the next outline. It was General Carl's. His chair hadn't been knocked over but pushed back. If nothing had been touched, then he had stood up from it before he was shot. Part of his chalk outline was on the carpet, and part was against the wall, like he had fallen and remained propped up against it.

Romey grew impatient and said, "Widow, bathroom first."

I nodded.

She walked over to an army-green door. It was narrow, like a door on a ship.

She opened it and stepped in. The bathroom was tiny. The same carpet as the office lined the floor. There was a sink that was maybe a foot square, a face-sized mirror, and a white toilet. The walls were completely bare, except for the mirror.

Romey flipped on the light and looked at her reflection in the mirror for a second. She took off her hat, which she was required to do inside the command building, only now that didn't matter. She did it anyway and held it in her hand.

She looked at the walls and said, "Looks like the same walls from the video."

She took out her phone and swiped and opened the video again. She compared the walls and the lighting to the still of Turik's face.

I stayed in the doorway and stared over her shoulder. I said, "It's the same."

She looked at the floor and then leaned down and looked behind the toilet.

I reached from behind her and lifted the lid. The toilet was empty.

She looked in with me and then stepped back.

I said, "Check the tank."

She opened the tank. There was a cell phone at the bottom. She looked at me and said, "Guess that's me."

"Don't. I'll get it. I've had worse jobs."

Romey said, "It's clean water."

"Was just trying to impress you."

I stepped in behind her, got a little closer than she might've expected. It was tight in there. However, I'd be lying to myself if I didn't admit that it was a little on purpose.

I reached past her arm and let my face get close to her hair. I could smell the products that she used. She smelled nice. It made the whole act of reaching into another man's toilet tank a whole lot better.

I felt around the bottom of the tank and fished out the cell phone. The water dripped and ran back down from it as I pulled it out. I waited for the dripping to stop and handed it to her.

She said, "Thanks. Let's get out of here."

I returned to the main room, and then she did the same.

She said, "It doesn't work now. Of course."

"You could put it in rice. Overnight."

"That doesn't really work."

"I don't know. I've heard it works."

"I doubt it."

"It might."

She didn't respond to that. She walked around me and stared at the chalk outlines. She asked, "Do you want me to go over how we believe it happened?"

I shook my head and said, "No. I think I get how you think it happened."

"Oh, really?"

"Sure. It's an obvious output. Turik entered the building with a loaded weapon—no problem there. He was a captain, and he had a relationship with Carl."

"Of course. He saved his life."

"Right, so he probably had carte blanche when it came to just walking in unannounced."

She nodded.

I said, "So he walked in, drew his gun, killed the secretary out in the waiting room."

She corrected me and said, "Receptionist."

"Right. Then he entered the office. The first victim was seated in the chair, facing the general a second before. Heard the outburst, stood up, knocked over his chair, and got shot."

Romey said, "In the heart. Instant death."

"Then Turik shot the general twice."

"First in the heart and then when he fell back, Turik shot him again in the head. Double-tap."

I nodded and turned back to the receptionist area. I walked out, and Romey followed. She kept the phone in her left hand.

I walked straight back to the entrance to the office. I stopped at the door. I said, "Turik would've stopped here because panic must've ensued at this point. Everyone would've heard the gunshots."

I looked back at Romey. She said, "Right."

"How many other people were on this floor at the time?"

"There were ten total. And twenty-three in the building at the time."

"That's counting the dead?"

"Yep."

"So three dead on this floor already at this point?"

She said, "That's the way it looked."

"Then what happened?"

"After Turik shot the three in here"—she walked past me out into the hall— "he checked the hall, but no one was out there. The other seven people were unarmed. Four were women.

Not that that matters. But no one else on this floor had a weapon. They weren't a threat, so he scrambled across the hall."

She walked and led me diagonally back to the colonel's office.

She said, "Turik knew that Warren wasn't here any longer. He knew that Warren had left the base and headed to South Korea. Therefore, he also knew that his receptionist wasn't up here anymore either. She'd been sent down the street to work in the school. Temporarily."

"This office was empty? And Warren was gone?"

"That's what I said."

"Then why was his office locked?"

She said nothing.

"If he left and packed up his things, then why lock it?"

"I don't know. Habit, I guess. Colonel Warren probably packed up a few days ago and moved out. He probably locked up before he left."

I asked, "Who was taking over his duties?"

"I have no idea. I don't run base logistics or staffing. I guess they were sending someone new."

I nodded.

Romey said, "So then Turik ran to the empty office and waited. As soon as he saw the two guards run in from the staircase, he shot them both in the back. A quick *Tap! Tap!*"

I smiled.

"Why are you smiling?"

"Just the way you say that."

"What's wrong with the way I say it?"

"*Tap! Tap!*"

"So?"

"I just never heard it like that before. I'd say, *Bang! Bang!* Not *Tap! Tap!*"

She said, "You're funny. So that's it. That's the way we figure it."

"You guys did some kind of forensic sweep?"

"Of course. We did the necessary. You see the chalk outlines."

"Is that the only way it could've gone down then?"

"I'm sure it's not the only way. But that's how it happened."

I asked, "How many guards were in the building?"

She looked up and thought for a moment and said, "Three."

"Where's the other guy?"

"The other woman was on the door. She's not allowed to leave that post."

"Not much security."

"Why the hell would we have more? This is virtually a forgotten installation, Widow. We're not exactly the highest plausible target for something like this."

I nodded and said, "So Turik hid in here and waited for the guards to run up the stairs. As soon as they were both up here, he stepped out and shot them in the back. What about the woman on the door?"

"Protocol requires her to go outside, wait for backup, and secure the yard."

"Did she see him shoot himself?"

Romey nodded and said, "And so did six other cops and about a dozen more Marines on the street outside. Including Kelly."

"I'm not questioning that he shot himself."

"Good. Because he did."

I said, "But what if it all went down another way?"

CHAPTER 24

"What other way?" Romey asked.

I said, "How about like this? Turik came into the building. He came up to visit with the general. He walked into the office. He asked to use the general's bathroom."

Romey started to say something, but I said, "I know. I know. COs don't share their private bathrooms, but Turik took a bullet for Carl. I bet he got all sorts of special treatment."

She said, "You're right. Go on."

"Turik goes into the bathroom. Locks the door. Sends Maya a video."

I paused, and then I started to walk to the corner of the entrance. I asked, "The guards who were shot. They weren't on the door, right?"

"No. I told you only one guard stands by the metal detector."

I said, "What if they were shot first?"

"I told you it looked like they were coming up to the hall to the sounds of gunshots."

"How good are your guys?"

Romey said, "I'm not going to answer that."

"Are they as good as you?"

"They are very good."

"They're Marine-trained MPs?"

"Of course."

"They got shot in the back, which means that, according to your story, Turik got the drop on them just by hiding across the hall. Why didn't they check the hall first?"

She stayed quiet.

I walked out of the office and Romey followed. I stopped at the opposite wall, halfway between the two offices. I looked at Warren's and then back at Carl's. I looked at the stairwell.

I said, "To me, it looks different. Your way is possible. Sure. It even sounds more practical. But it's a press release."

"A press release?"

"That's what we'd say in the SEALs as misinformation. Slang. We never disclose details of an operation."

"What about the operation on Bin Laden? The SEAL who shot him wrote a book about it. That's telling the story."

"Is that how it went down?"

She paused a beat and said, "Is he lying then?"

"Maybe. Maybe he's not even a SEAL. Maybe he's a decoy."

She said nothing.

I said, "What if he was never really shot at all?"

"So, what really happened to Bin Laden?"

"He was shot in Abbottabad. Don't you read the papers?"

"He was shot where?"

"Abbottabad, Pakistan, at night."

"I thought you said it didn't happen that way?"

"How would I know how it happened? I was on a beach in the south of France at the time."

She smirked a bit and said, "What a miserable job you had. So tell me how you see this whole thing going down."

"What if the shooter was here already?"

She stared at me.

I said, "Waiting in Warren's office? Across the hall. What if the shooter saw Turik come up the stairs and watched him go into Carl's office unannounced?"

Romey said, "Go on."

"What if the shooter was about to follow, but there were two MPs on this floor? They were already up here talking to each other. Maybe they were right in front of Warren's office. Maybe they were up here patrolling together. Maybe they were just in the wrong place at the wrong time. Maybe the shooter didn't want to confront them head-on." I stared at Romey.

She said, "Maybe."

"You know, in the field, operations never go as planned."

"Of course."

"So, if there was a second shooter and he had the opportunity to neutralize two MPs, then he'd take it."

She nodded.

I said, "Our shooter was supposed to follow Turik in and kill the target. He was probably supposed to shoot General Carl and then escape, using Turik as his patsy. Only he had an obstacle. Your guys were standing in the hallway—just by accident. So he took advantage of the situation. He watched them walk by, and shot them both in the back."

I looked back at the automatic glass door, and I asked, "How do you guys explain the broken glass?"

"Turik fired through it."

I nodded and walked over to it. I stopped when the doors started to open automatically.

I said, "Five feet."

She nodded.

"The doors are sensitive. They open at five feet," I said, and I waited. Romey looked puzzled as I counted the seconds, like one Mississippi, two Mississippi, and so on.

"What're you doing?"

"These doors stay open for about five Mississippis before they close."

"So?"

"That's a long time. In your story, Turik would've run across the hall here, and your MPs would've run up the stairs and not noticed the automatic doors were open to an office that was supposed to be closed."

She shrugged.

"Not likely. I think these doors were closed, and the MPs walked right by it. Maybe they were at that end of the hall, talking or patrolling. Maybe they were visiting the offices at that end. The shooter was already in Warren's office more than five feet from the doors. He waited for them to walk back by and shot them both in the back through the glass. Which is how he got the drop on them."

She said, "I hate to say this, but I think you're right. There's another aspect to the story that didn't quite fit with me before. I haven't told you."

I said, "The two dead MPs didn't even have their weapons drawn?"

She nodded.

"Turik's innocent. There's another shooter. Some guy was here. He shot your guys in the back. The gunshots would've been fast to dispatch both of them that quickly. The commotion may not have started yet. Certainly, the shooter would've had a head start on it. So he ran straight across the hall into Carl's office."

I picked up my feet and sprinted across the hall, reacting the way it played out. Romey followed behind me. I busted through the general's office door, which was just a regular door, and I pointed at the receptionist's desk.

I said, "He shot the receptionist the second he entered. He didn't even stop to aim. Was her body on the floor?"

"Yes."

"Was her seat knocked over?"

"Yes."

"She might even have been standing, wondering what the noise was. Maybe she was rising from her chair when he entered and plugged her. But he didn't stand still. He burst right into Carl's office."

I walked into Carl's office and pointed my hand outward like I was the shooter. I said, "He had known that there was another guy in here. That's how he shot him so fast. He saw him enter the office."

"Master Sergeant Thompson. He was meeting with Carl. A business matter."

I nodded and said, "He shot Thompson first and then double-tapped Carl. He might've even spoken to him first."

I walked over to the edge of the desk, and then I trailed around it and fired one last invisible round into the spot where Carl would've been shot in the head. I said, "The general was already dead before he hit the floor, right?"

"We think so. He was shot in the heart. Like Thompson and the receptionist."

"Those are professional hits. Why the double-tap in the head?"

"If you're right and there was a different shooter, then it'd be like that—a professional. Carl was the target. He got double-tapped."

I nodded and asked, "Was he shot in the head or in the face?"

"What's the difference? Both will kill ya."

"Which was it?"

"Face."

I nodded, thought for a moment.

"What?"

"You told me that Turik got a purple heart for saving Carl's life."

"Yeah."

I asked, "You told me that was in Iraq?"

"That's right."

"Are you sure?"

"I don't have the file in front of me or anything, but I think so."

I said, "I need to see that report."

"I can get it."

"Good."

"So, what next?"

"After our shooter killed Carl, then Turik came out of the bathroom."

She said, "After he hid his phone inside the tank."

"No."

"No? We found it. Remember?"

"No, it wasn't his phone. They would've taken his phone. And most people take their phones out and either play with them or set them on the table. And Turik did neither."

"What?"

"Back at the diner this morning, he didn't have a phone on him. I'd bet on it. They took it."

"Who? Who took it?"

"Them. The guys who made him go along with this whole operation."

"You sound paranoid. Them? We don't even know that yet."

"The big guy. From the diner. The giant."

"What about him?"

"He must've been Turik's babysitter. You can't let a patsy go out in public without one. They wanted him to be seen doing his regular things. The waitress told me that he came there three mornings a week before work. They wanted him to be seen wearing his camos and carrying his gun. They probably told him to look crazy. Which wouldn't have been hard, considering."

"Considering what?"

"The way they got him to go along with this whole charade."

"How?"

"Leverage."

"What leverage?" she asked. Then she said, "His wife."

I nodded and said, "There's no better way to get a Marine to go along with something so evil than holding his family hostage. I'd guess they took her and ordered him to help the shooter and then kill himself."

"I'm not religious, but isn't suicide a mortal sin in Islam? Like it is in Christianity?"

"Depends on who you ask. Jihadists would tell you that it's fine in the name of martyrdom, but regular Muslims would fight back against that. But …"

"But what?"

"Turik wasn't even Muslim."

"What? Sure he was."

"No. His sister told me that he disavowed it privately to her months ago. He's been atheist for years. He just claimed Islam so as not to be blackballed by his family."

"Then he killed himself because they gave him no choice," said Romey.

"Yeah," I said.

"What now? How do we prove any of this? And whose phone is this?"

"It's probably Carl's phone. Did you ever find his?" I asked.

"I don't think anyone even thought to look, but I'm sure we don't have it. I don't remember it being logged into evidence."

"Call Kelly. Ask him, would you?"

She nodded and asked, "Anything else?"

"Why don't you call him? I'm going to walk through one last time."

She nodded and went to the stairwell to make her call.

I walked down to the far end of the hall and walked the length of it all the way to the other end and then back again. Then I walked into Carl's office and looked it over again.

I retraced the shooter's steps back to Warren's office, and then I looked around it.

I started to wonder. How did the shooter get in here unnoticed?

CHAPTER 25

olonel Warren's office was a standard military office. There was a clean receptionist area, two plain chairs set out in front, a wall with a portrait hanging on it of a face I didn't recognize, and the door to Colonel Warren's office.

I walked over to the door and tried the knob again in case I had been wrong about it being locked, which had happened to me before. Sometimes I'd try a knob and think it was locked and then try it again, and it wouldn't be. I was tired, after all.

Warren's door was still locked.

The office was meant to be private, which meant that there was no window to look in on it.

I stared at the locked door and turned back to see if I could see Romey. She wasn't in my line of sight. It wouldn't take a warrant to get her to unlock the door. I was sure that she could simply get a key to it. But I didn't want to wait. I didn't need to have a warrant or go through official channels.

I faced Warren's door, stepped back, and pulled my right knee into my chest, not like a soccer kicker, more like a guy about to stomp on someone's face. I kicked it straight into the door, just to the right side of the knob.

The key to kicking in a door comes from pressure, and that comes from mass. Getting the right mass in the right spot will work every time. I had plenty of mass and knew where to put it to work. My boot heel and sole landed viciously against the door.

It fired open like a breach charge had exploded against it. Wood splintered and metal ripped. The door flung in so hard that it rebounded against the wall and started to come back before I even put my foot back down on the floor.

I stayed in the doorway, surveyed the room. It was dark. This office did have a window to the front of the building, but the blinds were drawn closed as if a Howard Hughes had been living in here with mason jars full of urine.

Romey was behind me. She said, "What the hell, Widow?"

"Sorry. I needed to see."

"See what?"

The office was full of framed photographs. Most of the ones on the desk faced away from me—toward Warren, if he had been sitting there. Some of them were facing the visitor. These were photos of Marines standing together in different training shots. There were a couple of photographs that were taken out in the desert. Iraq was my guess. Plenty of evidence of makeshift forwarding bases and military equipment.

One guy was in all of the photographs, first as a young man and then later as an older man. It was Colonel Warren, I guessed.

I stepped into the office closer to the desk. I reached down and grabbed a framed photograph off the desk at random. I turned it around, stared at the picture.

Romey repeated, "What?"

I turned back to her and showed her the framed photograph.

I asked, "If Warren left, why didn't he pack this photograph of his wife?"

CHAPTER 26

Romey said, "He didn't pack anything? Everything's still here?"

I looked around the office, set the framed photograph back down on the desk. I didn't touch anything else.

I walked behind the desk and looked out the window. I looked down at the sidewalk.

I said, "You can see the walkway up to the entrance from here."

I turned to Romey and said, "Our shooter was in here. Probably from the night before. Maybe only hours before."

"How did he get in here? Warren?"

"I'd say so. You need to call somebody. Find out about his orders to go to South Korea. Find out exactly where he's supposed to be."

"Do you think he lied?"

"I'd say so. I'd say he never had orders."

"He gave the shooter a key to his office?"

I stayed quiet.

Romey said, "Was he the shooter?"

"I doubt it."

She took out her phone and started dialing. She put the phone to her ear and waited. She said, "Hey. Listen. Send the forensic team back over here to the crime scene. We've got new intel."

Romey looked at me and decided to take the rest of the call out into the hallway. Before she crossed over the automatic glass doors, she pulled the phone away from her ear and looked at me. She said, "Don't touch anything else. They're going to sweep over this room. Better not to move anything. Let my guys do their thing."

I nodded. She left the room.

I turned back to the desk and walked around it. I inspected Warren's chair. It was tucked in neatly under the desk.

I felt the black leather. It was cold, as was the desktop.

There were papers neatly stacked to the left of the desk. I gazed over them quickly. They were typical military paperwork—nothing of interest there.

I pulled out his top drawer, which I found to be also typical of a colonel. He had kept everything that had a daily use in that drawer. I found a stapler, pens, and other office supplies.

I shut the drawer and then opened the second one. That's where I found what I was looking for.

I found a Taurus Millennium G2 handgun, which is a pretty nice piece. The last time I checked, this gun was retailing at around three hundred bucks. Not bad for a good, reliable, concealable weapon.

It is compact, but not tiny like other weapons. It had a twelve-round magazine and one in the chamber. The Millennium G2 is comparable to a Glock—a fine weapon.

The Millennium G2 wasn't a regulation service weapon, not that anyone would question a colonel in the Marine Corps. But I figured that this was Warren's personal weapon. It was probably off the books.

I looked up to see if Romey was still out of the office. I couldn't see her, but I could hear her speaking to Kelly on the phone.

Two thoughts passed through my head. The first was that I should tell Romey about the gun. It's the honest thing to do. The second was that she would most certainly bag it and tag it. She'd hand it over to her guys as evidence. Not that it was evidence of anything related to our case, but a gun found on-site and a possible implication that Warren was involved here would categorize the gun as evidence.

On the other hand, I had a third thought. If there was a professional shooter out there, and we were going to be trying to track him down, then I would need a gun. And I doubted that Romey was going to oblige and have one for me.

Way back in the day, I was a good cop. Not the best, but far from the worst. In my experience, there were the rules you followed and the rules you didn't. I know that not everyone agrees with that. And some guys break the wrong rules. To me, you just stick to what's right. Sometimes there are some rules that are just plain wrong. And I wasn't a cop anymore anyway.

I picked up the Millennium G2 and ejected the magazine and racked the slide. The chambered round ejected. I caught it. I stared into the chamber and performed a visual check. The gun was safe. It looked like it hadn't been fired recently. All thirteen rounds were accounted for. It looked in good working order, which I imagined it was.

I dry-fired it to make sure that it worked. It did.

I loaded the magazine, kept the extra round out, and chambered a fresh one. Then I ejected the magazine and stacked the extra round on top. I pushed the magazine back into the weapon. I gripped my hand around it. This model came with a pinkie extender on the tip of the magazine, which was good for a guy with large hands. Still, I had a three-finger grip on the gun. Not ideal for me, but my pinkie wasn't a problem. The extender didn't compensate for me the way that it might've for the next size hand down from mine, but it did give me a better grip on the gun than if there was no extender.

I slid the Millennium G2 into the right front pocket of my jacket.

I closed the drawer.

I saw nothing else of interest on the desk.

Romey came back in and said, "Anything else?"

"Warren's desk is full of office supplies and his work papers. We need to find him."

"I agree. I got Kelly coming over here with our forensic guys. They'll check everything out. They already collected everything in the hall and Carl's office. I'll make sure that they focus in here."

I said, "Not everything. They missed the phone in the tank."

She nodded and said, "Why would they even check there?"

"Someone should've realized that Carl's phone was missing."

"We would've. It's only been hours since the whole thing happened."

I said nothing to that.

Romey said, "What now?"

"Two things."

"Which are?"

"First, there's something else in that video that bothers me."

"What's that?"

"The phrase Turik uses. He says, *good measure*."

"What about it?"

"Earlier, when I was waiting for you near the flag pole, I was staring up at the flag, and I thought about a saying that we had out in the field. Not really a saying. It was just sort of spoken words. We'd often revel in the flag. Like it was a symbol of our patriotic religion."

"As it is to all military personnel. And all Americans."

"Not all Americans."

She said, "Most. The good ones."

"In the SEALs, there used to be some saying about how we served the flag *without measure*. It meant that the power behind the American way is immeasurable. Something like that."

She nodded.

"I think the Marines have something similar, but it uses the word *good*. Like *good measure*."

"I never heard that."

"Maybe I heard it from an old instructor. I think that Turik was saying that to name something specific. I don't think that he was just rattling off a Marine saying."

"So what could it be? About the flag?"

"No. I think it's the name of a mission."

She stayed quiet.

I said, "Get someone to research it. Will you?"

"What was the second thing?"

"We need to go to Warren's house. If he's involved, we need to find him."

She said, "Let's go now. We can wait downstairs."

I nodded, and we walked out to the hall, down the stairs, and out the front door in silence.

CHAPTER 27

We waited in front of the command building out on the street.

Romey said, "The agents who are here are British."

"British?"

"You know, like crumpets and James Bond?"

"They're a part of Her Majesty's Secret Service?"

"Or whatever. They got the accents."

Widow said, "Sounds like MI6."

"Who?"

Widow said, "England's Secret Intelligence Service. It's like their version of the CIA. How many guys?"

"Just two guys."

"So, what are they here for?"

Romey looked around the street. She looked in the direction of both checkpoints like she was checking her guys. Then she said, "You can ask them yourself when we head back to the station. I think they're still there."

Just then, we saw Kelly pull up outside the checkpoint to the south, as he had before when he picked me up. A police van followed behind him. I hadn't seen it before. They all passed the guards and rolled up to us. The van pulled around and off to the sidewalk and parked.

Four people got out. Two of them were women. All four of them were young. They looked like they were in their twenties.

Romey walked over to Kelly's window and said, "Don't get out."

He didn't.

She said, "We got some new info."

"What?"

"A video. From Turik."

"A confession?"

"No."

"What is it?"

"I'll show it to you later. But it looks like Turik is innocent."

Kelly said, "What? How?"

"It looks like he might've been coerced. Or at the very least, he had an accomplice."

"What do you want me to do?"

"Stay here with the team. Make sure they go over Colonel Warren's office."

She went on to explain to him the situation and my theory of what happened.

I stepped toward her car and looked at the checkpoints again. Some of the MPs stared back at me. I made eye contact with one of them. He looked me over suspiciously and then returned to talking to one of the other MPs.

I saw the forensic team go to the back of the van and pull out a bunch of gear. They wore protective eye goggles and plastic gloves.

I looked down at mine and pulled them off, stuffed them in my pocket.

Romey came over and said, "Let's go."

We got into the car, and she backed up, headed back toward the same checkpoint that we had gone through earlier. She said, "Where to first?"

I said, "Got Warren's home address?"

"Of course. It's on the computer."

"We'd better head over there."

"No reason to call South Korea then?"

"You can have one of your guys call to see if there ever were orders, but I doubt it."

Romey headed toward the gate.

I said, "How are you going to get past the media?"

She said, "Don't worry about that."

And she smiled.

CHAPTER 28

Romey said, "Can I make a confession?"

I looked over at her and said, "What?"

"I always wanted to outrun the press. When I was a little girl, I had always pictured myself growing up to be Marilyn Monroe. You know, like a celebrity?"

"She's a little before our generation. Don't you think? Shouldn't you have tried to be more like somebody current?"

"Like who? Madonna?"

"I don't know. I always had more of a thing for Pamela Anderson."

She shot me a look that said something like, *You would say that*. But she didn't say it. Instead, she said, "What about Princess Leia?"

We neared the exit gate. But she continued to talk. She said, "I thought guys from my generation had a thing about Princess Leia in the gold bikini?"

"She's pretty nice. But Star Wars is a little before my age too. No, good ole Pamela was more my speed."

She said, "That figures. You got a thing for the plastic look."

I said, "Hey, nothing's wrong with plastic. I had toys when I was a kid. They were made outta plastic."

She shot me another look. This one, I didn't know what it said. It wasn't quite an aggressive look or an *I'm not surprised* look, but more like something in the middle.

The guards at the gate recognized her car immediately and saluted. We slowed in order to weave in and out of the staggered concrete barriers that blocked anyone from speeding through the gate.

We came face-to-face with a street full of media. The day was turning into night. The sun, which was still just as hidden as it had been the whole day, was setting somewhere to the west. I knew that for sure because the overcast was turning into full dark, and fast.

I'd heard it all said about California: overcrowded, overpriced, and overarrogant. But it does have one of the most beautiful sunsets in the world. I'd seen the sun set from every hemisphere, and arguably, nothing beat the fast drop over the Pacific Ocean. Especially a California sunset from this part of the state, where I could see the mountains, the far-off coastline, and the ocean.

This wasn't one of those occasions. Even without the overcast and the high altitude, I still would have been unable to see the horizon because of the crowds of reporters and cameramen.

As soon as the police cruiser cleared the gate, Romey switched on the light bar and the siren.

The blue lights flashed and rotated, ricocheting weakly back off the clouds and trees and snow. Some of the reporters moved, some stayed where they were, and others rushed to the front of the car. That's when Romey hit the horn, which was a deafening, horrible sound, like a dying animal.

Once, I had been camping in the mountains in Yukon. It was early morning, and I was lucky to be awake already when a grizzly bear chased a buck into my camp. I watched the bear kill the buck and drag it off. The screams the deer made were best described as the horn on a police car—loud and blood-curdling.

The brazen reporters pushed on the car and the hood, several of them knocking on the glass, vying for attention. They were all screaming questions at us. Romey kept screaming at them to back off.

I did nothing.

It took about five minutes to push all the way through them. It reminded me of being caught in protests in Yemen once. We had a team of four SEALs all in street clothes. We piled into a taxi, trying to escape the local police. That mission worked out.

Romey finally cleared the reporters. But by the time we reached the end of the pack, many of them were piling into their vans and turning around to give chase.

I said, "Exactly how big is Hamber?"

"Why?"

"I've only seen the main strip, and it's tiny. If this is the entire town, these guys will find us pretty easily."

"Don't worry. We'll take the back roads. Hamber is spread out."

"Like LA?"

"Come on, Widow. This is a country town. It's spread out like country towns are."

"I'm from Mississippi. Remember? I know how that works."

Romey sped up after we broke through the last barrier of people. The sirens wailed, and the blue lights rotated and reflected from tree to tree.

She said, "I stayed in Jackson once. It's a wicked small place."

I stared over at her. She'd let out a deep Bostonian accent. I said, "You do speak like someone from Boston."

She returned to her generic American accent and said, "It took years to get rid of it."

The car bounced and wound around the road.

I looked back and saw the nearest media van about two-thirds of a mile behind us. Which was a nice head start, but on an empty country road, it would be very easy for them to spot us. I said, "Better speed up."

"Don't worry."

Romey jammed the accelerator down harder, and we pushed farther ahead. It was only a matter of minutes until we lost them. And then we were in the downtown area.

Romey switched off the sirens but kept the light bar on.

I asked, "Why did you lose the accent?"

"When I first joined the Corps, the enlisted made fun of me."

"I would guess that you wouldn't be bothered by what others thought."

"I'm not. But the officers did it too, not in front of me but behind my back. So when I was approved to go into the MPs, I took classes in my spare time. The kind of voice coaching, stand-in-front-of-people kind of thing."

"Public speaking?"

"Right. They taught it as an elective at a junior college. It was one night a week. I didn't care about the grade. I just went until I felt like I learned all the tips that I was going to learn. Then I applied them."

I nodded and stared out the windshield.

"How did you lose yours?"

I glanced over at her and said, "I didn't."

Romey turned the wheel and moved over to the inside lane. We drove through the downtown area quickly. It was a Monday night in a small town, but it was the end of the day shift for most people. The day workers had probably clocked out about an hour ago, meaning that most of them had already headed home. However, the roads still seemed a little too abandoned.

I asked, "Where's everyone? Why are the streets so dead?"

"Hamber's biggest employer is Lexigun."

Which I already knew.

"The owner died a couple of days ago. Today was his funeral. The employees are off for a day of mourning. He was a beloved figure here. His family can be traced back to the days of the first settlers who pushed out this way. Back in the eighteen hundreds."

"Fifteen hundreds," I said.

"What?"

"California was discovered and explored and settled way back in the sixteenth century, not the nineteenth."

"There wasn't an America in the seventeenth century."

"Not true. There wasn't the United States of America, but there were the Americas named after explorer Amerigo Vespucci soon after Columbus sailed the ocean blue in 1492. And there was a California, as in the State of California."

"Hell, if we're going to be that specific, then actually, the Native Americans had already discovered it. They were already here, right?"

I smiled and said, "Technically, Asians discovered it."

"What?"

"Where do you think the natives came from? Twelve thousand years ago, they crossed from Siberia over a land bridge to Alaska."

"You don't got a girlfriend, do you, Widow?"

"It's a little hard to keep one."

"I bet."

We turned off the highway down a two-lane road called Lamey Road. Romey drove on for another mile, weaving around the snaking road. I looked out the window and saw nothing but trees.

She slowed the car and came up to a three-way stop. She didn't stop, but she did look every which way with great attention. There were no other cars in sight.

She took another left, and after another mile, I saw streetlights. And then off back from the road, I saw house lights.

Each house was completely different from the next. Some were brick and big. Some had cheap siding and were smaller. But they were all quiet.

We crossed another stop. This one a four-way, but one of the roads clearly led to a dead end.

She took the opposite direction, and we came to a subdivision. There was a single wooden sign off in the corner of the entrance. The name was generic, Hamber Pines, which was ridiculous because there were no pines anywhere in sight.

We drove into the subdivision and veered to the right.

Romey killed the light bar and took it slow.

The houses were all two-story cookie cutters, nothing special about any of them. Each had the same brick, the same scarce trees, and the same lot sizes. There were only four basic designs. They appeared to be on a rotation; not one was next to its equivalent setup.

The only real differences between the houses were the vehicles in the driveways and the number addresses posted on the front porches near the doors.

Romey said, "Help me find it. I've never been here before."

And she gave me the address. I looked right and she looked left. I guessed that we were already on the right street because she only gave me the numbers.

Most subdivisions are addressed with odd numbers on one side and evens on the other side, like odds to the left and evens to the right. This one was all weird. Odds and evens were mixed in together. No reason to bank on an approach of following a pattern of looking on the odd-number side for Warren's physical address.

After several minutes, Romey said, "There it is."

We pulled up. She parked at the end of the drive and left the Charger running.

She said, "Stay in the car."

"What? No way!"

"Widow, you're not a cop anymore."

"What about this badge?" I asked and reached down and touched the laminate that she had given me earlier.

"It's not really a badge. Warren will know that. Best if I go alone."

"Not happening. Don't even fight me on this."

She nodded and said, "Okay. I'm not giving you a weapon."

I nodded, didn't mention the G2 in my jacket pocket.

She said, "Stay behind me a bit."

We got out of the Charger. I shut my door. She left hers ajar. We walked up the drive together, keeping our steps as quiet as we could, but also trying not to look sneaky. We didn't want to alert anyone who might be watching that we were sneaking up on the house.

I stayed close to Romey, a couple of feet behind her. I reached into my jacket pocket and blindly flicked the G2's safety selector to fire in case I needed to deploy it fast. The G2 comes with an extra safety measure that requires a key to unlock the firing block, but I had dry-fired it back at his office, so this wasn't a concern. But I didn't really have to dry-fire it to know. A Marine colonel wasn't going to hinder his backup weapon's firing ability by keeping it on safety lock.

I glanced down and followed Romey's hand. In one quick movement, she unsnapped her gun holster. She kept one hand on the butt of her gun, and the other she used to pull out a small flashlight. She didn't switch it on, just kept it stationary. I saw her look at every visible corner of the house, the porch, and then she scanned the windows. She was a good cop.

I did the same. Basically, I double-checked each spot for something she might've missed. I saw no one.

The windows were all dark, except for a single large window on the right front side of the house.

The porch light jumped on as Romey stepped up on the first step. It wasn't from someone inside turning on a light. I figured that it was a motion sensor light. It was a bright light. It lit up the whole porch, the steps, and halfway down the driveway.

I scanned the windows and the corners again, fast. I still saw nothing—no sign of life.

Romey said, "Be ready."

I wasn't sure that she meant to say it to me or at me, like I was one of her guys. Maybe it was muscle memory. Maybe it was something that she said to Kelly just before they encountered a potentially dangerous situation.

I said, "You be careful."

She stepped up onto the porch and moved slowly, but not too slowly—like she was stepping through a minefield, only she didn't want anyone to know she was stepping through a minefield.

She came up to the front door, which was a big white thing with long, vertical glass windows on each side. There were drapes covering them. They didn't budge as I would've expected if someone was home and wanted to peek out to see who was on his porch.

Off to the side was a long bench painted white, like the door. On the other side was a series of potted plants. Nothing special.

At one end of the porch, near the corner, I saw two bowls that were empty. I assumed that they were set out to feed a local neighborhood cat or maybe a stray.

Romey said, "Here goes."

She rang the doorbell and waited.

I listened carefully. There was no answer and no sign of movement inside.

She rang the doorbell again. No answer.

Then she started knocking, hard. She said in a cop voice, "Colonel Warren. Open up."

She waited several long moments and repeated the whole action. There was still no answer, no sign of movement.

She tried the same actions again. And again, there was no answer, no sign of movement.

She said, "What now?"

"We go in."

She thought for a moment and said, "You know I can't do that."

I said, "You can't. I can."

"I don't know, Widow."

"Look, we know that Warren lied about leaving. We know that someone shot your guys from his office. We can't wait for warrants."

"I never did something like that before."

I said, "You're a good cop. You should stay out. Let me handle it."

She said, "Maybe if we had probable cause, then I could enter."

I said, "Give me a few minutes, and I'll find some probable cause."

She nodded and said, "I still can't give you a gun."

"Don't worry about it. I won't need one."

"What if the second shooter is in there? You could get shot at."

I faced her and thought for a moment. I said, "Then at least you'll have probable cause."

She smiled and said, "That's not funny."

"Don't worry. I've been in many situations like this unarmed."

"What kind of job did you have?"

"You help me find the guys who forced a good Marine to kill himself and take the fall for this, and I'll tell you."

She nodded, and then she asked, "Should I stay here?"

"Yeah. You hear something, shoot the lock."

"I should radio for backup. We can watch the house from the car. No one will get away."

I said, "That's a bad idea. Until we know more, let's keep this to ourselves."

"Right. If someone got to Turik, made him kill himself, and to Warren, then there's no telling who else might be involved."

I didn't say anything to that. I'd already figured that part out. I think she had too. She was just saying it out loud. I'd worked with cops like that before. Some people think better when they hear themselves say the words out loud in front of a colleague. I figured that it was her way of coming to terms with it, like she didn't want me to think that she was crazy.

I said, "I'll check around the back."

She nodded.

CHAPTER 29

I left Romey standing on the porch, under the light.

I approached the side of the house, hugging close to the brick wall. I went west, past the garage, which was a two-car thing with an automatic door. It was closed.

I didn't want to walk on the other side of the house because, in my experience, people always walked out of their house through the garage or the back door when trying to avoid someone who's standing at their front yard. And back doors are usually built either at the exact center of a house or near the garage.

It would've been a bad idea to go the other way and risk someone exiting the back door, trying to flank us. They would certainly go around the garage. It was human nature.

I passed the driveway and looked around the neighborhood. No one was outside for several houses. At the end of the street, from the direction that Romey had driven us in, I saw a garage door open. The light inside and the sound of the car disturbed the deadly calm of the suburban street.

I waited near the corner of Warren's garage until the neighbor's garage door had shut all the way and the car was out of sight. Then I looked back at Romey. She was standing there, watching me.

I couldn't pull the G2 out yet. I didn't want her to see it. So I had to take the chance to jump around the corner. This would be the most dangerous part, I assumed.

I leaped around the side of the house like a kid jumping out from a hiding space to scare his little sister.

No one was there. No dark figures or bad guys with guns. But there was plenty of darkness. The only light nearby was from the neighbor's backyard, and it was dim. It was too dim to help me, which was fine by me. I liked to work alone and in the dark.

I stepped forward into the darkness and pulled out the G2. I kept my finger in the trigger housing, but the weapon pointed at the ground. I didn't want to shoot someone by mistake.

I stepped quietly but not slowly toward the back of the house. I slid along the wall until I came to a window into the garage. I tried to peer in but saw nothing. There was no light. I left the window and moved forward.

Ten seconds later, I came up to a chain-link fence. I stepped to the left and peered around the corner of the house into the backyard. I only had about a one-hundred-eighty-degree line of sight if I counted what was already behind me.

I reached down and unlatched the gate's locking mechanism. The latch creaked open, giving away my position to anyone who was close enough to hear it. I quickly entered the back-yard, then stopped and waited.

The yard was silent. The house was silent.

I set the gate back slowly. I didn't latch it back. I just leaned it shut.

I continued nonstop to the corner of the house and then around the side. There was still nothing but silence. The backyard was so silent that all I heard were my own footsteps in the shallow snow and grass.

In the distance, I could hear the hum of a heating unit, one of those big ones. The motor on it hummed quietly, and the fan spun almost as quietly.

I imagined that to most people, these were the sounds they heard every night. They were the sounds of safety and comfort. They were the things that made them feel normal, like getting up every morning and heading to jobs that they hated. It was all a part of the daily ritual of taxpaying citizens. This wasn't for me. I liked having the freedom to travel and go where I pleased, how I pleased. No one told me what to do or where to go. Not anymore.

All the windows on the back of the house were pitch black, except for the light coming from the glass slider on the deck.

I walked up the wooden stairs cautiously. The wood creaked a little more quietly than the gate had but still worried me, because the house was silent enough to allow anyone to get the warning that there was an intruder on the back deck.

I kept the gun down by my leg, out of sight. I didn't want to get shot because someone saw the weapon. If Warren was actually home and just pretending not to be, then he could legally shoot me for entering his house. I wasn't sure about entering his yard. I didn't know California's laws on property and trespassing.

It didn't make any difference because no one seemed to be home.

I looked in the back through the slider. There were loose-hanging, vertical blinds, but they were pulled open.

I saw no one. The light was a dim lamp on a table back near the far wall.

The house had an open design. I looked left and saw an empty kitchen. I looked right and saw Colonel Warren's living room furniture. The rooms were empty.

A flat-screen TV hung from a wall to the right, in front of the sofas. It was switched on, but there was nothing on the screen. It was just some generic wallpaper, like the thing had a display setting that switched on after no activity had been sensed for a long time. I'd seen PCs do the same thing with a screensaver.

I scanned the room again to be sure, and then I tried the slider. It was locked, which is what I expected.

I looked around the back deck. There were more planters, some cheap patio furniture, and a barbeque grill on wheels.

I reached down and grabbed one of the smaller planters and dumped out the plants. They slid out and fell on the back deck. Then I chucked the pot through the glass.

The slider shattered. The sound was loud. It echoed into the darkness of the backyard.

I crouched down, weapon ready. I waited.

First, I waited for someone to come running out of the dark hallway, but no one did. Then I turned and looked left and looked right. I studied the neighboring properties on both sides. I saw nothing.

I could hear a dog bark down the street. Then another one joined in, but still, no one came out to see what the noise was.

I stepped over the broken glass, and across the threshold into the house, which also meant that if Warren was innocent in all this, then I'd just entered the legal territory of getting shot as an intruder.

I aimed the G2 out in front of me. This time, I pulled my finger out of the housing, just in case someone innocent was

WITHOUT MEASURE   **177**

home. While I didn't want to get shot, I also didn't want to shoot the wrong person.

Still, no one came out of the darkness.

I checked the kitchen again quickly. Nothing there. I studied the east wall of the house. The kitchen was the farthest point. I walked to the hallway, staying crouched.

My eyes adjusted as best as they were going to, and I started to head down the hallway. I came to another hall that branched off. One direction led to the front door, and the second led to two doors. I walked toward the two doors. The first was a bedroom. It was unoccupied. There was a crisply made bed inside and an empty closet, and an en suite bathroom, which was small. The door was open. I saw three pieces: a shower, a toilet, and a sink.

I turned back to the second door. I walked closer and started to smell something. It was faint.

The door had a dead bolt and a lock on it, which made me assume that it led to the garage. None of the locks were locked.

I opened the door and darted through it. I was prepared to shoot if I needed to.

That preparation was unnecessary because I came face-to-face with a powerful stench.

I knew that smell. I searched around for the light switch and flipped the light on.

A couple of panel lights slowly came to life.

The building was a basic suburban garage. A long tabletop lined the back wall. Tools were hung in neat fashion along a wall rack. A set of metal lockers that looked like they were recycled from a military base stood in the corner. And two plain cars were parked inside. They were obviously his and hers—one Ford and one Mazda.

The Mazda was a little red thing that looked like I wouldn't even fit in it. The Ford was a newer Taurus, white. I assumed it was Warren's.

They both had military stickers, but the Taurus had the proper identification to signal to the guards at the gate that it was Warren's car.

I stepped down in a single drop over a two-step stair and stood in the cold garage.

I ignored the Mazda altogether and walked around the long hood of the Taurus and back to the trunk. I walked to the trunk because that was the source of the stench—no doubt in my mind. It was obvious because there were flies fighting to get in. Hordes of them were on the trunk lid.

I looked up at the ceiling and saw a hole leading to the attic. A low wind noise blew through it. It wasn't big enough for anything other than a small rodent to come through. It was the point of entry for the flies, I guessed.

I didn't touch anything.

I scrambled back to the driver's side door. I tried to open it, but it was locked.

I reversed the G2 and swung it at the window like a hammer. For the second time in one night, I heard the echo of shattering glass.

I reached through the broken window and popped the trunk. It clicked open.

I walked back around to the trunk and opened it the rest of the way in one fast motion like I was removing a Band-Aid.

The smell intensified and wafted over me like a bioweapon. It felt like I was being gassed. I was reminded of sixteen years ago when my old SEAL trainers shut each of us into a room and gassed us with tear gas as a part of SEAL training. This wasn't a new tactic of training soldiers, but what was new about it was that they filled the room with the rotting carcasses of pigs, which made it feel terrifying, to say the least.

I looked down at the contents of the trunk.

I was staring at two very dead bodies.

CHAPTER 30

The two dead bodies were half covered in shadow from the trunk lid of Warren's Taurus. They were folded over and piled neatly in the trunk like luggage. The top body was a male, and the bottom was a female. Both were older, probably in their sixties. And both were covered in blood.

I kept the G2 in my hand because I hadn't checked the upstairs yet. But I was sure that whoever had piled the bodies into the Warren's car was long gone.

I reached down and turned the male's face toward me. It was Warren. I recognized him from the photographs on his desk. He was a lot older than in the pictures, but it was him.

He'd been shot in the head. The bullet had been fired straight into his forehead and at point-blank range. That was evident because there were huge powder burns all over his face, caked in blood.

I reached down past him and grabbed the head of the female. I twisted it and faced it up.

It was Warren's wife—no doubt about that either because the face was exactly the same as the one from his photograph of her.

She'd been shot in the forehead as well. It was the same execution style, the same point-blank range; only her death had been much earlier than Warren's. The blood on her had dried up, and the powder burns dried up in it. She had been dead for more than twenty-four hours. I was sure of that.

I laid her head back down gently. I leaned down and studied their bodies. They were killed with the same gun, muzzle to the forehead. The wife had bruises on her forehead like a gun had been pushed hard into it.

She had two black eyes. Her face was a mess of dried blood and mascara. I imagined that Romey's forensic teams would find gunpowder and probably evidence of tears as well.

Suddenly, I heard a pounding sound behind me, like a loud knocking.

I stood up straight and spun around, pointed the gun in the direction of the sound.

It was Romey knocking on the outside of the garage door.

She said, "Widow? Are you in there?"

I called back to her. I said, "Yeah. Go back to the front door. I'll open it."

She said, "Okay."

I walked back through the garage door to the hall and checked the spare bedroom again. I didn't hear anyone else in the house, and I was pretty sure that no one was there, but I'd also known a few cops who were shot by not being thorough enough.

I went down the other hallway to the foyer and stopped at the bottom of a staircase. I pointed up it with the G2. No one was there. No sounds or lights were there. I flipped on all the light switches that I saw. All the lights above me fired on, even the staircase light.

I looked back up the stairs—still no sign of life.

Romey banged on the other side of the front door.

"Hang on," I said. I held the G2 down by my side—no reason to hide it from her anymore.

I unlocked the door and she pushed it open. She had her gun out.

Romey stepped into the foyer and glanced up the stairs. She stood up on her tiptoes like she was trying to see as much as she could. She asked, "Anybody here?"

"The garage."

She looked at me and then at the G2. She asked, "Where did you get the gun?"

"Technically, I stole it."

"From where?"

"Warren's office."

Romey waited for a second, and then she asked, "It was his backup?"

"Found it in the desk when you were out in the hall. On the phone. I figured that I might need one."

"I don't know how I feel about that, Widow. It's a senior officer's personal weapon."

"Don't worry. He won't be filing a formal complaint or anything. He's dead."

She paused a beat, and then she asked, "Garage?"

"Yes. Shot in the head. Wife too. They're in the trunk of his car."

"Oh no."

"Shot by the same shooter who killed five Marines on your base."

"Did you check the whole house?"

"Not yet. But we won't find anything else. Not the shooter, anyway. He's long gone."

She said, "We'd better have a look anyway."

I nodded and said, "The only part left is the upstairs."

"You seem to know what you're doing. You lead the way."

I led Romey up the stairs, gun out, but pointed at the floor.

Upstairs, we found two bedrooms, a bathroom, two walk-in closets, and an upstairs laundry room. All the beds were neatly made. All the closets were well organized. Shoes were arranged in neat order along the back wall in one of the closets. The other room was more of a master bedroom. It was a little bigger and a lot more feminine.

Romey stared at the feminine room.

I said, "Looks like the Warrens were sleeping in different bedrooms."

She nodded and said, "Doesn't necessarily mean that they had marital problems. It could just be an old-fashioned thing. My grandparents slept in different rooms."

"I don't think it had any bearing on what happened to them."

We left the upstairs and moved to the garage. Romey went straight to the Taurus's trunk. She gasped at the way they were packed in there.

She said, "They look terrified."

"I'm sure they were. They saw it coming. The killer executed them right to their faces."

"I didn't like Warren that much. No one did. But he was a Marine. He didn't deserve this. And Mrs. Warren. Her only sin was staying married to an old creep like him."

I said, "What about Turik?"

"I didn't know him, but I feel bad for blaming him."

"If the shooter used Warren's wife as leverage to make him cooperate, then it's safe to say that Turik was in the same boat."

She nodded, said, "We never found his wife."

I said, "Judging by the difference in decomposition, gun powder burns, and dried blood, I'd say that Mrs. Warren died long before the Colonel. Therefore, we can presume that the shooter never had any intention of leaving them alive."

She nodded.

"We can also presume that this is more than one guy."

"Of course, at least one guy babysat the hostage."

I said, "It's four. At least."

"Four?"

"One with Mrs. Warren, one with the Colonel, and two more. One with Turik's wife and the one with Turik."

"Four," she said in the sound of doomed realization. She added three more words. She said, "That's a conspiracy."

"We need to find Mrs. Turik."

"We already went to Turik's house."

I asked, "You searched his entire property?"

"We looked everywhere. There's no sign of her."

Romey paused a beat and said, "We didn't look for a grave."

"There wouldn't be one. These guys left the Warrens in the trunk of their own car. They knew it would get searched eventually. They're not concerned with exerting the effort it takes to dig a grave. Besides, they could've easily just shot her and left her in Turik's living room. Your guys would've chalked it up to Turik killing her before he left for work this morning. They could've framed it in any number of ways. They could've made it appear like she found out about his plans and tried to stop him. They would've assumed that once he'd killed her, there was no turning back. Your guys would've assumed he killed her, went to work, and murdered five Marines in a bout of insanity, then killed himself. It all plays out the same."

Romey asked, "But what about the Warrens?"

I said, "That's the part that doesn't make sense. Not at first. Why go through the trouble of setting Turik up and then leaving the Warrens practically out in the open?"

She said, "They wanted Turik to look like a terrorist. They wanted Turik to be seen as an ISIS terrorist." Then Romey paused and said, "The media. Oh God!"

"What?"

"There's a press conference."

She looked at her watch and said, "It's too late. They gave it an hour ago."

I asked, "If you're here and the general and colonel are dead, then who gave the conference?"

Romey paused a long, long beat. I watched her face turn flush. She said, "It wasn't from the base."

"Where was it?"

"The White House."

CHAPTER 31

"Why was it there?"

Romey said, "The White House wants to look tough on terror."

My whole career and life, politicians have always done what politicians do. Politics is not a game of governing as much as it is a game of theater. It's more like watching a play where everyone wants to be the top dog.

I said, "George R. R. Martin had the right title."

"What?"

"He's a writer."

"Never heard of him."

"He wrote a series of epic fantasy books. The first one's called *A Game of Thrones*. It's a great title. Makes sense here. I was just thinking about politicians."

"I didn't know there was a book. I love the show."

I said, "I didn't know there was a show."

"You really do live under a rock."

I stayed quiet.

Romey said, "What do we do now?"

"We can't help Turik's reputation now. If the White House has made a statement, then the cat's out of the bag."

"We can't just walk away?"

"We're not."

"So what then, Widow?"

I said, "What's Turik's wife's name?"

"Fatima."

I didn't say anything.

She said, "It means happiness, I think."

I shook my head and said, "*Farah* means happiness. Fatima is the name of one of Muhammad's daughters."

We headed out of the house, back to the car. I slipped the G2 back into my jacket pocket, and Romey holstered her Beretta. I said, "We need a photograph of her. Can you get me one from Turik's house?"

"We can go there now."

"No. Call Kelly. Have him pick one up. He can scan it and send it to your phone. We need some fast answers."

"So where to?"

"I want to know who's here."

"Who's here? Widow, what are you talking about?"

"The guys from MI6 that you were talking about earlier. They're foreigners. That means they came with someone important from another country. I want to know who. And what's he got to do with this?"

"How would he have anything to do with this?"

I didn't answer that. Instead, I said, "Take me back to the base. I want to chat with him."

Romey said, "We can't leave yet. I'll have to wait for Kelly and the team to get here. Also, I'll have to call in the locals. This is a crime off base, and technically, Mrs. Warren falls under their jurisdiction."

I asked, "What time is it?"

Romey looked at her watch again, more out of habit, I guessed because she had only just looked at it. She said, "It's nearly twenty hundred."

"Call the locals first. They'll get here faster. They can wait for your guys. Then you can take me to the base."

Romey didn't respond. She just got inside the Charger and started to make her calls. I stood outside the car for a moment. I stared up at the clouds. The nighttime chill stormed across my shoulders and neck.

I started to think that if they'd never found Fatima's body, she was probably still alive. But what would they be doing with her?

The answers to that question entered my mind, and I began to get angry, which was good because I didn't want to think about how exhausted I was.

CHAPTER 32

Romey made her calls, and we waited for the local cops. First, a couple of patrolmen showed up in two Ford Crown Vics. They were professional with Romey during the first part of the conversation. But when she told them we had to leave, they quickly fast-forwarded through professional courtesy and patience straight to hostility. At this point, they were giving her grief about jurisdiction and what she was doing inside the house in the first place. That gave her a problem, and I had been so clumsy that I hadn't even thought of it or a way out of it. Then again, I doubted that she'd lie to them anyway.

Instead of answering that question, she ignored it. She cited a bunch of military statutes, and then she informed them of federal ones as well. She argued about how she had every right to be there and to leave. She argued that technically it was just as much her crime scene as theirs. According to statute so-and-so, the military was in the right, she had told them.

She was impressive and totally bullshitting. But I said nothing about it. I was on her side.

In the civilian world, a tough female cop might've been just about equal to a tough male cop. No question. But in the end, a tough female Marine outranks a pair of tough male patrolmen any day.

Romey got in the car and said, "Buckle up."

Which I guessed was her way of saying we were about to drive away—fast.

* * *

Romey got us out of the subdivision and back to the base in less than twenty minutes, which was impressive. The crowd outside the base didn't seem to care as much about us reentering as they had when we left. I guessed that was because the White House had already given a statement and called the base shooting possibly an act of terror. I hadn't seen the broadcast. I didn't know what they called it. I'm sure they would've condemned it and used strong language, probably the word *terrorism*, but then again, I wouldn't bank on it. Missteps in White House language have led to more mistaken conflicts than almost anything.

We went through the gate, and saw Kelly and two more military police cars behind him.

Romey stopped on her side of the road, and Kelly stopped on the way out. They talked through open windows.

Kelly asked, "Where are you going?"

"Back to the station."

"What about the Warrens?"

Romey said, "The local cops are there now."

"Aren't we keeping this all in-house?"

"It's too late for that. We'd have to cooperate with them anyway."

Kelly asked, "We didn't have to at Turik's house?"

"We didn't find any dead bodies at Turik's house."

Kelly didn't answer that.

Romey said, "Go by Turik's first and get me a photo of Mrs. Turik. Send the rest of the guys over to the Warrens' place. Try not to step on the locals' toes."

Kelly nodded and looked straight ahead for a moment; then he looked back at Romey. He asked, "You really think that Turik's innocent?"

"It looks that way. It looks like forced cooperation. Probably."

Kelly said, "Even if it's true, he still knew about their plans. He still helped."

Romey said, "We don't know that for sure."

I said to Romey, "Let's go."

She said, "Get over there, Kelly. I need that photo."

Romey buzzed her window up, and we drove off.

We took the same turns and stopped at all the same stops as before. I said, "You know he's not totally wrong."

"About what?"

"Turik isn't completely innocent. Maybe he didn't know that they were trying to murder Carl, and maybe he did. We may never know that."

"As far as I can tell, he was forced to help."

I said, "That doesn't make it right. And he killed himself. Not sure if they asked him to do that or if he did it out of guilt."

Romey said, "Maybe he thought we'd blame him. If it was his gun."

"Was it his M45?"

She nodded and said, "Ballistics confirmed it was."

"That's just more evidence that he's a little guilty."

"How's that?"

"Cause I saw him with his M45. This morning, remember? It was holstered at his side. That means that sometime after I saw him and after he entered Carl's office, they took it from him."

Romey pulled the police Charger into the lot of the MP station and parked in her space. She shut off the ignition and opened her door and got out. I followed her up through the doors and back into the station that I had been in only this morning.

Romey said, "We don't know the M45 that you saw was his. We only know that his was used to kill Carl."

I said, "It was his."

"How do you know?"

"That's not an easy weapon to come by."

She nodded and led me back down the three open rooms that they were using as different departments.

I said, "How come you guys have such a big department here?"

"Big?"

"Yeah. You got some state-of-the-art equipment here and a lot of manpower for such a small base."

Romey said, "As you know, this is a training base. Among the people we train are cops. We handle a lot of the forensics, information hunting, and analysis for the whole state."

I nodded—that made sense. The Marine Corps was like the rest of the military, and the government for that matter. They liked to compartmentalize and specialize things in one location—more efficiency.

I said, "Where are the MI6 agents?"

"I don't see them."

Romey stopped in the second area, and we headed to the right. She walked over to a small door that I hadn't even noticed before and pulled it open. It led to an echoing stairwell. It was all concrete and steel, like a fire escape stairwell.

It looked newly constructed.

She said, "Come on."

I nodded and followed her. We walked upstairs to the second floor. I looked up the shaft and saw that the stairs ended on the third floor, which I figured must've been roof access.

I said, "I didn't even know that this building had a second floor."

"It doesn't look it from the outside. We have no windows. It makes it feel more like a bunker than a police station."

"More like a prison to me."

She held the door open for me and smiled.

I stepped through the door and realized why she was smiling.

The second floor was smaller than the first floor. It looked to be about half the length. The walls were concrete, with no coverings to make it even look like an office building. The reason for the bare-bones look was because on the main passage, to the right, were jail cells—two of them.

"This is a jail?"

Romey said, "It's just two holding cells. Which we hardly ever have need of, but we must have them. One of our features in this remote mountain location is that from time to time, we hold prisoners who are being transported. We also

function as a stop between here, Camp Pendleton, and wherever. Marine bases have these all over."

I nodded.

She said, "My office is also on this floor."

I followed Romey past the cells to another door. She opened it, and on the other side, I saw a couple of empty desks and one that had a man seated in it. He was a desk sergeant. His nametape read, "McKee."

McKee stood up and saluted her as she walked in. Romey waved him back down and asked, "You're still working?"

"Yes, ma'am."

"Cut the formalities. This is Jack Widow."

McKee offered his hand for a handshake, which I took. I said nothing.

Romey said, "Where are our special guests?"

"They requested a couple of rooms for the night. We have them staying in Harriton."

Harriton must've been the name of one of the dorm buildings that I saw on the way in.

Romey asked, "Did you have the floor cleared out?"

"Of course, the guy from State insisted."

Romey said, "Call down to Gibson. Find out if she got me anything on *good measure* yet."

McKee said, "Do you want your messages?"

"Save them. Before you call Gibson, call over to the State guy and tell him we're coming over to talk to the agents."

McKee said, "They said they were going to call it a night."

Romey looked at her watch and said, "It's twenty forty-five. They're not asleep. Just call them."

McKee said, "They said it like they didn't want to be bothered. Not like literally."

"Just do it."

McKee nodded.

I smiled. The order of command and the way business is done all came screaming back at me from the past. Luckily, I'd never had an office. At least, I'd never been to it if I had one. I had always been more of a guy-in-the-field type. I didn't understand people who worked behind a desk. I guess it all made sense to them, since those were their jobs. They chose desk jobs. It was part of their careers, and someone had to keep up with paperwork. I just wasn't the paperwork type.

Romey said, "Let's go in for a minute first."

I nodded.

She stopped at her office door, reached into her jacket pocket, and took out her keys. She unlocked the door and we walked in.

Romey's office was just like I pictured it. I saw the reverse side of an open laptop sitting on a desk. Behind the desk were neat cabinets, wall photographs, diplomas, and military certificates of appreciation and recognition. All signed by commanding officers. All proudly displayed, but not overexposed like she was trying to compensate for something. It was all pretty standard for a high-ranking officer. I had seen it all before. And I'd probably see it again.

The thing I did notice was how clean her office was. Military life held high standards of cleanliness for all of its occupants, but this was something even overboard for the military. Her office wasn't just clean; it was immaculate. If cleanliness was next to godliness, then Romey was trying to start her own religion. Not that I'd mind joining.

Inside, she didn't request that I sit down across from her, but she did sit in her own chair. She started typing on her laptop, logging in, I guess. I didn't watch her use her password, but I wondered if it was the same *Boston81* password that she had used on the tablet earlier.

She looked up at me and said, "Hopefully, we can get something on *good measure*. If you're right, we'll find it."

I shrugged.

She went onto her laptop like she was checking email. I sat down and waited, which took me back decades to when I was a child waiting in my mother's office. She had been a small-town sheriff. She was murdered. I didn't want to think about that, so I changed the subject in my mind.

I said, "Romey, let me use your phone?"

She looked up at me and started to speak, like she was going to ask me why or object. I figured that she had a thing about personal space and letting a total stranger use her phone, but she said nothing. She leaned back in her chair and pulled her phone out of her pocket. She handed it to me.

I asked, "Is there a passcode?"

"No. I use it too much to lock it."

I nodded. I took the phone and stared at the tiny keyboard again. I didn't want to ask for help, just embarrassing, so I used my pinkie finger and dialed Maya's phone number from memory. Just before I could hit the call button, the phone rang in my hand.

Romey looked up at me. I read the name on the screen. I looked up at her and handed the phone back to her. I said, "It's Kelly."

She took the phone, answered it. She said, "Kelly, what's up?"

I said, "Put it on speaker."

She nodded and said, "I'm putting you on speaker. Widow's here."

She switched the BlackBerry to speakerphone and set the phone on the desktop between us.

I heard Kelly's voice. It was staticky. He said, "Guys. We've got a bit of a problem."

Romey said, "What is it?"

"I'm here at Turik's house, and I've been over the house with a fine-tooth comb."

"And?"

"I can't find a single picture of Fatima Turik anywhere."

CHAPTER 33

"Nowhere?" Romey asked.

Kelly's voice became more staticky, like he was on a radio and not a cell phone. He said, "Nowhere. I looked all over the place. I found photographs of Turik and some military pictures from Iraq, but not one photo of his wife. It's weird."

I nodded.

Romey said, "You double-checked?"

"I double, triple, and quadruple checked. There's nothing. It's like she doesn't exist."

I asked, "Do you know anyone who knows what she looks like?"

"I did."

I stayed quiet.

She said, "General Carl knew what she looked like."

"He's not going to help us. Turik didn't have any other friends here?"

"He was a quiet guy. He kept to himself."

I nodded.

Romey said, "Kelly, just forget it. Go to the Warrens' and help there."

Kelly said, "What do you want me to do there?"

"Just help out. The locals don't have the forensics that we've got. Supervise it. And be professional."

Kelly said, "Yes, ma'am."

"We're working on something here. I'll call you later." But Kelly had already hung up; the line was dead.

Romey said, "What the hell does it mean?"

I shrugged.

"Did they get divorced, maybe?"

"No. I don't think so. She must've been the leverage that they used against him."

"Why doesn't he have any pictures of her?"

I said, "Maybe they're all on his phone. A lot of people don't keep photo albums anymore."

"Yeah, but he would still have them in his house. He's got other photos."

I didn't respond.

She asked, "Is it a Muslim thing? Like how they make their women cover up. Maybe they aren't supposed to take pictures either?"

I shook my head and said, "Well, I know they're not going to flaunt revealing beach shots, but there might be some proper family photos, maybe in a drawer somewhere. Of course, since he's not a Muslim, it doesn't really matter what's allowed."

"How are we supposed to ID her body?"

"She's supposed to be Middle Eastern. So I guess she won't look like anyone else from here."

Romey nodded.

I said, "Give me your phone again. I was trying to call Maya. She can tell us what Fatima looked like. Maybe she's got a picture."

Romey nodded and gave me the phone. I redialed Maya and waited through the ring. But I didn't have to wait long because she answered before the second.

"Widow?"

"It's me."

Maya said, "I have been hoping to hear from you."

"Are you back in San Francisco?"

"Yes. We are here, safe and sound."

"Good. I want you to stay home tonight and tomorrow too."

"Why? Is something happening? They're saying he's a murderer on TV."

I heard the fearfulness in her voice. I closed my eyes, pictured the terror in her eyes. I pictured her fear for her brother's reputation for her own reputation. More than that, I feared for her life, for Christopher's life. Now that Turik had been named as the shooter, it would only be a matter of time before someone connected Maya Harris, a known atheist, to a Muslim and ISIS terrorist.

I shook off this fear and said, "Just do it, okay? Keep Christopher home from school for a couple of days."

She asked, "Are we in danger?"

I said, "No. Nothing like that. Better safe than sorry."

"So what have you found? Please tell me you found some-thing to clear my brother."

"I can't talk about it right now. We're still investigating."

I heard her sigh from over the phone line. I didn't wait for her to say anything else. I said, "Maya, I need a favor."

"Sure."

"I can't explain it right now. So don't ask any questions, okay?"

A long, long time ago, I learned a trick or two in dealing with witnesses, way back from the NCIS. One of those tricks was to make them feel like they were a part of our investigations. It could prove critical to the success of an operation.

I was coaxing Maya into thinking that the success of proving her brother's innocence could hinge on her staying quiet.

She said, "Of course. What do you need?"

"I need a photograph of Fatima. Do you have one?"

Maya was silent for a long second. She said, "I think so. It's in my email. Jimmy sent it to me once. He loved her very much."

Then Maya seemed to come up with her realizations about why I was asking, and she asked, "You found her body? Need someone to identify her?"

"No. No. Nothing like that. We just need a photograph of her. Can you send it to me? On this number, okay?"

"Sure. I'll do it as soon as we get off."

"Good. Thank you, Maya. I gotta go now."

"Wait," she said.

And I waited.

Maya said, "Have you made any progress?"

"I really can't talk about it."

I heard the strain in her voice, and Romey looked at me. She mouthed the words, "Tell her."

I said, "Maya."

"Yes?"

"I can tell you that your brother was innocent."

She didn't speak for a moment, and then she said, "Thank you, Widow."

I said, "Don't thank me yet. I've still got work to do."

"Thank you," she said again. "Without you, we'd have no chance of anyone believing us."

"You just keep yourself safe, okay?"

"Okay."

"I'll call you tomorrow."

I listened for a goodbye, but Maya just hung up the phone.

Romey said, "How did she sound?"

"We gotta get these guys."

Romey nodded and said, "We will. We're right behind them. We'll figure out who they are and send the cavalry after them."

Not the cavalry, I thought. I wasn't interested in arresting them, but I didn't tell Romey this.

Just then, Romey's office phone rang. She answered it and said, "Yeah?" And then her face turned to an expression of intense listening. She was quiet for a long time, listening to the speaker on the other side, and then she said, "You're sure?"

She was quiet again, and finally, she said, "Okay. Good work."

Romey hung the phone up and looked at me. She said, "That was one of my Marines."

I nodded.

"She spent the last few hours looking up any operations called *Good Measure*. Or with the tag words *good* or *measure*. Of course, both came up, but not with those specific words together. And none that were Marine ops."

I said, "It doesn't mean that there was no op. You just can't find it."

"If there had been an op called *Good Measure*, then we would've found it."

"You couldn't access my files. So maybe this was the kind of black op that you can't access."

"The difference is that your files are sealed due to your job. Carl's and Turik's files wouldn't be."

"The operation might be."

"What for?"

"If it was an agency black op or joint mission."

"What agency?"

I felt my brows furrow. I said, "The *agency*."

"I guess that makes sense. Carl used to run ops in Iraq during the war. I guess some of them probably were CIA missions."

"I wouldn't be surprised if it were in other places."

"What other places?"

"The agency runs missions all over the world. Ever heard the phrase *We were never here*?"

She nodded.

"I did operations all over the world. A lot of unfriendly places."

"Doesn't the CIA use the SEALs for dark ops like that?"

"Depends. Not always. They might use Marine forces. Sometimes it's a matter of convenience."

"It must be nice to shop around for who does what mission."

I said, "They don't usually care. It's not their butts on the line. I've been around the block, and I can't remember more than once ever seeing a CIA case officer close to a hot spot."

"What the hell do they do during missions?"

"Those guys are usually thousands of miles away monitoring the operations on a laptop over pizza in a hotel room."

"That's a disgrace."

I said, "They don't get paid the big bucks to do dirty work."

"What now?"

"Now, we go ask our guest about *Good Measure*."

"I'm not so sure you'll get access to him."

I asked, "Why do you think that?"

"He seemed important."

"What's his name?"

"I told you. I never met the guy. Just the agents and the guy from State."

I said, "Let's go have a chat with all four of them."

CHAPTER 34

Romey and I waited for another five minutes, and she called out to McKee about meeting with the British Secret Intelligence Service. He said that they had declined the meeting and then she ordered him to call them again. Which he did, only now they were ignoring his call.

I said, "Take me over there."

Romey said, "You have to behave. I still have to work here."

"Don't worry."

Romey didn't respond to that. She got up from her desk and led me back out of her office. She turned and locked it.

She stopped at McKee's desk, and he started to stand and salute again. She waved him off again. I guessed that he did that all the time, which was a good policy to have. In the military, you never know when your commanding officer might be in a bad mood and looking to take it out on someone. Proper behavior and following the rules in the military can mean the difference between pay grades, and good assignments versus bad ones. I know. I'd had plenty of COs threaten to send me to work in a military shack in the middle of Antarctica more times than I can count.

Romey told McKee to get on the phone and call them one last time, which he did. While we waited, a text message came to Romey's phone. She pulled it out and looked at the screen. She let out a murmur or a sigh like she had seen something that stunned her. She looked up at me and handed the Black-Berry to me.

I took the phone and looked at the screen. It was a message from Maya Harris. It was a photograph of Fatima Turik. I wasn't sure, but I think my jaw dropped. And I thought this because Romey made another sigh and a face like she was jealous.

I realized that she had been stunned by the photograph because it was stunning. Fatima was stunning.

She had dark skin, but I wasn't sure that she was an Arab. Maybe. I had guessed that she was Muslim because she was Turik's wife. I had assumed that she was the kind of Muslim who covered up everything, the kind who subscribed to the old, more dogmatic version of Islam.

Fatima Turik wasn't just pretty; she was downright gorgeous.

Romey said, "The camera definitely loves her."

"I'll say."

The photograph was of Fatima in a bikini and sunglasses. She was next to Turik by a nice size in-ground pool.

I asked, "Is that from Turik's backyard?"

"I think so. He has a pool."

"So much for the burka."

Romey said, "I thought it was called a hijab?"

"No. That's the one that only covers the hair and neck like a veil."

"What's the difference?"

"Burka covers the whole body. It's that black thing."

Romey said, "No, I mean, what for? Why have the difference?"

I shrugged and said, "I guess the more modern versions of Islam don't have to cover up completely. Most of the Muslim world live in the hottest part of the planet."

"So if they can choose, then why go with the old thing?"

"Beats me."

"Thought you were an expert?"

"Why would I be?"

"You seem to know a lot about the subject."

I said, "I know very little about it. I know a little about a lot of things, but not a lot about any one thing."

She shook her head and said, "I don't believe that."

I said, "So Fatima is a beautiful woman. No wonder Turik married her."

"We should've asked Maya for more information."

"Let's find her alive first. At least be able to give Maya some good news."

Romey nodded and turned back to McKee. He finally put down the phone and said, "No answer still."

Romey said, "Forget about it. Let's just go over there."

I nodded and followed Romey back to the stairwell and back out of the building to the lot. We got in her police Charger and fired it up and headed toward the Harriton dorm.

CHAPTER 35

The wind howled as we stood in front of the Harriton dorm building. The streets were still completely deserted. The chill factor picked up, and the wind carried it along.

I felt the precipitation in the air. It was so thick that I could smell it.

Romey said, "I think it'll start snowing soon."

"Or raining."

"No way. Not this time of year. It's going to snow."

I didn't argue. She would be the expert, not me.

Romey led me up a straight cement walkway. The grass was still from the weight of the snow, which was just heavy enough to anchor it from the wind.

I looked over the sky. The base had been built high and was surrounded by forest, but there were no trees on the base. I could see the sky clear enough. It was still overcast and dark gray.

We stopped at a set of big double doors. Romey pulled out a keycard and swiped it to unlock the doors. Inside, I saw a hallway that was short but wide. On the farthest end was a staircase that led up. Off to the right was a single elevator.

Romey said, "Elevator."

I nodded, and we went over to the elevator. She hit the call button.

We heard the cables far above creak, and the elevator came slowly down the shaft. Then we heard the ding sound from a floor counter on the left of the elevator doors. It dinged until the elevator reached us and the doors slid open.

We got on, and Romey hit the button for the top floor. We rode in silence except for the scraping noises that echoed in the elevator shaft.

On the top floor, Romey led the way. She said, "They're at the end of the hall. There are a couple of suites on this floor that are for officers who come here to train."

I nodded. I didn't expect that the State Department would put some foreign diplomat in with the enlisted. Spare no expense.

We stopped at the end of the hall, and Romey knocked on the door. We waited for a long moment. She raised her hand to knock again but was interrupted by the sounds of unlocking dead bolts and the chain on the door.

The door opened, and a short, stocky guy in trousers and a button-down shirt answered. He opened it all the way. I glanced him up and down quickly, as he was doing the same to me, also quickly. In fact, he was faster than me, which was impressive because he had more ground to cover than I did.

He looked at Romey and then back at me. He asked, "What you want?"

I heard his accent quite clearly. I'd heard many, many comments in my life about men with British accents. And not just in America. I'd heard women from all over the world make comments about how they loved British accents. I'd heard it in South America, Mexico, Australia, Russia, and all over Europe. The one place I never heard anyone talk about it was in the UK. Why would they? Everyone had an accent there.

I'd heard women everywhere describe the British accent as the most pleasing accent to listen to. Some had even used the word "sexy" to describe it.

This guy didn't have one of those kinds of accents. His was Irish and a very slurred dialect, which was like listening to a train wreck. But I understood him enough to know what he was saying.

Romey said, "We need to speak with you."

"Okay. Go on."

"We need to speak with you inside."

The guy didn't look back at the rest of the room. I shifted my vision and looked past him. Not a slow look and not quite a glance either.

There were two other guys in the room. One had his back to us. He sat far off in the corner. He was bald and was reclining on a chair with his feet up on an open window. He was smoking a cigar. He was the asset. No doubt.

The other guy was standing in a kitchen, leaning against a counter, his hand behind his back.

"Yer not getting in here," the guy said.

Romey said, "I'm not asking you."

The guy said, "Surry, love. Yer not comin' in."

Romey looked the guy square in the eyes. She was giving him the professional evil eye that I'd seen cops try before. It was a good weapon to have in her arsenal. It reminded me of the looks that she'd tried on me when she and Kelly arrested me this morning. It was a good technique, a good effort, but useless. The guy wasn't budging.

Romey asked, "Where's Eastman?"

"Who dat, love?"

Romey turned her face sideways and said, "Don't call me that."

"Who are ye referring to?"

"The guy from State? You know? Your babysitter?"

"Oh, he's here."

"Where?"

Just then, we heard a door open from out of our line of sight, and a medium-sized man stepped out of the bathroom. We heard the sound of a flushing toilet, and Eastman had a towel in his hand like he was using it to dry his hands. Why had he decided to carry it out of the bathroom? I had no idea.

He walked up behind the agent with the Irish accent and said, "Major? What's this about?"

Romey said, "We need to speak to the asset."

Eastman held on to the hand towel and put his hand on the shoulder of the MI6 agent. He said, "I'll take care of it."

He stepped out into the hall, past the agent, and shut the door, which wasn't a good sign.

CHAPTER 36

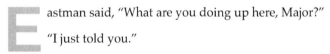astman said, "What are you doing up here, Major?"

"I just told you."

"You know that you can't come up here and question a foreign diplomat."

Romey said, "I'm conducting an ongoing investigation. I can talk to whoever I damn well feel like talking to."

Eastman said, "Okay. That's enough, Major. I outrank you in this matter."

"You don't outrank me in any way imaginable!"

I raised my hand up like a mediator and asked, "Who are you?"

Eastman looked up at me. He wore a tie, a button-down shirt, and a pair of blue trousers. All of it was ironed and creased professionally. There wasn't a wrinkle that wasn't supposed to be there. He even wore cuff links. He wore every part of a professional suit except his coat, like he wasn't supposed to be too comfortable in front of the foreign guy.

Eastman said, "Who are you?"

I said, "I asked first."

Eastman thought for a moment. He broke eye contact with me and looked at Romey, just a quick glance. Then he said, "My name is Miles Eastman. I work for the State Department."

I said, "There, was that so hard?"

"And who are you?"

"My name is Jack Widow."

I was watching his eyes to give away exactly who he was. As in, what was his real position? I had met State Department officials before. There was a wide range of people who worked for State. Sometimes they were professional diplomats working in foreign embassies. Sometimes, they were representing American interests in foreign markets. Most of them had been good, hardworking people doing a hard job. Then there were two other types. The first was a lackey. No real explanation needed for that, but basically, a lackey was an errand boy or, in this case, a babysitter.

Then there was the second type of State Department official. This was the type who claimed to be a lackey but actually was something else entirely. Normally, this was a dangerous type of guy. Usually, it was a guy who had a cover as a State lackey. These guys were usually CIA or NSA or some other alphabet agency that operated in the dark. These guys were typically up to no good. The question that I always asked myself was: Were they up to the type of no good that was in the best interest of the country? Or were they more on the illegal side?

Luckily, Eastman was the former type of lackey. I knew instantly because he recognized my name. A CIA agent wouldn't have reacted at all, even if he had seen my file. He would've acted all cool, like it totally didn't matter who I was, like he wasn't impressed.

Eastman started trembling, not a terrifying reaction, not overblown, just enough for me to notice it. He said, "Widow, I know about you. What are you doing back here?"

I said, "That's good that you know who I am. It'll make this easier."

Eastman repeated his question, only not to me. He turned to Romey and said, "What the hell is he doing here?"

She stayed completely quiet.

Good cop, I thought. I said, "I'm here to see your asset."

"I'm afraid I can't let you do that."

I looked at Romey and said, "Didn't you forget something?"

She looked at me, puzzled.

"Didn't you forget something, back in the car?"

She looked at me with some kind of expression on her face that I assumed was supposed to give me a signal, but I couldn't read it. I wasn't her partner. I imagined that she and Kelly probably had a whole slew of expressions that basically made up their own secret language.

I nodded like I did understand. She said, "I did." She looked at Eastman and said, "I'll be right back."

She turned and walked away. She got all the way down to the elevator. Eastman watched her the whole way. Then he looked at me.

I said, "That elevator is slow."

Eastman said, "What are you doing?"

"I told you. I'm going to talk to your asset. We have some things to discuss. Are you going to help me?"

Eastman looked back over my shoulder like he was praying Romey would come back. I stepped in front of his line of sight. He was an average size, average build. Nothing was particularly interesting about him. He was so forgettable that I almost second-guessed my earlier assumption that he was a real lackey because a great CIA agent would've been good at pretending. But he was the real deal.

I said, "She's not coming back for at least ten minutes. Which gives me enough time to get in there and talk to the guy I need to talk to."

"I told you. I can't let you do that."

I reached out and bunched up his collar. He watched my hand like he was witnessing a baseball bat swinging at his face in slow motion. He didn't strike me as the kind of guy who had ever been in a fight before. I'd be surprised if he ever had.

I lifted him by the collar, fast, and jerked him up off his feet and slammed him into the opposite wall. I clamped my left hand over his mouth. I didn't want him screaming. I didn't want a couple of British MI6 agents running out of the room.

He mumbled something underneath my hand.

I said, "I can't hear you. In fact, I don't want to hear you."

He stopped mumbling and stared at me. I could see the fear in his eyes. You can't fake that, not so easy. He was definitely a real lackey, which meant that he really was just here to babysit these guys.

I said, "I gave you a chance already."

He didn't murmur anything back.

I said, "Would you like one more? And before you answer. I'm going to explain the situation. Got it?"

No response.

I said, "Nod if you understand."

He nodded. His feet were off the ground.

"New evidence has come up. Turik didn't kill those Marines."

He murmured again.

"Shut up!"

He stopped.

I said, "I don't care why you're here. I don't care about you. I don't care what the White House wants the story to be. I don't even really care what you guys tell the public."

He was watching me.

"What I care about is that Turik didn't kill those guys. What I care about is eight dead people. What I care about is a good woman and her son. What I care about is finding an innocent wife."

He nodded.

I said, "You read my file. I'm sure that as soon as you saw that Romey had interrogated a person of interest, you checked me out. Is that right?"

He nodded.

I said, "Good. Then you probably saw a bunch of top-secret clearances and redacted information?"

He nodded.

"That means that I'm not a very nice person to have as an enemy. I gotta tell you something else."

He stayed still.

"The thing that I'm most eager about is getting the guys who framed Turik. You can understand that, right?"

He nodded again.

"You can say that I've got some pent-up anger. You want me to take that out on you?"

He shook his head.

I said, "Good. I want you to make this meeting happen. Got it?"

I uncovered his mouth, and he said, "I got it."

"Good."

I put him down.

Romey came walking back from behind me. She said, "You know what?"

No one answered.

"I didn't need anything from my car after all. Did I miss anything?"

I said, "Eastman has been kind enough to agree to let us chat with his asset."

She said, "That's great. Thank you for seeing it our way."

Eastman said, "You got it. I just want to help."

I reached out and Eastman jumped back. I said, "I'm just fixing your shirt." Which I did.

"Thanks." Eastman turned, walked slowly back to the door like he was contemplating whether he should call out to the agents. In the end, he decided against it. He knocked on it.

The Irish agent opened and said, "Yer both still here, love."

Romey said, "Don't call me that. Last warning."

Eastman said, "Let them in."

The agent looked at Eastman and then at me. He said, "You look a little under duress. Everything okay?"

Romey said, "Just let us in."

The Irish agent ignored her and said to Eastman, "You don't call the shots here. I'm going to have to ask you all to leave."

Just then, the man who had been smoking a cigar rose from his chair and stood up. He looked back at us. He said with a British accent, "Let them in, Raymond."

Raymond said nothing to that. He stared at me for a long second, like a pit bull.

Romey didn't wait for him to open the door. She pushed through, past me, past Eastman. I pushed past Eastman and followed behind her.

I stopped in the kitchen, looked around. The setup was nice for a military dorm. It looked more like a five-star hotel, not that I knew how to distinguish a five-star hotel from a four.

The kitchen had all new appliances, a double oven, and a gas stovetop. The fridge was big, double doors. It was stainless steel and tucked neatly into the wall. White tile backsplash with a big farmer's sink jumped out at me next. All the counters were clean. The only thing the kitchen was missing was an island.

The other agent was still leaning on the back counter with his right hand tucked behind his back. I looked at him and said, "You can take your hand off your gun."

He looked at me just as ferociously as Raymond had.

The man who seemed to be in charge said, "Do it, Connell."

Connell listened and moved his hand from out of sight to the front. He left it down by his thigh in plain sight.

The man in charge said, "My name is Malory. Shaun Malory."

The name didn't mean anything to me. I didn't recognize the guy by face either. I didn't recognize him by name, but Romey had a different reaction.

CHAPTER 37

Romey looked closely at Malory. She walked to the center of the dorm room and stared at him. She said, "You're the British admiral for the navy."

Malory said, "Well, First Sea Lord is the official title, but I haven't had that job in years."

I said, "Really? You're the highest military official in the UK?"

Malory looked at me, reached up, and puffed his cigar. He said, "Again, I don't have that title anymore."

Eastman interrupted us in a way that made him seem like he was desperately trying to make himself known, borderline overcompensation. He said, "Now he's the deputy prime minister."

I looked at Malory and said, "You're not the deputy prime minister. That's a woman right now."

Malory said, "It's not official, but I will be. The prime minister is stepping down, and the current deputy is expected to move up. Of course, with our politics, you never know."

I said, "I thought the current prime minister was popular?"

"Shows that you pay little attention to England, Mr. Widow."

No one said a word, but I was sure that Romey had noticed that Malory knew my name, which caught me by surprise as well. I said, "I'm surprised that the First Sea Lord would know my name."

Malory said, "Former. Again, I'm no longer the First Sea Lord."

"In our country, prominent people retain their titles. Even if it is a formality."

Malory said, "As they do in the UK as well. So Mr. Widow, how can I help you?"

I looked at Romey and then back at Malory. I said, "I think that you know."

Malory didn't speak, but Eastman said, "You'll have to be more specific."

Again, he seemed to interrupt even though he must've known that he wasn't invited to speak.

Malory said, "Shut up!"

Eastman looked like someone had crushed his ego, but he didn't respond. Malory looked at me and said, "I'm afraid he's right. You will need to be more specific."

I glanced at Romey, who was staring at Malory, and part of me thought that she was watching the cigar, fighting back the urge to tell him that there was no smoking allowed in the building. I was fairly certain that smoking wasn't allowed nearly anywhere on base except in designated areas.

I asked, "What is *Good Measure*?"

Malory puffed on his cigar and exhaled smoke in Eastman's direction. He looked at Romey, and he must've seen the same angst in her eyes as I had because he said, "Please forgive the cigar, Major Romey."

She nodded.

Malory looked at me and said, "Mr. Widow, why don't we talk somewhere else."

Romey said, "I'm coming too."

This seemed to be against what Malory intended, and he looked at Eastman.

Eastman said, "If she goes, then I go."

I said to Romey, "Stay here. Let me talk with him alone. Don't worry."

She didn't react how I had thought. I was afraid that she'd see it as a move to exclude her because she was a woman. In many ways, the old male politics of the UK was alive and well.

She didn't react that way. She knew that I'd tell her anything that was relevant anyway. She said, "Fine. But I'm not waiting up here. Too much musk."

I nodded.

Malory said, "Raymond, grab my coat. Meet us by the lift."

Raymond didn't answer back, but he did hop to it.

I said, "Good service." I had directed it to the Irish agent, and he took note of it. He shot me an evil look but held his tongue.

Raymond went to a closet and grabbed Malory's coat and his own.

I followed Romey and Malory out to the elevator.

Romey said, "I'll be at the car."

I nodded and watched her press the elevator button. We all stood there in silence until the doors opened.

Malory said, "It was good to meet you, Major Romey, finally. Farewell."

Romey nodded and got on the elevator.

Malory said, "Let's take the stairs."

"Where we going?"

"The roof."

Raymond came out with Malory's coat and held it open like a butler. Malory slipped one arm into a sleeve, followed by the other.

The three of us walked out to the stairwell and up to the roof.

CHAPTER 38

T he Harriton Dorm was only around three stories, but the ceilings were high, and the roof was technically the fourth floor, and the base was devoid of trees. Except for only a few other tall buildings, I could see most of the base from the roof.

I didn't know how many acres Arrow's Peak Marine Base was on, but I guessed that I could see at least most of the occupied portion.

To the east, I saw a runway and several plane hangars, which I assumed to be empty. But I couldn't be sure. There were two helicopter pads. One had a Bell-manufactured AH-1 -Super-Cobra attack helicopter parked on it. I assumed it was a training model. I couldn't see close enough to be sure, but it appeared to have its side-mounted cannons removed.

The roof was a large, open space. Except for the entrance to the stairwell, there was nothing else up here but several rows of air-conditioning and heater units. Some of them whirred and droned, and others were hushed and dormant.

Malory walked over to one ledge and leaned over the cement barrier. He looked over the side. He pulled his cigar up to his lips and realized that it had burnt out, or the wind had blown it out. He clenched his lips around it and felt around his pockets.

He glanced at Raymond, who pulled a gold Zippo out of his pocket. At first, I was sure that Raymond was going to light it for him, but he didn't. He tossed the lighter to Malory.

Malory lit his cigar, puffed on it twice to make sure that it was lit, and slid the Zippo into his coat pocket.

He said, "Mr. Widow, what are you here for? I was told that you had left."

I looked at Raymond.

The agent moved away from us and stood about ten feet behind me.

Malory said, "Look at the magnificent view from up here."

I moved closer, stood next to him at the ledge. We both looked around the distant tree line, the mountain peaks, and the gray sky. I looked down at the street below, saw Romey sitting on the hood of the Charger. She was on her phone.

Malory didn't repeat his question. Instead, he pointed at the gate. He said, "Look at them."

I looked.

He said, "Your American press is virtually unmatched in the entire world. You know that?"

"Virtually?"

He puffed again and looked at me. He said, "Ours is better."

"Better? Your media covers what gown the queen is going to wear to a party. They talk about Prince Whoever sleeping with What's Her Face."

"That's true, but so does yours."

I stayed quiet.

Malory said, "What's your angle here, Widow?"

"My angle?"

"Yeah, what do you want?"

"The truth."

Malory paused and said, "The truth is complicated."

"What're you doing here?"

He didn't answer.

I said, "Why did you come here the same day that Turik and Carl were murdered?"

"Turik wasn't murdered."

"You're right and you're wrong."

"How's that? Turik killed himself."

I said, "What do you think happened?"

"Turik went crazy and killed my friend."

I didn't respond.

"I'm here to bury my dear friend. General Carl and I went back a long way. And Turik murdered him. Now, I'm here to bury him."

I said, "Turik didn't kill anybody."

CHAPTER 39

I asked, "What is *Operation Good Measure*?"

Malory didn't respond to that either.

I said, "Turik is innocent. We found evidence. Turik was coerced into cooperating. It looks like he may not even have known what for until it was too late."

"How do you know this?"

"The evidence is overwhelming. Plus, we have a video."

"A video?"

"It's him. He's saying to look into *Good Measure*."

Malory looked away.

I said, "Which I assumed was a mission. Some kind of black ops mission."

He stayed quiet.

I said, "Only Romey couldn't find a mission with that name. And she's pretty good."

I stepped away from the ledge and turned my back to Raymond. Then I said, "But she didn't find anything even with those two words."

I glanced back at Raymond. He was in the same position, staring at us.

Malory looked at him and said, "Leave us."

Raymond said, "Sir?"

"Just go wait in the stairwell."

Raymond said, "Sir, I can't."

"Do it! Go!"

Raymond looked at me and then nodded. I watched him go back to the stairwell.

I said, "You knew my name, like you had learned something about me. I assume that Eastman looked me up and shared my records with you?"

"He told me about you."

"Did he tell you everything?"

"He told me enough."

I asked, "The State Department sent you with a babysitter. They didn't have much time to prepare, which means that you came here abruptly. Therefore, you're telling the truth about Carl being your friend. He was killed, and you came here immediately. The problem is that England is a long flight. So how the hell did you get here so quick?"

"I was already on my way. I arrived in California yesterday."

"What the hell are you doing here?"

He said, "Carl asked me to come."

"Why did he ask you to come?"

"He said that he was afraid of someone. He said that someone knew what we had done."

I asked, "What did you do?"

CHAPTER 40

Shaun Malory was staring over the side of the building again.

At first, I thought that he was stuck in a trance, and then I realized that he was actually thinking of jumping.

I said, "Hey."

He looked back at me.

I said, "A woman's life is on the line. Whatever you did, it's just us here. No one else."

"Just us?"

"I'm not with the military police."

"You're wearing a badge."

"It's not a badge. It's more like a visitor pass. Besides, I couldn't arrest you anyway. You're not American."

He said, "Did you see the TV?"

"No."

"Your president went on TV and called Turik a terrorist. Said that he murdered those people in cold blood. Murdered my friend. Killed himself. Now, you're telling me he's innocent."

"Seems like you already knew that."

He didn't respond to that.

I said, "Tell me, why did Carl call you here?"

Malory took another puff of his cigar and said, "*Good Measure* isn't what Turik said."

"I heard him. It's what he said."

"No. It couldn't have been."

I stayed quiet.

Malory said, "Turik said *God Measure*, not *Good Measure*."

He took a long series of puffs from his cigar and stared at the view. He said, "Operation *God Measure* was an off-the-books mission. British and US Special Forces. That's what I was back then."

"When?"

"It was twenty years ago. In Syria."

"What the hell were you doing there?"

"This was long before the civil war and all. And we weren't there. Not technically."

I moved back beside him on the wall.

Malory said, "The Iraq War was on everyone's TV sets, and my country had competing interests in the Middle East."

"With whom?"

"With everyone else. Even with you."

"Not me."

"The United States."

I nodded.

He said, "The war was over, and the rest of us, that is, our populations, didn't want to hear about the Middle East again."

I said, "Skip the history lesson. Tell me about *God Measure*."

Mallory scratched his ear and said, "Carl and I were friends for a long time. He was a captain back then. I was an intelligence officer."

"MI5?"

He nodded.

"Twenty years ago, we were operating in Jordan. There was a militant group called Jeme alha-Tawhid Jihad. Which means *State of Religion and Jihad*."

I shook my head and said, "No, it doesn't. Its translation is *Organization of Monotheism and Jihad*, not State. That came with ISIS. And it's Jama'at al-Tawhid wal-Jihad."

"You know of it?"

I shook my head and said, "Only that it's the origin of ISIS. We've been fighting in the Middle East for more than three decades. Every SEAL knows about ISIS, some more than others, but in general, we all understand it."

"Do you know the details?"

"Just some of it."

"Let's just call them ISIS. That's what they would become."

I stayed quiet.

Malory said, "ISIS was originally the brainchild of a Jordanian man. Did you know that?"

"I thought it came out of Al-Qaeda?"

"That's where the power behind it came from, but no. Originally, it was born in Jordan. Our trusted ally."

He took a puff from the cigar and blew out the smoke in a slow, lethargic breath. He said, "We were spying on a guy named Owen. He was a Brit banker. On the surface, he didn't seem important. The only significant thing about him was that he used to work in our government. Back in the nineties. Maybe the eighties too."

"What happened to him?"

"We killed him."

Malory puffed again and looked back at the roof entrance. He asked, "Ever heard of Edward Hunter?"

"Can't say that I have."

"He was an American. He was a journalist in the 1950s. He worked in Miami. He's best known as an anticommunist. He was also rumored to be a CIA agent."

I nodded.

He said, "And he was. He was an agent. He wrote an article about Chinese torture and manipulation called *xǐ nǎo*. Do you know this one?"

I looked down at him and then over his shoulders at the lonely streets below. I said, "I don't know Chinese. I don't have a lot of experience in that theater."

"It was a series of tortures designed to convert people into becoming allies of the People's Republic. They tried to convert POWs into siding with them, even coercing them to do things that they didn't want to do, like give up State secrets, even assassinations."

I felt my head cock involuntarily like I did not believe what I was hearing. And I said, "Are you talking about brainwashing?"

Malory said, "Mr. Widow, *xǐ nǎo* means *washing the brain*."

CHAPTER 41

I said, "You gotta be joking?"

"I'm afraid I'm serious. That's what they were trying to accomplish."

"No way!"

"Your government did the same thing. If you study American history, then you'll recall the CIA trying to master brainwashing back in the seventies."

I said, "I remember. And even then, they found it a crazy idea. We had all kinds of crazy ideas back then."

"It was your country that dreamed of space exploration. That used to sound crazy."

"The Russians made it to space first, not us."

"But it was still an American idea."

I said, "I'm not sure about that, but still, brainwashing? Come on."

Malory said, "Think about it. ISIS tries to convert their captives all the time."

"You mean somehow ISIS has perfected something that my government couldn't?"

"Who said they didn't perfect it?"

I stayed quiet.

Malory said, "The CIA tried narcotics. The Chinese used sleep deprivation and torture. The Germans tried vocal propaganda. And the Russians use misinformation. In some cases, they even support it with evidence. It can be quite effective."

I didn't respond.

He said, "Even kidnappers have some success in warping the minds of their captives. Ever heard of that?"

I said, "Stockholm syndrome." I nodded along. I had heard of that. I had even seen it to a certain extent. It was a real phenomenon.

"The chemicals, the propaganda, the misinformation, the torture, and Stockholm syndrome all combined can be quite effective. Don't you think?"

"Are you saying that Turik was brainwashed? I already told you that he was innocent."

"Not Turik. Someone else."

"Who?"

He didn't answer that, not yet. He said, "The banker, Owen, that we followed into Jordan. He was supplying a man named Abu Musab al-Zarqawi. Ever heard of him?"

"The founder of ISIS."

"Yes. Back then, he was a part of something else—small time in comparison to later. We had good intel that his group had started to implement a brainwashing program. It was working. They were using it on young recruits. Young men with nowhere else to go."

"That's not proof of success. All of those Jihadist groups use the plight of young, impressionable people to convert them. Conversion isn't the same as brainwashing."

"Not all of these young groups were Arab. They were trying it on other groups. They were trying it on young Brits."

"Which is why you were interested?"

"Yes. Owen was funding the whole damn thing. And he was bringing over names."

I asked, "Names?"

"Potential targets. They were working on a very special list of names."

"Who?"

"Young adolescents. You know the young are the most fragile, the most receptive to their brainwashing techniques. Brits and Americans too."

"What Americans?"

"They looked for teenagers who had prominent parents. It all started with those who showed signs of rebellion. Do you have kids, Widow?"

"I don't."

"Well, let me tell you they are very impressionable when they are teenagers. Just think back to when you were one."

Which I did. I closed my eyes for a moment and tried to imagine. I remembered growing up with no father. I remembered how close I was to my mother.

Malory said, "Music, movies, drugs, there are a lot of things that can influence our kids today."

"I always had a thing for rock. I remember my mother wouldn't let me listen to some CDs. But I don't remember it being an influence on me. I became the man that I am because of her hard work. Nothing would've changed that."

"Widow, I can tell you firsthand that you can lose a child just like that."

He looked away, and I got the sense that he meant the word firsthand. I stepped forward and asked, "What happened?"

Malory was looking away in a deep, deep stare, but I sensed that tears were welling up in his eyes. He said, "I had a daughter. I lost her."

"How?"

"We followed Owen into Jordan, as I said. That's when we learned he was in contact with al-Zarqawi. We arrested Owen after. He told us that he had no choice. He told us that al-Zarqawi had taken his kid hostage. He told us that they would kill his boy. We told him to play ball and we'd save his kid. We told him that if he went along, we could save his son. We even offered him immunity in exchange for al-Zarqawi."

I said nothing.

Malory said, "He went along with it. We had him wired. They were to meet in a safe place that we had already staked out. Well, al-Zarqawi saw us coming a mile away. They killed the boy, killed Owen, and most of my squad. We were left with our pants down."

"What else?"

"We retaliated in good British fashion. We bombed al-Zarqawi's home in Zarqa. Only he wasn't home. But his three daughters and two sons were, not to mention his wife and brothers. The children were from two months all the way up to fifteen."

Malory paused a long beat and said, "I quit after that. I didn't want to be in the service anymore."

"There's more than that?"

Malory nodded and said, "Fast-forward five months. I had a daughter. Young. She was nearly ten. My wife had left us both long ago. So it was just the two of us. I was in the Navy at this point. I was stationed in Portsmouth. I was deployed at sea for six months when it happened."

Malory turned back to me. He wasn't sobbing, but I did see a single tear running out of his eye. He said, "My little Millie was taken. The captain pulled me into his private quarters and told me that the police had found my sister and her husband dead in their home, and my little girl was gone."

I asked, "Al-Zarqawi?"

"Of course!"

"How did you know?"

"He sent a message. He sent an email—a video file of her playing in the backyard of my sister's house. Millie was swinging and playing around. The email was signed in that ISIS symbol garbage like their black flag. There were no words. No demands. No ransom. Just the file."

"What did you do?"

"I tried everything that I could to get her back. I used all kinds of resources behind the backs of my superiors. Years later, in 2006, we found al-Zarqawi. This time, I wanted to pull the trigger myself. The brass wanted to bomb him. They wanted to let the Americans do it.

"I had a good friend in your Marine Corps. So I asked him to help. Carl knew the whole story. He had an agenda of his own as well. The CIA had learned of ISIS's brainwashing programs and had learned that, like the Chinese, they were having some success with it. They wanted to put a stop to it. Although, I always thought that they wanted the research for themselves. However, I didn't care. I wanted al-Zarqawi dead. So I convinced Carl to help since my country wasn't going to."

A cold breeze gusted across the roof, and I shivered. It was a quick movement.

Malory said, "In 2006, we went into Baqubah, Iraq."

"You went personally?"

"I did. Carl had to lead us because he didn't want to take the chance of losing control of the story. So he chose a small crew. We went in at night. It was a remote location. The risk was minimal. Al-Zarqawi was meeting with one other terrorist who was on your US target watch list. They didn't trust each other, which was good for us, and they only brought a couple of guys with them. We went in and found al-Zarqawi. I shot him in the head. We killed the whole crew. It was only four extra guys. It was easy in and out."

I asked, "So what went wrong?"

"What went wrong was that we lost one guy in the process."

"Who?"

"On the way out, we got shot at. The tactical situation of the location meant that we had to chopper in about three miles away."

I asked, "The visibility?"

"Right, they were meeting in the middle of nowhere, but they were staying in a house on a hill. The trees were all shaved down for miles. We had no aerial cover, which meant that we had to land far away and walk in. On the way out, we came across resistance. A twenty-man crew. They opened fire on us. We lost a guy. It was a Marine. He was shot."

"And you left him?"

"He was dead. We saw him die. He was shot right in the chest. And we weren't supposed to be there in the first place. We tried to recover his body."

"What the hell happened?"

"We were overcome by enemy fire. They had truck-mounted cannons. So we retreated to the LZ. The chopper had to circle for a long time. We waited until morning. We were bogged down in marshy land. We waited until the coast was clear, and the chopper came in. We took it out."

I said, "We don't leave a man behind. If he's dead, we go get his body even if the mission is off the books. I don't believe that the other Marines went along with it."

"Carl said the same. So did Turik. And we went back. We had to cover up the mission anyway."

I stayed quiet. I was trying my hardest not to punch Malory. I didn't like hearing that a Marine was abandoned by his brothers.

Malory said, "So we bombed the compound and killed the rest of the crew. We spent days sifting through everything."

"Go on."

"We found all of the dead soldiers, the trucks, the firepower, and the men that we had already killed. They were still dead; only now they were blown to bits."

I waited for more.

Malory said, "But … we never found the Marine's body."

CHAPTER 42

"What does that mean?" I asked.

Malory didn't respond at first. He started to speak, but I interrupted and said, "You left an injured man alive?"

"That's right. And I'm greatly ashamed of it. We all were."

Malory looked out again over the landscape. This time I wasn't sure if he was contemplating his sins or something else.

I asked, "Were?"

He said, "The Marine we left behind, he lived. I know that Carl and Turik both felt terrible about it. I don't know how they ever explained it to their COs. I guess that Carl was a high enough rank to make up some story."

"Who was the guy?"

"His name is Danner."

"Mike Danner? The son of the guy who just died?"

"That's the one. He was a POW for nearly ten years. Five years ago, your government found out that he was alive."

"Five years ago?"

"It took them five years to get him back. It was supposed to happen five years ago. It was supposed to be all hush-hush until the media got hold of the story. Guess how they did that?"

I shook my head.

Malory said, "Members of your American Congress. The opposition party, as in my country, is quite brutal. They found out that your president at the time was secretly negotiating to free Danner. Only that didn't happen until the next cycle of administrations. Your politicians are as bad as ours."

"Danner spent ten years as a POW?"

"He was only released about six months ago."

I stayed quiet.

"Now, you understand my interest in the brainwashing. How long would it take for ISIS to brainwash a captured US Marine?"

I didn't answer.

Malory said, "Ten years would be extremely admirable if he lasted that long."

"It'd be admirable if he lasted half that long."

He nodded and then he said, "Widow, the others from the mission…"

"Yeah?"

"There were six of us. Originally. Danner, Carl, Turik, myself, and two of my guys."

I nodded.

He said, "They're all dead. Except Danner and me."

CHAPTER 43

The rooftop was chilling over, and the temperature dropped, and snow started to fall. It was slow, tiny flakes. Christmas had already passed, but the measured snow made me think of perfect Christmas weather.

Malory said, "It's beautiful here. I'm in London now. It's not as dreary as your American movies make it look, but it's a far cry from calm winter weather like this."

I said, "I know. I've been there."

Malory turned to me. He said, "I'm so sorry."

I stared at him.

He said, "Before I shot him, al-Zarqawi told me he enjoyed killing my daughter. He said that she was a pleasure to … a pleasure to rape."

This time a huge tear formed and balled up and streamed out of his eye and down his face.

I stayed quiet.

"My revenge drove me to risk my friends' lives. We left Danner behind. Ten years, he suffered. I ruined his family's lives. I ruined Carl's life. Turik's. I should throw myself off this roof."

I grabbed him by the arms and said, "You're not doing that!"

He nodded.

I said, "You're going to come clean. Tell the Marine Corps what happened. Turik isn't guilty. We know where Danner is. He's probably at his house right now. You're going to tell Romey the truth. Then she can arrest him."

"What about me?"

"What about you? After we catch this bastard, then you can spend the rest of your life feeling sorry for yourself."

"My government will throw me in prison."

I let go of him and said, "That's your problem."

Silence came between us for a long moment. Malory said, "What now?"

"Let's go downstairs. You can tell all of this to Romey. She's worked this case very hard. Give her the satisfaction of setting this right."

Malory stared at me for a long moment. He had a look on his face that reminded me of someone or of something, and I couldn't quite place it. He searched my eyes for something, but I did not know what. He was a different person than he had been a moment ago, like something changed inside him. His pupils seemed to see right through me, like I wasn't even there.

He had that same look on his face that I'd seen on Turik's fourteen hours ago.

Malory turned, not fast; it seemed like everything was in slow motion. He grabbed the cement wall, planted both hands on it, and jumped over the side.

CHAPTER 44

The snow was still calm, but I was not.

I ran to the ledge and stared over the side. Three stories below, I saw that Malory's dead body was on the walkway leading to the front door. Blood was seeping out from underneath him. He had landed like a snow angel, except one leg was bent back and folded behind him. His arms were spread out like wings. His lifeless face stared back at me. It only took a few moments for the blood to pool so far out that it filled the spaces under his arms and looked like his missing wings.

He looked like a phoenix; only he wasn't rising again.

Romey stared up at me from the police Charger. Her eyes were wide. I stared back at her, frozen. I didn't know what to do. She broke our stare and ran over to Malory's body.

She must've checked him for signs of life. But she found none. She looked back up at me. Horror was in her eyes. She thought I threw him over the edge.

I turned, stared at the rooftop door. It was the only way off the roof. Well, not the only way, but I wasn't following Malory.

I did the only thing that I could think of.

I ran.

CHAPTER 45

Nothing beats the impulse to run from the police like the need to survive.

My mother had been a sheriff, and her father before her. I had grown up in a cop family. She had always told me to never run from the cops. *Always do as you were told* had been her philosophy, but this wasn't the time for that kind of thinking. In a day filled with misinformation and everything else, no way was anyone going to believe me that he threw himself off the roof.

Romey might believe me. But no way was Raymond going to.

I knew that Mike Danner was the bad guy. He had spent ten years in the Middle East as a POW. He had been transferred from one terrorist organization to the next until ISIS got him. He came back to the US and used Turik to kill Carl. He used Carl to lure Malory here. And now he had killed him too without pulling a trigger, but the job was done, nevertheless.

Malory had said that he was the only one left. He had said that there were British sailors too. He had told me that they were all dead. He was the last.

I bet that the dead British sailors were killed by Danner.

The trucker that I had ridden in with the night before had told me that he was hauling bullets for Lexigun, Danner's father's company. Malory had spoken of brainwashing. ISIS was trying it. Only they had succeeded, to a point. I could only imagine what it was like being tortured and brainwashed for ten long years.

I could only imagine what Mike Danner's mind was like now.

I wasn't sure about mind control, but brainwashing over the course of a relentless ten-year period filled with ISIS propaganda made it all seem rather convincing.

Brainwashing may or may not work, but certainly, they could've convinced Mike Danner to betray his country, his father, and his friends. Malory's squad did abandon him to those monsters.

Mike Danner was the key.

Suddenly a new thought entered my mind. If Danner had converted to ISIS, what did he plan to do with a small arms manufacturing company?

I didn't have time to worry about that because I heard a noise from the rooftop access door.

The door swung open, and Raymond stood there with a confused look on his face. He was confused because he was counting the people on the roof, and his brain was registering that his count was one short.

CHAPTER 46

The one short was, of course, his asset, Malory.

I had known MI6 agents in my past. In my experience, they were highly trained, highly resourceful, deadly, and not to be trusted any more than American CIA agents.

Whatever Raymond's official title was, he had stopped counting and now was staring me down with cold eyes. He had his pit bull look again.

I turned toward him and did the only thing I could think of.

I sprinted straight at Raymond, no holding back.

Raymond was fast and well-trained, but in any situation, the advantage always comes from the element of surprise, which I had. It may have only been a couple of seconds, but I had it all the same.

Raymond drew his weapon, but by the time it was out, I was barreling down on him.

I rammed him straight back into the stairwell. He slammed into the wall and let out a loud groan that surely was heard by anyone on the third floor and maybe the entire damn building because it echoed down the stairwell.

Two things happened that I was grateful for. The first was that Raymond hadn't broken his neck. I didn't want to kill the guy. I didn't even want to hurt him, but no way would he have given me the same courtesy. As far as he knew, I'd just thrown his boss off a roof. He would've shot me first and asked questions later.

The second thing I was grateful for was that he had dropped his gun. I picked it up while he was still dazed. It was a Glock 17. I racked the slide and ejected a chambered round. I tried to catch it, but I missed it. It bounced off the cement floor and rolled off the edge. I heard it bounce and rebound and ricochet down the stairwell.

Quickly, I ejected the magazine. It was fully loaded with nine-millimeter parabellums, which was one of my preferred rounds to have. I inserted the magazine back into the gun and racked the slide again. I pointed it at him.

He was still on the ground but completely dazed.

I said, "Stand up!" My old cop voice came back. It was like riding a bike.

Raymond said, "You're not getting away with this."

I ignored him and said, "Get up!"

He stood up slowly.

I said, "Faster." And I rushed toward him, bunched up his collar, and threw him in the direction of the roof access door. I said, "Move!"

He stumbled forward onto the roof. Then he said, "What're you gonna do, throw me off too, mate?"

Raymond started to turn around to face me; only I wasn't in his line of sight anymore.

I slammed the door on him.

I heard him rush toward it. The door had a fire exit push-bar handle, which meant that once it was pulled all the way shut from the inside, then it was locked from the inside.

I heard him huffing and puffing on the other side, but I had no idea what he was saying because of that accent. He had become virtually incomprehensible.

He sounded like he was screaming complete gibberish, which I assumed was also laced with Irish profanities.

I spun around and ran down the stairwell. I didn't wait to see if each landing was safe; I just kept going. Which made me think of Mike Danner. After he shot Carl and the others, he must've rushed down the stairwell at the command building the same way.

Then I thought of the cameras at the exit gate. I was certain that if Romey's guys checked those, they'd see Warren's Ford Taurus leaving. They'd probably see Mike Danner sitting in the seat next to Warren.

Before anyone knew what was going on, Mike Danner had killed five Marines and coerced Turik to run out the front door and kill himself. Which distracted the MPs on-site long enough for Danner and Warren to walk right out the back, get into Warren's Taurus, and drive off.

No one thought twice about it, maybe because not many knew that Warren was supposed to have shipped off. Or maybe there was too much commotion to think about it.

Colonel Warren had thought that he was saving his wife's life by going along with Danner's commands. Turik had thought that he was saving Fatima by doing the same. But that was all a lie.

Danner probably killed his own father. Or perhaps his father *had* committed suicide. Maybe he had found out that his son had become something else. He wasn't the same Marine who shipped off. He'd returned an ISIS fighter.

I stopped at the second floor, didn't run down to the first floor. I heard the door from the floor above me swing open, which was Connell, I presumed.

I opened the second-floor door and walked through it. I stuffed the Glock 17 into the waistband of my jeans, covered it with my jacket. I had two handguns now, which was better than one. But the Glock 17 was by far the better of the two.

I casually walked down the hall, past the dorm rooms. The floor was relatively silent. I heard television sets and ambient building noises. I also heard snoring.

I figured that most of the guys had been bored. Boredom was often the worst part of being under base lockdown.

I walked to the elevator. I had thought that Romey might be on it. So I pressed the call button. The elevator opened and was empty. I stepped in and pressed the ground floor button.

Before the doors closed, I did one last thing.

I pulled out the Glock 17 and fired it into the empty corridor.

CHAPTER 47

The Glock 17 is a great handgun.

It's one of the most reliable and has all the necessary stopping power for ninety-nine percent of street combat situations. However, like most guns, it's not quiet. In the echoing walls of the Harriton dorm building, among the sleeping and relaxing Marines on lockdown, a single gunshot from a Glock 17 is very loud. I might as well have blasted a shotgun into the corridor.

I heard Marines yelling and heavy doors flinging open and bare feet running on the tiled floors.

The elevator doors opened on the first floor, and Romey was standing there, her Beretta drawn. I was a little scared that she'd try to arrest me, but I also knew that she was more level-headed than, say, a British agent who had just had his asset fall off a building.

She looked at me and said, "What the hell happened?"

"Come on. Let's get to the car."

"Widow, I can't leave."

I grabbed her by the arms, which wasn't planned and also not the best move to make. But she didn't fight back.

I looked into her eyes like a long-lost lover, and I asked, "Romey, do you trust me?"

She faltered for a second, like the question was a stun grenade. Then she said, "Of course."

"I'm glad you said that. Then trust me. We need to get out of here. I'll explain later."

She didn't question me. She said, "Okay."

We ran out to the double doors of the Harriton dorm.

Outside, I already saw flashing blue lights coming at us from the direction of the police station.

We jumped in her Charger, and Romey hit the gas. She drove faster than she had so far. She whipped us around corners, taking different routes than before. She reached for the switch to the light bars.

I stopped her, my hand covering hers, gently. I said, "Leave them off."

She nodded. We continued to speed from one street to the next. We passed the chopper, the landing strip, and the command building. One checkpoint remained. The other MPs probably ran toward the commotion at the Harriton dorm.

They watched us fly by but probably didn't think anything of it. Romey was their ranking officer, after all.

We were headed to the gate when Romey slowed the vehicle. I said, "Be careful."

She nodded and didn't say anything.

I said, "Don't worry. If this goes bad, you can always just tell them I took you hostage."

She gazed over at me quickly and then back to the MP at the gate. She asked, "Are you?"

"Of course not."

"It looks bad, Widow. It looks like you threw him off."

"I know. But you know I didn't."

"I know that. But why are we running?"

I said, "Get through the gate first."

She nodded. She slowed the car more. She was about to keep driving through, but the guard at the gate held up his hands. He waved her to slow.

She said, "Widow, what do I do?"

"Better stop. See what he wants."

"He's gonna want to know why we are rushing out of here. He's gonna want to know why a foreign diplomat was thrown from a roof and we are leaving the scene."

"One way to find out."

The MP walked up to the window. I recognized the guy. It was Berry from earlier. Berry saluted Romey and said, "Ma'am."

Romey leaned across slightly out the window and said, "Berry, I'm in a rush. Make this quick, Marine."

She sounded agitated, which didn't require good acting on her part.

Berry leaned down and looked at me. Then he looked around the car briefly. He looked once more at Romey and looked like he was staring at her chest, but not in the kind of way that I had earlier. I had snuck a peek at her frame; only I wasn't so obvious about it.

Romey spoke in an angry tone. She said, "Can I help you, Marine?"

"Ma'am, I don't mean to be a first-class jerk here, but you're not wearing your seat belt. Neither of you are. You know that's regulation. It doesn't matter what your rank is, ma'am."

Romey looked over at me. I saw relief sweep across her face. She looked back at Berry.

We both put our seat belts on. And she said, "Berry, step aside. We're conducting an investigation here."

He nodded and stepped back and saluted her again. We drove off through the gate and fought through the remaining media.

CHAPTER 48

We left Arrow's Peak in Romey's rearview, along with the media. They didn't seem inclined to follow us.

Romey said, "They never radioed over the system about Malory."

"Maybe they're trying to keep the media in the dark. Lots of those guys have radios and police frequencies."

"Or maybe, they don't want to alert me that I'm wanted as your accomplice."

"Maybe."

"That's not funny, Widow."

"Don't worry. You'll be cleared soon enough."

Romey said, "Where the hell are we going?"

I said, "Do you know where Lexigun is?"

"Of course."

"What about where Michael Danner lives?"

"That's easy. He lives at Lexigun. It's an industrial complex, and their house is behind the property."

I said, "Good. That'll be easier."

"What's going on?"

"Malory told me about *Good Measure*."

"What was it?"

"It wasn't *Good Measure*. It was *God Measure*."

She said, "Stupid name."

"I don't know. It's a Brit thing. I guess. *God Measure* is what Turik said, not *Good Measure*."

"So, what was it?"

"It was a joint mission. Only you wouldn't have found it because it was a joint mission between General Carl and Malory."

"Like a private mission?"

"It looks that way. It's so off the books I doubt anyone left alive in either government even knows about it. At least not all of it. I'm sure that Eastman knows something. Plus, whoever his bosses are."

Romey drove on. She kept her lights and siren off, but kept her speed up. Not as fast as before, but fast enough.

I said, "The short of it is that before being a politician and the First Sea Lord in the Royal Navy, Malory was an MI5 agent. There was a traitor to the crown who led his team to Jordan and a terrorist. They attempted to kill the terrorist, only it all came out of bad intel, and they ended up killing his children, wife, and brother instead."

"Bombing?"

"Naturally."

"Doubt the terrorist forgot that so easy."

I said, "He didn't. He abducted Malory's daughter."

"Oh God!"

"Yeah, gets worse. He taunted Malory with video files and emails. He only told me about one, but I doubt that was it. There were probably years of it."

She nodded, said, "Then what?"

"Carl and Malory are old friends. Not sure how or how long. But they've been friends a while. They had a scratch-my-back-and-I'll-scratch-yours sort of thing, I'd guess. So Malory was told by his government to drop it, which he must've pretended to do. And the years went on. Eventually, Malory found al-Zarqawi."

"Zarkada?"

"Al-Zarqawi. He's the terrorist."

She nodded.

"Doesn't matter. He's dead."

"They killed him?"

"Yeah, but there's more."

"What more?"

"Al-Zarqawi was in some remote location. Malory went in with a joint team of special forces."

"British and Marines?"

"Yep. Carl agreed. I guess he saw it as an opportunity to kill a big fish. Or a promotion. Or both."

"So, he took Turik in with him?"

"Turik was there. Malory was there. A couple of Brits, who are dead now, by the way."

She looked at me, breathed out. Then she said, "Hang on." She came to that four-way stop on the highway that I had seen in the morning, and she took a right, headed north. She said, "Lexigun is this way."

I nodded and said, "There were three Americans on the mission. One's still alive. Guess who?"

"Michael Danner?"

I nodded.

She said, "Is this in 2006?"

"Yes."

"That's when Mike Danner went missing. When he ran away from a post, they said he walked off or got lost or something. Then he was captured by ISIS."

"Only he didn't walk off. That was a bullshit story concocted by whoever."

Romey said, "Maybe Carl?"

I said, "No. It sounds more politician-made to me. Probably from someone on the Hill or in the White House or the Pentagon. Even the generals there are basically politicians these days."

I glanced ahead and saw a street sign for Lexigun. It must've been the only thing on this road.

Romey said, "Michael Danner came back like a year ago. I think."

I said, "Six months ago."

"His father. He died like two days ago. They said it was suicide."

"I doubt it. He probably found out who his son really is now. Danner would've been highly monitored. Doctors around the clock. They probably dismissed his father if he ever complained about his son being different. They probably told him to give Mike some time. And so on."

"Or maybe he killed himself. Maybe he couldn't take who Mike had become."

I said, "Maybe."

I didn't tell Romey about the brainwashing. I wasn't sure that I believed it myself. I wasn't sure that she didn't already suspect that he was different. Ten years in captivity will change anyone. I was sure she knew that.

She asked, "Do you think he converted?"

"Converted?"

"I've heard that ISIS makes you convert, renounce your own religion to become Muslim."

I nodded and said, "Unless you already are Muslim. ISIS kidnaps more fellow Muslims than anyone else. Can't convert someone who is already a believer."

She didn't speak.

We saw the drive to Lexigun. The street ahead twisted and turned in another direction, which meant that I was wrong. The road led to more than one thing, which I wasn't interested in.

Romey said, "What about his daughter?"

I said, "Millie? I guess she's been dead a long time now."

"You sure?"

I didn't answer that because, on the one hand, I'd love to find out that she made it out alive. But on the other, I hoped that she was dead. I hoped that she had died a quick death before horrible things started to happen to her.

Romey said, "I guess that's why Malory jumped. Everyone else is dead. He wanted to complete the circle."

"Not everyone's dead. Danner's not. Not yet."

We came to a security gate, which was a chain-link thing with a guard hut in front of it, like the Marine base. But there was no guard on duty.

"Everyone's probably still at home. Still mourning for Mr. Danner, Sr."

I nodded.

She asked, "Now what?"

"Best I go alone."

"No way! You wouldn't let me go alone back at the Warren's house. So I'm not letting you. Not this time."

I said, "You sure?"

"I'm already out on a limb. I need to see it through."

I nodded and popped open the passenger door and climbed out. Romey did the same. We stood in front of the car. I said, "Wish we had backup. Can you trust Kelly?"

"Kelly?"

"Yeah, call him. Tell him off the radio to help us."

"Forget that!"

"You don't trust him?"

"I trust him. He's a good Marine. I don't want to risk his career too. Maybe we can just wait?"

"Nah, we can't wait to sort all this out. If Fatima is alive, then we need to get in there."

Romey said, "Plus, what if they're planning something with the ammunition?"

"Like what?"

"I don't know, a dirty bomb or something?"

I looked at the gate, but the road ahead wound into a sea of trees. I couldn't see the plant. I only saw the lights in the distance. I said, "I guess they could use something in there for a bomb."

"Doesn't it bother you? ISIS is basically controlling a weapons plant."

"Not really."

"Why the hell not?"

"Because the only thing that would scare me is if this was a nuclear plant. Or they had something nuclear in there."

"They might."

"No way. We got guys who log and check and monitor that stuff. The Department of Energy knows every little stick of uranium that's in our borders. Believe me. They probably have a database of all of it on the planet. They'd know if there was anything like that here. Not to mention the DOD, the FBI, and probably a thousand other organizations."

"What about something bio?"

I thought about it a second and nodded.

"They might?"

"Anything is possible. We'd better get in there." I walked to the gate and looked up at a surveillance camera that was staring back at me.

Romey said, "Hope no one's watching that."

"They probably aren't. Everyone's home. Day off, right?"

"Yeah."

"Besides, this place belonged to Danner's old man long before he got released. That means that ninety-nine percent of them are innocent. Maybe even a hundred. It's hard to convince any old American to betray his employer or his country to join an ISIS terrorist."

"You think it's just Danner in there?"

"I doubt it. We know he's got at least three guys with him, probably more."

Romey asked, "Who are they?"

I shrugged and said, "Could be ISIS. Could be hired mercenaries. Either way, they're all dead men walking."

"We should take them alive."

"I'm not promising anything."

She nodded and didn't mention it again.

The gate was locked, but it looked like it was operated by a button inside the guard hut. The hut didn't have any doors on it or glass for windows, which was good because we could just walk inside it. The bad thing was that the gate lock was operated by a computer. That was locked, and I didn't have a password for it.

Romey said, "What now?"

"Guess we'll have to break in the old-fashioned way."

"Climb the fence?"

I turned to her and smiled and said, "We ram it."

CHAPTER 49

Before we rammed through the gate, Romey and I stood over her trunk, which we had just closed after rifling her weapons out of it. We laid what we had on the lid for inspection. We stared at them.

I said, "That's it?"

"That's it."

We had a Glock 17, an M9 Beretta, Warren's Millennium G2, and a beautiful Benelli M4 Super 90 semiautomatic shotgun. The latter was a fantastic weapon with incredible stopping power. I'd love to use it.

She saw the way I looked at the Benelli and said, "Sorry," because the Benelli she had didn't work.

I asked, "Then why the hell do you have it?"

"I told you we're a training base."

"Are you being trained?"

"Of course not."

I said, "I don't get it."

"It's not meant to be used."

"I get that. Why are you carrying it in your trunk instead of a real one?"

"Don't get mad at me. I didn't know we'd be here."

"All right, then."

She said, "We can fool someone with the M4."

"As long as you don't have to fire it, sure."

She said nothing.

I said, "Just put it back in the trunk."

She did.

We returned to the Charger's front seat, and she revved up the engine, held the handbrake. Then in one quick burst, we rocketed toward the gate—the Dodge Charger with the ramming package on the front—quite a car.

We rammed straight through the gate.

Romey didn't stop. She kept the headlamps on low and floored it around the winding drive.

The Lexigun Complex was like any other small armament manufacturing operation. The only real security was the outer perimeter. Once we were inside, the complex wasn't like a big plant. It was industrial and monotonous. There were a few different service drives that zigzagged and intertwined through the complex.

We drove the main one, which happened to be dimly lit enough to light our way, but dark enough to not draw attention to us.

We passed several brown-and-white buildings with zero windows in sight.

Romey said, "This place is so dull."

"Worse than a Marine base?"

"Arrow's Peak isn't so bad."

She followed the longest, straightest road, which passed several other smaller buildings and parking lots. All empty of life, but we did see a huge loading area with trucks backed up to pick up outgoing shipments. Everything was turned off.

I said, "Keep going. There must be a house on the property."

We drove for another three minutes, and we found a thin strip that looked like a secret driveway. And it was. We saw a mailbox at the end.

Romey said, "That must be it."

"The house is farther, behind those trees."

"What now?"

"We park and walk. We can't go up the driveway. It's a single car width. They'll see us coming."

She looked around and saw another pair of long hangars. She drove past them and parked in a gravel lot. We left the car and started to walk up the drive.

I said, "Here, take the G2."

She looked at it and said, "You keep it."

"That's unfair. I think you should have it."

She said, "It's not fair now. I've got a Kevlar vest on. If I get shot, I'll live. Besides, you'll need the extra bullets. I won't."

I smiled.

We made it halfway up the drive, and we saw the house up ahead. It was a big two-story ranch-style house. There was a double-car garage with two vehicles in it and two more parked out front. I knew there were two in it because the door was open, like someone had just gotten home and wasn't planning on staying long.

The vehicle on the end, closest to us, was a single-cab white pickup. The tailgate was down, and the bed was empty. There was a toolbox attached to the back.

I looked at Romey and said, "That's the truck I saw this morning."

"When?"

"The big guy. From the diner. After Turik left."

"Maybe he's here."

I said, "He's here."

We continued up the drive.

There were high roofs, which meant high ceilings. There might've been a basement. That wasn't clear. There were lights on, scattered about in different windows. The front door was a huge iron door that must've been ten feet tall. It was a double door painted black. Two stained-glass windows about the size of my torso were on the upper part of each door.

The house had a huge, grand chimney. It was constructed of rocks and stones as big as my hands. Smoke rose out of it.

The house had outside lights that weren't tied to motion sensors. But they were already on. We cast long shadows back down the driveway behind us.

There was a medium-sized porch with some stone steps leading up to it.

We neared the top of the driveway. Romey started to approach slowly up a stone walkway that led to the front door.

I grabbed her arm and said, "Wait. Let's check out the garage first."

"Okay."

I led her farther up the driveway. We walked alongside the pickup. Again I said, "Wait."

Romey stopped.

We both had guns drawn and ready to fire.

I looked over the pickup. First, I looked into the interior and then back at the bed. I tried to open the toolbox, but it was padlocked.

Then I tried the passenger side door. It was unlocked. I opened it and leaned in.

Romey asked, "Widow, what the hell are you doing?"

"Looking for help."

"What help?"

I didn't respond. I opened the glovebox and found something promising. I found a forearm sleeve packed with eight shotgun slugs. I smiled.

The forearm sleeve is like a gauntlet. This one was a black nylon and polyester mix with Velcro straps so that it could be adjusted to fit any size arm, even mine. I lifted it out and showed it to Romey. She smiled back at me like I had said "Jackpot" without using words.

I slipped the forearm sleeve over my left forearm. Then I leaned back out of the truck and looked on the floorboards and under the seat. I hopped back out of the truck completely and popped the seat off its latch and pulled it forward.

I was met with exactly what I didn't want. It was empty. There was no shotgun to put the slugs in.

Romey said, "Check the other vehicles."

Which I did. There were two cars and one SUV. All three were locked, but I could see into all of them except for the trunks of the cars—no shotgun in sight.

Romey said, "There's gotta be some better firepower here somewhere. Their house is literally on the same property as their gun company."

I shrugged and said, "Let's get inside."

"Which way? We shouldn't go straight through the garage. Right?"

I didn't answer. I said, "Check the door."

Romey walked out in front, and I readied the Glock. I aimed down the sights at the center mass of the door to the house.

Romey crouched down low, out of my line of fire. She reached up and touched the doorknob. She looked at me and nodded.

I nodded back.

She twisted the knob and stopped. She looked back at me and shook her head. She said, "It's locked.

"Damn it!" I whispered.

She rejoined me near the cars. I said, "We should try the back door."

"What if it's locked?"

"Then we bust in."

"They'll hear us."

I said, "Then we go loud."

She nodded.

I said, "Let's go."

We walked out of the garage and around the side of the house. Romey had her flashlight on her belt, but we weren't going to need it. There was plenty of light from the house to light up our path.

The house was a beautiful house up close. The entire thing was constructed from rock and what looked and felt like real timber.

The backyard had no fence.

Romey and I circled around the side and stopped at the back corner. I was first, so I peered around the corner.

The backyard was full of snowy trees and darkness. There was an in-ground swimming pool. It was a long thing with two regulation laps roped off for swimming. The water wasn't frozen solid, but I assumed it was icy cold. It was deep too. I couldn't see the bottom. It was too dark.

Close to the house there was plenty of light, but its reach only went out about twenty feet. And then I saw nothing but darkness.

I led the way, and we walked to the first window with light coming from it.

I stopped and looked in. The room was a large downstairs bedroom. I saw a made bed and a chest of drawers and a closet—nothing of interest.

I led Romey past that window, and we walked past several more large windows. No lights.

We made our way to the back door, which wasn't a door at all, but a glass slider. It was already open like someone was enjoying the night air.

We heard voices coming from inside.

I stopped and signaled for Romey to do the same. We crouched down on our heels, and she leaned toward me.

I whispered, "Let me take a quick peek."

"Okay."

She stayed behind me, and I walked over, slowly, to the open slider. I heard the voices. It sounded like all men, and they were talking casually, like at the end of a workday.

I hugged the wall. The light coming out of the room didn't look like normal artificial light. I realized that as soon as I got right alongside the open slider because the light on the ground was flickering. It was mostly from the fireplace. That's when I realized the reason I couldn't make out clear words: they had the fire going too.

I tried to look in without giving myself away. I made a quick peek, not even a full second. It was just long enough to take a quick mental snapshot of the layout of the room. I moved in and whipped back.

I closed my eyes and tried to picture what I had seen. I saw a huge, open room. There were high ceilings with timber beams. I saw rock pillars. Far off in the distance, I saw a kitchen with two big islands. I saw a dining room table.

I tried to picture the rest of the room. I had also seen couches, sofas, and chairs.

I saw two guys seated, both drinking beer. Both were talking and having a good time.

I saw no one else in the room.

Romey was behind me, waiting for my information. I snuck back over to her and said, "Two guys. Possibly armed, but no weapon in sight."

"What are they doing?"

"They're chatting it up."

"Like hanging out?"

"Yeah."

She said, "These guys are already celebrating like they got the job done."

"Terrorists are just like anybody else. They hang out on their downtime, just like we do."

"They think they've gotten away with murdering eight people, and now they're hanging out drinking?"

I shrugged and said, "It'll make this part easy."

Romey said, "Let's take them alive. I want the arrest."

I said, "I can't believe it, but I think it might be that easy."

"What about the others?"

"I only saw two. I have no idea where the others are."

"Maybe they are in another part of the house? A basement?"

I said, "Maybe, but it sounds pretty quiet in there."

"Maybe they're out."

"They'll be back."

Romey stood up and readied her Beretta. She said, "Let's arrest these idiots."

I nodded and said, "You lead the charge."

Romey smiled, and we got into position outside the slider. She counted off to three with her lips, and we charged in.

"Freeze!" she screamed.

And that's what they did. They were completely frozen. The two guys on the sofa stayed where they were with horror and shock in their eyes all at the same time.

I walked close to them, only about two feet away, and shoved the Glock in their faces. I asked, "Where's Danner?"

They didn't answer.

I called back to Romey and asked, "Is this him?" I pointed the Glock at the guy on the left.

Both guys were young, very young. I would guess that both were midtwenties. Which told me that neither of them was Danner because they wouldn't have been old enough to have been involved in Malory's story.

The one on the left was white, and the one on the right was Arabic, which also told me that most likely, the one on the left was closer to being Danner than the other.

Romey said, "Neither one of them."

I grabbed the white guy by the collar and jerked him up off the sofa. Romey kept her Beretta aimed square at the other guy.

I asked, "How many more here?"

He started shaking and said, "No one."

I hit him square in the face with the butt of the Glock. His nose broke, and he winced, and he grabbed it with both hands.

He said something, but it was unintelligible because of his broken nose.

I said, "How many!"

"One. Just one, upstairs," the Arabic guy said.

Romey said, "Where's Danner? Where are the others?"

"They're all out. They'll be back any minute."

I asked, "How many of you are there?"

The Arabic guy didn't answer. I dropped my grip on the white guy and walked up to him. He remained seated on the sofa.

I pointed the Glock into his kneecap and said, "How many?"

I could see the fear in his eyes, which made me think of Mrs. Warren and how horrified she must've been. The guy said, "Six. There's six of us."

I smiled because I knew he was telling the truth.

Romey said, "You guys work for Danner?"

He nodded.

I looked around the room, kept the Glock pointed at his kneecap.

The room was a huge living room with all of the typical furnishings and fixtures that a normal family would have. There were bookshelves lined with books and photographs. There was a big oak coffee table, with a bucket of ice that had beer stuffed in it. Then I saw something else.

On the center of the coffee table was a Qur'an. A big leather-bound book like it belonged in a museum and not in a family home.

I asked, "That's Danner's?"

"Everything here is."

"How are you two involved? You're too young to be ex-military. Unless you're both flunkies."

The white guy was rolling back up on the sofa. He held his nose back and said, "We're part of ISIS." He said it like he was proud of it, like he wore their flag with pride.

Romey asked, "How's that possible?"

"What, because I'm white, I can't serve Allah? Praise be to him."

Romey stared at me, disbelief in her eyes.

The white guy said, "Ever heard of the internet?"

I asked, "You were recruited?"

He nodded.

"They were probably contacted on social media. Facebook or whatever. ISIS has been doing that for years. American kids are easy to talk to these days. Recruiters go online and pretend to be lost souls, make friends with young Americans who actually think that they are lost souls, and they just talk them up," I said, and I looked back at Romey.

"They're homegrown?"

"That's probably what Danner's old man found out. Danner's probably here to recruit fighters and sympathizers for ISIS. You know? Taking advantage of our youth."

The Arabic guy had rage surging up in his face.

I said, "Don't even think about it. I'll plug your knee."

"You won't do that. Cops have rules."

"Kid, do I look like a cop?"

He looked at me, up and then down. He looked at Romey, and then he let the rage go.

I asked, "The guy upstairs, is he deaf or something?"

The white guy said, "She's not a guy and she's asleep. Sleeping pills."

I looked back at Romey, who said, "Widow, it's Fatima."

CHAPTER 50

Romey handcuffed the two guys together. It turned out to be lucky that there were only two because she only had two pairs of cuffs.

We left them cuffed and walked to a grand staircase just beyond the living room in a huge foyer.

Romey ran up the stairs. I stayed close to her and ready to shoot anyone who came out at us. But there was no one. We found four bedrooms upstairs. The first three were completely empty and dark. The last one had a figure sleeping in a California king bed on top of the covers.

Romey switched on the light, which only turned on a lamp next to the bed. No overhead lights. There weren't even any light fixtures on the ceiling to turn on.

She didn't hesitate. She ran straight for the figure and rolled her over.

I walked quickly to an open door, Glock pointed straight out. I leaned in and flipped on the light. It was an empty master bathroom. It was very nice. Marble counters. A huge walk-in shower with rainforest showerhead.

The weapons business had been lucrative for the Danner family. That was for damn sure.

I looked back at Romey.

She had a huge smile on her face. She said, "It's her. It's Fatima. She's alive."

CHAPTER 51

wondered why Fatima was in Danner's bed, but I didn't say anything to Romey about it. I didn't want her wondering too. I could already imagine why.

The guy had said, "She's asleep. Sleeping pills." Which implied that they had been keeping her drugged, maybe with worse things than sleeping pills, but she looked alive and didn't have a scratch on her, which was good news.

Romey slapped her lightly on the face a few times and said, "Wake up. Wake up."

After a moment, her eyes rolled open like she had been woken from a deep sleep.

"She's coming to."

I nodded. Romey was excited. She had wrongly accepted that Turik had been guilty of murder and treason. She had accepted it like everyone else. And now we had a small win. She had found Turik's wife, and she was alive. She seemed in good health. Of course, the hospital and cops would insist that she get a rape kit, which would tell an entirely different story. I presumed so, anyway. But she was alive. She had all ten fingers and all ten toes, which was far more than I could say for previous captives that I'd come across in my life.

I said, "We should move downstairs."

Romey said, "We should call Kelly."

"You sure that's what you want to do?"

"What else is there? We got them by the balls."

I said, "I mean, you sure you want to call this in and say we found them alive?"

"We can't murder them. We got two of them now. Their testimony will be enough. Let's get her downstairs, and we can call Kelly. My guys will get here with a literal army of armed cops. We can ambush Danner when he comes back. It's over."

I nodded.

Fatima opened her eyes completely and was in shock. She acted like she didn't know where she was, which might've been true. They probably took her and drugged her.

She spoke in a disoriented voice. She asked, "Who are you?"

"My name is Dominique Romey. This is Jack Widow. We're here to help. I'm a cop."

Dominique? I thought. That wouldn't have been my first guess.

Fatima looked at me like she recognized me. Her eyes widened, which I guess meant that she was scared by my looks.

I said, "Don't worry. We're the good guys."

Romey said, "Take your time, okay? We're here to help you. No one's going to hurt you."

Fatima looked back at Romey and then burst into a fit of over-the-top gratitude. She grabbed Romey tight and hugged her like her life depended on it.

Romey said, "Listen, there're still some bad guys out there. They're supposed to be back any minute. So we need to get downstairs."

Fatima said, "Okay." She paused a long beat, and then she asked, "Where are the rest of the police?"

Fatima had a strange accent. I couldn't place it, but that was because it wasn't out in the open. It was almost like a hint or trace of something familiar to me. I couldn't place the Middle Eastern accent. Of course, that wasn't surprising because they spoke with thousands of accents and dialects. The Middle East was part of Africa, part of Asia, and arguably part of Europe. It was a melting pot, a converging point of a multitude of cultures and languages and accents and different incarnations of basically the same religions. And I was no expert.

Romey said, "Don't worry. They're going to be here soon. We just need to call them. So let's get moving. You can rest downstairs. Okay?"

Fatima thought for a long moment. Then she said, "No! No! There were some of them downstairs."

"It's safe. We have them locked up."

Fatima grabbed hold of Romey, tight again like a bear hug. She begged over and over. She said, "Please? I can't see them again. The things that they did! I can't. Please?"

Romey looked up at me. I shrugged.

"Okay, honey, but I need to call in the reinforcements. We're going to go back downstairs."

Fatima said, "Please don't leave me alone."

That accent. It popped out again at me. Where is that?

"Okay. Don't worry. We'll be right back."

I said, "I can stay here."

Romey said, "I need you downstairs. The others could pull up any second. You'd better search around for weapons and whatever else you can find. We may need to hold them off."

I nodded. She was right. We didn't really know that there were only four others out there. The two idiots downstairs might've been lying.

We got up and left the room. Romey turned back and said, "I'll be right back. You just rest here."

Fatima nodded.

Romey said, "I meant that. The signal up here isn't the best. I'll have to go outside to call."

I nodded and said, "Okay. I'll check out the rest of the house."

I watched her walk out the slider to the backyard. She stopped and stood near the pool, pulled her phone out, and started dialing.

I checked the two guys handcuffed together. They were still secure. I kept the Glock out, ready to fire, but I was sure they had told the truth that no one else was here.

I checked the rest of the downstairs, which was easy because all that was left were two doors. The first was a half bathroom, and the other opened up to a cold, cement staircase that led down to the basement. The light had been off. It was pitch black. I flipped the switch, and two hanging light bulbs, both about twenty feet apart, fought to come on. They finally did, and I made my way down into the cavernous basement.

There was no sign of life.

The basement was half a storage area, like most basements were, and half something else entirely. The second part was the most interesting to me. But before I checked it out, there was one thing that I had to see first.

There was a wall with a small arsenal displayed behind glass. I walked over to it, flipped another switch, which lit up the wall by a single bright halogen lamp from the floor.

I had never seen anything like the guns on the wall. Not in a private collection. There were antique Colts, Peacemakers, rifles, and even muskets that looked like they were from the American Revolution. But there was one thing that I had to have.

There was a World War II Ithaca M37 Trench Pump-Action Shotgun. I knew it was World War II because the damn thing still had a bayonet on the end of it, which was a long spear tip that must've been a foot long and what Romey would've described as wicked sharp.

I smiled, stuffed the Glock 17 back into the waistband of my jeans, and pulled down the Ithaca. I pumped it. It sounded useable, which it probably was. It was hard for me to believe that Michael Danner, Sr. would've polished it, oiled it, and taken such good care of it if it didn't work.

The Ithaca M37 is named after the city where it was originally made, which is Ithaca, New York. And it is a fine, fine shotgun. It was trusted by American armed forces in every war from World War II to Vietnam, and then police departments all around the country, even to this day. There are few substitutions.

I flipped it and looked into the port on the bottom. It was empty. Good thing I was prepared. I loaded it from the shells on my forearm sleeve. It held seven shells, leaving one in my forearm sleeve.

I didn't stop smiling until I went back to the other wall.

CHAPTER 52

I stopped smiling at the other side of the room because of what I found.

There were two metal desks, two comfortable cushion desk chairs, and two desktop computers that looked very, very expensive.

Lined across the wall near the desks were huge terminals like something where Google would store its important information.

What is this? I thought.

On the other wall, there was a single huge map of the world, and next to that, there were a couple of smaller ones. All were political maps with drawn borders and red lines and complicated legends explaining what the symbols meant.

The thing that really stood out to me was on a bulletin board.

I approached the board and studied it. It was completely filled with pinned photographs with words written in Arabic, which I couldn't read.

I recognized three of the people from the photographs, but there were others that I assumed could be Carl and the British sailors. One was of Turik. It looked like it was taken from his home. Fatima was in it as well. She was the second person I recognized. The last was Malory. And the others I didn't recognize. But all were dead now. All had big red Xs over their faces like they'd been crossed out. All except Fatima and Malory. I supposed it was because they didn't know that Malory was dead.

This was like a vision board for assassination. They had done some heavy planning for this operation.

I stepped back. There was a table next to the bulletin board. It was in the corner. It had personal items on it, like family photographs. I almost dismissed them until I looked at one. It was a photograph of a familiar face; only I wasn't sure who. I wasn't sure where I had seen that face before.

The good news was that it was a black-and-white picture that was clipped out of a newspaper. I reached out, left the Ithaca down by my side. I scooped up the picture and shattered the glass against the table. The noise was loud in the basement but the echo was dead in a matter of seconds.

I pinched the picture with fingers from one hand and dropped the frame. I flipped the picture back around. It was a folded-up, cutout newspaper clipping. I opened it all the way.

The caption told me why the guy was familiar. I had seen him before, long ago, way back in 2006. It was a photograph of al-Zarqawi. It read that he was dead. Killed in an American bombing, which I knew to be a cover-up.

I guessed Danner was straight-up converted to ISIS. This was his basement. Which also made me think about his poor father again. The guy probably came down here, found all this stuff. He might've actually killed himself out of shame. Then again, Danner was a traitor to his country, which was a hard line to cross for any former Marine. But once it's crossed, there's no going back. Killing his own father would've been just as likely as his father committing suicide.

Then I saw another clipping that was just out on the tabletop. I picked it up. It was from an Iraqi newspaper. There was a photograph of a living al-Zarqawi. It was full length. He was smiling. It looked more like it was taken in Europe than in the Middle East. I stared at it. It was London, no doubt about it. I could see Big Ben behind him. It was far in the distance and over his shoulder, but I'd recognize that huge clockface anywhere, which was odd, because surely he was on a no-fly list. Then again, anyone can get a false passport and go anywhere. You only have to have the right connections.

In the photograph, al-Zarqawi wasn't alone. He was holding hands with a girl—a teenage girl. She had dark skin, brown hair, and was maybe fifteen or so.

There was writing too. This clipping had plenty of the actual article left over. Only it was in Arabic. It was probably anti-American propaganda.

The caption was also in Arabic, but the date wasn't. The date was from 2005. Al-Zarqawi was alive and well.

I thought about Malory, remembered what he had told me. The brainwashing. The murder. The bombing of al-Zarqawi's family.

Then I thought about the date: 2005. I remembered Malory's daughter.

They had killed al-Zarqawi's children. He had taken Millie hostage. He had tormented Malory with emails, saying nothing, only sending him photos and video files.

I had imagined the video and photographs to be the worst-case scenario. I had imagined rape and child abuse and horrible things done to a little scared girl.

Here was a photograph of al-Zarqawi holding hands with a teenage girl. She wore a hijab, a head covering over her hair, like Marilyn Monroe would, trying to be in disguise—trying to hide in plain sight.

The girl in the photograph could be Millie.

Then I thought about Turik. There had been no photographs of his wife at their house.

No one had ever seen her in town.

Malory had gone on and on about brainwashing. Brainwashing can take years, he had said. ISIS had been successful to a certain point. But what was brainwashing really, if not simply finding young minds and twisting them with propaganda, and repeating it—for years?

Brainwashing.

CHAPTER 53

Several things happened all at once.

The first was that I heard, loud and clear, a vehicle outside on the drive. Heavy tires dragged along the pavement, a full-sized engine hummed, and the body rocked on its suspension. It was a truck or SUV, and it was pulling in, pulling up, and pulling close. I imagined headlamps sweeping over the driveway. I closed my eyes and backtracked in my mind. I imagined them sweeping and washing over Romey's parked Charger. Which they easily could've spotted. And they would've noticed it because even though we had parked it back in a nearby lot, it was still a military police Charger and didn't belong here. And I didn't know what direction they had driven in from.

I heard the slam of the parking brake, the death of the ignition, and three pairs of heavy boots hitting the driveway and scuffling in a heated panic. They knew we were here.

The next thing that happened was that I heard voices above. Male voices. The angry voices of the two guys who'd just been handcuffed.

I didn't wait to hear anything else. I turned and ran up the stairs.

I knew there was a chance of the two guys that we had hand-cuffed already being free, which meant that they were waiting for me at the top of the stairs. It also meant that Romey was a prisoner, which I had to assume anyway.

I would've liked to have a drone readout on the enemy positions. I would've loved to have been briefed on the enemies' capabilities, on Danner's skillset, on the giant's history. I would've loved to at least had the opportunity to have reconned them first. But I didn't have any of that information.

All I knew was that there were six hostiles upstairs, counting Millie Malory.

The good news was that two of them were American and young and dumb, which equals inexperienced. But the bad news was that the giant had looked competent, maybe even a specialist.

I already knew that Danner had been a Special Forces Marine, ancient history now, but still dangerous. The last guy, I didn't know.

The worse news was that I was outnumbered and outflanked.

The worst news was that they had the high ground, and they had Romey.

I ran up the stairs, loud, but my sound was muffled by theirs. I had listened to their boots running and stomping and busting through the front door. I heard them stomping into the huge living room.

I stopped at the door between them and me.

I knew the hallway beyond the door was tight. It was too tight for all of them to stand in there. Danner or Millie, which-ever was the real leader here, wouldn't let them get bottle-necked in there. That would do them no good.

They could kick open the basement door and lob a grenade in —if they had grenades, which I doubted. Maybe there were some that were somewhere on the property, but I doubted it. Grenades aren't meant for resale to the private sector. Then again, I wasn't sure if Lexigun had a government or military contract.

I waited. I had no other choice.

Finally, a voice called out, "Widow."

It was a muffled voice, but distinguishably a man's voice, not Millie's.

It was far from the door. It sounded like it came from down the hall, back in the living room. I assumed it was Danner's.

I took a chance and called out. I said, "Michael Danner."

He said, "That's me. You're in my house. You know? That means I can shoot you."

Try it, I said to myself.

He called out, "Widow, we have your women."

He had said "women," plural. He thought that I still believed Fatima was innocent and not Millie Malory.

I closed my eyes. I recalled the mapping of the living room in my head: couch, sofa, and chairs. The front door opened up into it. They had walked past the kitchen, past the dining room set. They were probably facing the hallway in a half-circle pattern. Spread out.

Good, I thought.

Danner said, "We know you're armed. Why don't you open the door? Toss out the weapons."

I said, "How do I know you won't shoot me when I open the door?"

Danner said, "You don't. But don't worry. No one's outside the door. I'm sure that you can hear all of us from down there. You know we're in the living room. This is my house, Widow.

I grew up here. I know you heard us all stomp in here. If one of us was in the hall, near the door, you'd have heard it."

I listened to his voice, noted the pitch and tone. He was telling the truth.

I didn't respond.

He said, "Widow. We've got the women. We're going to shoot them."

I said, "Shoot them."

Silence.

I said, "Especially Millie."

Silence.

I heard Millie's voice. She called out, "You know?"

Keep them talking. Maybe Romey had made that call to Kelly.

"Of course."

"How did you know?"

I said, "Your father."

Silence.

She said, "He knows, then? Good. I want him to know."

I didn't respond. I kept my eyes closed, tried to picture where they each stood. Millie was the farthest back. She was probably near the slider. The giant had the heaviest footsteps. I could hear him to the west, standing with his back to the fireplace. Danner was smack in the center of the room.

Danner shouted, "You have till the count of three, Widow. Then we kill her. Throw your weapons out."

I went to the door, kept the Ithaca ready. The basement door opened inward. I jerked it quick and crouched down. I was ready to blow a hole in the first face I saw standing there, but there was no one there. I pulled the Ithaca back and checked down the hall, fast—quick lean out and lean back.

Danner had told the truth. There was no one there. I saw them all standing in the living room, just how I had pictured.

I didn't see Romey, but I pictured her behind the group, being held at gunpoint by Millie.

Danner said, "Three."

Silence.

"Two."

I said, "Okay. Okay."

I tossed out the Glock, not close enough for them to pick up without stepping forward.

Danner said, "Toss the G2 out!"

They must've scared Romey to death for her to give up my second weapon.

I said, "Romey?"

"She's here. Toss out the gun."

"I want to hear her voice."

Silence.

"She can't talk."

I peeked out and said, "Why not?"

I saw Danner. He was a regular-looking guy. Average height. A muscular build, but not more than three days a week in the gym. He was standing between the two young guys from earlier. Next to the white guy was another white guy. He was the same age as Danner. He was tall but shorter than me. He had a good build. He was holding an M4 Carbine with a scope on it, which would cause him problems at this close range. It looked like a small- to medium-range scope. In such a tight hallway and short distance, it would take an extra second to aim through it. Then again, he probably would simply look over it. I was only around thirty feet away.

Behind him and a little to the ten o'clock position was the giant I had seen this morning. He was standing in front of the fireplace. He had a shotgun as well—a Remington 870. It looked like a Marine Special Purpose. He had it leaned against his shoulder, casual. The three more-experienced guys were playing it cool. The younger two were nervous. I could see it in their eyes.

I couldn't see Millie or Romey.

I said, "Why can't she speak?"

"Show him. Take a look."

I hugged my back close to the open door and stopped. I breathed in and breathed out. I was a little nervous about sticking my head out again.

I looked at my arm. I stopped and pulled the forearm sleeve off, tossed it onto the floor inside the basement. I didn't want to give away that I had the Ithaca. Although, I suspected that Danner one hundred percent knew about it.

I stepped out halfway and back again—faster than before.

I cringed at what I had seen in that fraction of a second.

Danner had stepped aside and let me see Romey. She was behind him, about ten feet—her back to Millie.

Millie stood behind her like I had thought, but she wasn't holding her hostage with a gun to her head.

She was pulling on a garrote that was tight around Romey's neck.

Romey couldn't talk because she couldn't breathe.

CHAPTER 54

A garrote is a vicious weapon. It is made from a simple wire; usually, piano wire works best. It is a tool simply made for silent killing. There is no other use of a garrote.

It's not like a survival knife or a firearm, which has multiple purposes: self-defense, hunting, or survival.

A garrote, like the one that Millie had, was more in the same category as a gas chamber or an electric chair. Its sole purpose is to execute.

I clenched my eyes shut tight. All Millie had to do was pull tight enough, and Romey was dead in seconds. The wire on a garrote is so sharp I've heard of guys accidentally slitting the throat of the target open. Often, victims would bleed out before strangling to death. It was horrible.

Danner said, "Toss it out. Make sure it gets closer to my guys this time."

I said, "How do I know you won't just shoot me when I step out?" I thought, *Did you get Kelly on the phone, Romey?*

"You don't. I promise if you give up, you'll both live longer."

That didn't reassure me, not one bit. Living longer in the hands of ISIS or ISIS wannabes was equated to dying a slow, painful death.

I said, "Okay. Just don't hurt her."

I tossed the G2 down the hall to their feet.

I heard one of the guys walk over, bend down, and pick up the G2.

Danner said, "Moment of truth. Come on out, Widow."

Which I did. I stepped out with the Ithaca M37 in my hands. The stock was buried deep in my shoulder. I aimed down the sight.

Danner saw it, recognized it, and he started laughing.

So did the other, nameless guy I had seen before, and so did the giant.

I stepped slowly down the hall. I tried to get closer.

Danner and laughed even harder.

The walk down the hall was a nightmare. It was like walking down the long mile on death row. It was like walking to your own funeral. It was like walking into the light and finding out that the light was actually hell.

I felt my nerves. I felt my insides tightening up. I felt that tiny, deep voice that we all have inside speak to me. It was that voice that keeps us alive, that warns us before danger, before death. It was the voice that prevents us from pointing a loaded gun at ourselves. It was that voice that tells us to keep our hand out of the fire.

I kept walking. The walls seemed to close in on me. My fatigue had slammed me straight in the gut, and the idea of walking to my own death combined with my fatigue to confuse my mind.

I tried to concentrate on breathing. I was taking the risk of my life. I was taking a leap of faith. I was counting my odds, and with every step, they got worse.

There were six enemy combatants in the room ahead of me. There were five guns in the room ahead of me, at least. There were five triggers and five fingers on them.

Danner slowed his laughing and looked at me. I was twenty feet from them, halfway down the hallway.

I thought, *Keep walking. Keep moving. Keep them laughing.* I asked, "What's so funny?"

I already knew the answer. I knew why he was laughing. I knew why he thought I was a fool.

He said, "That gun."

Keep walking. Keep moving. Keep them laughing.

I kept the Ithaca aimed at them. I swiveled it from side to side, imagined shooting each of them—fast. Imagined getting the drop on each of them. Seven fully loaded shells. Six targets.

I said, "What's so funny about the gun?"

The two young guys were the only two with their hands on guns that were pointed in my direction, but they didn't fire. They were more confused than I was, but I wasn't confused at all. I already knew why Danner was laughing. I knew why he didn't shoot me. I knew why he let me walk this far.

Keep walking. Keep moving. Keep them laughing.

Danner said, "That old gun."

Ten feet.

He said, "You can't shoot that."

Six feet.

Danner smiled and said, "That old collection down there. There are no bullets. That old thing isn't loaded. My father never kept it loaded, and he always kept the bullets at his office. He never kept them in the house. He was afraid I'd kill myself. Joke's on him though, isn't it? I killed him. And I didn't need bullets."

I gave them a look like I was defeated, like I thought the gun was empty. I lowered it and dropped my head.

Danner laughed again. The giant laughed. The other guy laughed. Millie laughed behind Romey. And the two young guys lowered their guns and started laughing.

Then, in a sudden burst, I jerked the Ithaca back into its position, stock buried deep in my shoulder, my finger on the trigger and my eye aiming down the sights.

I smiled and said, "I loaded it. I took the slugs from the white truck outside."

CHAPTER 55

The thing about old shotguns like the Ithaca M37 is that they're a lot like modern shotguns. They have the same pump action. They have the same design. They have the same grips. They take the same ammunition. Some of the modern versions even still have the same loading bay on the underbelly.

The one thing that was great, that was awesome, about older shotguns like the Ithaca M37 and a handful of others is a feature called slam fire.

When a modern shotgun fires, the shooter has to pump the action and pull the trigger. Then he has to release the trigger and repump and pull the trigger again. He repeats this cycle. That's how modern shotguns work, a basic concept. But not the World War II Ithaca M37.

This Ithaca M37 can slam fire, which means it follows all the same steps as the modern shotguns, except one. The shooter doesn't have to depress the trigger and pump again and then pull the trigger again. Once he fires the first time, the shooter can simply hold the trigger down and repump the action, hard and fast. This results in all the power and force and destruction of a shotgun without all the fuss of pumping and squeezing the trigger over and over again.

I had heard of a guy who could fire a fully loaded shotgun using slam fire in less than one second. I had personally never seen it, and I wasn't sure what the world record was. I wasn't even sure that there was a world record.

I wondered if I could beat it.

At that second, everything went into slow motion.

I pumped the Ithaca—once. A loud *Crunch! Crunch!* sound echoed, and it was soon drowned out by the loud *Boom!* from the blast of the first slug.

I aimed to the left and squeezed the trigger. The young Arab guy blew apart like spontaneous combustion. Blood splattered back on me. It was wet and hot.

I swiveled on my feet in a clockwise position. The second guy was the guy I had never seen before. He was fast. He actually started to raise the M4 Carbine up toward me. But I was faster.

Crunch! Boom!

He blew apart, the same as the first guy. His torso exploded. A shattered ribcage exploded from under his skin. More hot, wet blood splattered everywhere.

The young white guy had been standing close to him. He, too, had been hit. And he was also blown apart; only a little less of him left his body and a little more of him remained than the other guy.

The giant had only enough time to open his mouth wide in utter shock, which was the last thing I saw of him, because the next slug tore his face off and the top part of his head. His brains exploded onto a framed portrait above the fireplace.

Crunch! Boom!

I'd like to say that I looked Danner square in the eyes. I'd like to say that we had a man-to-man face off—good guy versus bad guy. Maybe slug it out like two characters at the end of a movie, but that didn't happen. Can't face off with a man who was just blown in half.

Crunch! Boom!

Danner exploded right from his center mass. His body was still attached in the way an outline is drawn before an artist fills in the middle with color. He actually blinked once before he was dead.

He fell back onto the coffee table. He landed on the Qur'an. I could see the leather-bound cover of the book exposed through the huge, gaping hole in his torso.

I flicked up fast and aimed at Romey and Millie.

Millie was screaming, in sheer terror. And I couldn't blame her.

The room looked like a whirlwind of death had swept through and exploded five people, which was an accurate recount of what had happened.

Romey couldn't scream, but I could see she was also horrified.

I released the trigger and pumped the next live shell in and ejected an empty casing.

Crunch! Crunch!

Millie had stopped screaming, but I could see the terror in her eyes, which I wasn't sure was because of what I had just done to her crew, or because she knew that she was next, or both.

I said, "It's over, Millie."

She tried to speak, but nothing came out.

I said, "You got no way out."

She jerked hard on Romey with the garrote. They both moved backward toward the open slider.

I saw Romey's eyes roll back. Her face started turning blue.

I said, "You kill her, and you're going to get worse than your boyfriend."

Millie said, "We're getting out of here. Stay back."

I said, "Who's we? There's no *we* left. Just you."

She said nothing.

I kept my aim on her. She stepped back and I stepped forward. She continued to step back, towing Romey with her. And I continued to move closer.

She moved outside. I moved outside.

The snow fell gently around us. She kept going. The swimming pool was right behind her. It was maybe ten feet. She kept stepping backward, and then it was five.

I said, "Your dad. He killed himself tonight. You got them all. Let go of her. No one else needs to die."

"He wasn't my father! My *ab* was!"

Ab was the Arabic word for "dad" or "papa"—I wasn't sure which, but I knew it was one or both.

"Al-Zarqawi?"

"Yes! He was my real *ab*!" she said. That accent finally came through. It was a mix between British and some Middle Eastern dialects. Which made sense. She had been ten years old and living in England. And then she had spent the rest of her life living as the daughter of the man who kidnapped her. She had experienced Stockholm syndrome, the real deal. Brainwashing, as Malory had said.

I heard sirens in the distance. They were faint, but I knew that sound well. Romey had gotten through. Kelly was on his way, a little late, but better late than never.

I looked at Romey; she was a deep shade of blue. If I didn't do something now, she wasn't going to make it to see Kelly ever again.

I said, "Al-Zarqawi was a nobody! He was a goat-loving nothing!"

"You don't know what you're talking about!"

"I'm glad he's dead! Do you know how he really died? You must. Your real father killed him. Shot him in the head."

"You shut up! Malory wasn't my father!"

I looked at Romey again. I was out of time.

Just then, the sirens blasted from the driveway to the house, and blue lights flooded the sky above us.

Millie saw them and looked up.

I charged. I moved as fast as my fatigued body would move. I ran full speed at them both.

I released the trigger and raised the Ithaca up in the air. I held it like a spear and rammed it straight up and over Romey's shoulder.

Turned out that Danner, Sr. had kept more than the Ithaca in good condition. He also kept the bayonet razor sharp.

The long, ancient blade flew over Romey's shoulder and square in the face of Millie Malory.

She didn't speak. She didn't scream. She didn't react. She didn't have time. I don't even think that she saw it coming until it had already stabbed through her cheek and pierced her brain. And even then, I'd never know if it registered.

I let go of the Ithaca, and the bayonet stayed in her face. Blood had splattered out and across my face, converging with what was already there. Which I could only imagine was more blood and human fragments.

Millie let go of the garrote, and Romey fell forward.

I caught her. She fell into my arms.

I watched Millie's dead body stay standing for a moment, the Ithaca M37 sticking out like an extra appendage, and then she tumbled backward into the swimming pool. Her body splashed and bubbled and sank down into the darkness.

I pulled the piano wire off Romey's neck and flung the garrote into the pool.

I looked deep into Romey's eyes. She started to pant.

I picked her up, held her in my arms. I said, "Breathe slow. Take your time."

She breathed in and breathed out. Her eyes rolled back down, and she breathed the air like it was a drug that she couldn't get enough of.

I looked at her neck. There was no blood, but the skin was black and bruised from the wire.

I looked deep into her eyes for what seemed like an eternity. She was staring back at me. She tried to speak but couldn't.

Tears were rolling out of her eyes, from either the pain or the fear of dying, or both. No one would blame her.

I smiled at her and said, "Dominique is a funny name for an Irish girl from Boston."

She laughed, only it was muted, and she started coughing violently.

I said, "Okay. Okay. Take it easy."

She grabbed my forearms, tight. Her fingers dug into them. She pulled herself up and hugged me.

CHAPTER 56

I rode with Romey to the hospital back on base. Only the staff there suggested that she be moved to Bridgepoint Marine Base, which was hundreds of miles to the south. They had a bigger facility there and were far better equipped to take care of her.

She was choppered out minutes later.

She needed X-rays and blood work. The emergency room doctor at Arrow's Peak had said that he believed she had deep internal lacerations and needed proper care.

Kelly had taken us back to Arrow's Peak. He had the sirens blaring and the light bar flashing all the way back. He had pushed through the media fast and had barely stopped at the gate.

I was in a hospital bed, which I hadn't needed, but Kelly had insisted I get checked out.

The doctors and nurses were shocked when they saw me. One, because I was covered in blood and internal body matter. And two, because none of it was mine.

The doctor had told me I seemed completely fine. He had made a sarcastic remark that I had forgotten. It was something along the lines of *fine on the outside, but your mental faculties are a completely different matter,* which was probably a slight at what I had done.

I was too tired to comment back.

I sat upright in the bed. I was no longer in my clothes. Nor was I covered in blood or anything else anymore. They had insisted that I take a shower before anything else.

Then they forced me to wear one of those hospital gowns.

I sat up in the bed because even though I was exhausted and the bed was very comfortable, better than a bus station bench, I just didn't want to stay in the hospital.

Kelly walked in. "How ya doing, Widow?"

I looked at him and said, "Tired."

"You should sleep."

I stayed quiet.

He paced for a moment. He had his cap in his hand. He walked to the wall opposite the bed, just in front of a chair, and leaned against the wall.

I said, "Sit down."

He started to object, but then he sat down. He said, "I owe you an apology."

"Don't worry about it."

"No. You saved Dom's life. And I owe you for that."

I stayed quiet.

He said, "I wanted to go with her, but this whole mess."

I nodded and said, "Somebody's gotta clean up. It's a hard job. I've been there."

"I know. I'm sorry I doubted you." He looked at the floor and then back up at me. He said, "I just don't know where to start. We blamed Captain Turik. The White House went on TV and told the public about this. They named him."

"You can walk that back. People make mistakes."

"I guess, but will anyone listen?"

I shrugged.

"All these dead people. It's all bad. No one wins."

"We did. Justice did."

He nodded and said, "Is there anything I can do for you?"

I said, "Malory?"

"We'll take care of that. No one will blame you."

"There's a British Secret agent stuck on the roof at Harriton."

"We got him. Anything else? You name it."

I said, "You can call Maya Harris. Tell her that her brother died a patriot. Tell her he was a good Marine."

"I'll do it tonight."

"Good."

"Anything else?"

I shook my head. I asked, "How hard would it be for me to see Romey in Bridgepoint?"

"You can ride with me in the morning."

"You going to be able to make it away from all this to drive there?"

He said, "Oh, yeah. They're sending someone to replace me."

"You want to be replaced on this? I'd think it's good for your career. You and she will both get promoted. You could get your own command."

"Nah, I'd rather be by her side."

Then I saw in his eyes what I had been too blind to notice before. He loved her. They weren't just partners in the Corps. They were partners in life. They were together. That's why Romey had pushed him away from this whole thing. She wasn't worried about him not believing us; she was protecting him in case I was lying.

I smiled and said, "You can come back for me. I need to sleep."

He said, "You got it. I'll wake you up. It'll be a while. Probably dawn. And don't worry. You can give a statement and everything tomorrow. No rush."

He got up from the chair and started to walk away.

I said, "Kelly."

He turned back.

I said, "You're a good guy. Romey's a lucky woman."

He smiled and said, "Thank you. I appreciate that."

Then he paused a beat and said, "You must've been a great cop. You should take it up again."

He switched off the light and left.

CHAPTER 57

Sticking around isn't my thing.

Something else that I didn't like doing was getting stuck in one place. And giving statements; answering questions for a case like this would only lead to more questions and more sticking around and more being stuck in one place.

I waited an hour after Kelly left, and I got up and left my room. At first, it was cold without any clothes and only a skimpy hospital gown on. But it only took about ten minutes of searching the halls of the hospital to find a room with the sounds of a snoring patient in it.

I slipped into the darkness on tiptoes, even though I hadn't needed to. This guy was fast asleep.

Some could've probably accused me of committing all kinds of crimes tonight. The lowest on that totem pole would've been stealing clothes. But I needed to wear something out. I wouldn't get far on a base full of Marines on high alert while in my birthday suit.

I found some wadded-up clothes on a chair and put them on. It wasn't a tailored look, but the pants fit. The waist was too big, but the guy had a belt. I tightened it all the way, and the pants stayed on. The shirt and coat were a different story. The shirt was a long-sleeved thing, but the sleeves only covered the tops of my forearms, and the coat was more than snug.

I managed to get it all on, and I think I was actually stuck in the coat. I would have to rip it apart to get it off later.

I lucked out on the shoes because this guy only had slippers, but they fit—mostly.

I walked out of his room and down the hall to the fire stairwell. I got out of the building without a fuss. And the base was still under lockdown, so walking around outside was easy enough.

I stopped at a building that had a double glass door and stared at my reflection. That's when I realized the guy I stole the clothes from wasn't a guy. They were female clothes: a pink shirt and a yellow coat. The jeans were also a woman's— a large woman's.

I smiled.

I couldn't leave through the gate. So I walked down the main street. I stopped at the same flagpole I had seen earlier.

I saluted it.

Then I headed farther down and to the fence. Luckily, Arrow's Peak was an old installation. The fence was nothing special. I scaled it without much effort, without anyone seeing me.

I walked up to the end of the crowd of media and merged in with them.

An hour later, I was sitting next to a nice enough trucker. I was in his eighteen-wheeler headed north. He didn't ask about the clothes. I guessed that he'd seen weirder.

I stared out the window at the snowy treetops and the mountains.

I wanted to sleep, but he wanted to talk.

ONCE QUIET: A PREVIEW

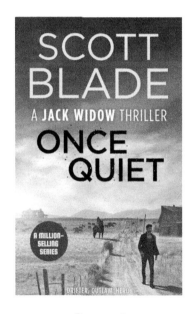

Out now!

ONCE QUIET: BLURB

A secluded Montana ranch...

A family under siege...

A seductive wife...

And Jack Widow.

Jack Widow has enjoyed a quiet life on the road. But a lifestyle like his costs money. A low bank balance causes Widow to take temporary work on a dying cattle ranch in northern Montana.

Widow works for the Sossaman family, taking orders from a beautiful wife. Quickly, Widow grows attached to her and her two sons. But his attachment to her may be more than a simple attraction.

Two strange things are going on around the ranch. The first: the husband is in a mysterious coma for the last ten years. The second: someone is watching the ranch. Someone with sinister intentions. Someone with a murderous agenda.

Fans of **Lee Child's Jack Reacher, Tom Clancy, Vince Flynn's Mitch Rapp,** and **Mark Greaney's Gray Man** will love the Jack Widow Action-Thriller Series.

Readers are saying...

★ ★ ★ ★ ★ Once Quiet is an all-out action thrill ride that delivers!

★ ★ ★ ★ ★ Jack Widow latest installment is fraught with tension and action.

CHAPTER 1

The four watchers were only supposed to watch, not intervene, not interfere—no matter what. They were told this, ordered this. They were only supposed to take notes and observe and record and remember, for their client, who had convinced them she was an officer of the law. After all, she had a badge, an important one, too. It was an accredited shield of justice, a silver badge in a formal leather case, like in the movies.

It looked real enough.

They had been following her instructions for the last ten days without deviation. Even though they were told only to observe, they were used to having more than just field glasses with them. They had expected more. An agent of such a top-shelf investigative organization would certainly have access to a big budget. But that's all they were given: a pair of field glasses, a phone number—her personal cell, and an address of the family that they were to watch.

She never gave them a budget. She was using them and that showed the whole operation wasn't legal. It wasn't by the book, which was fine by them. They weren't fans of the law anyhow, but they respected her motives. Family is family. They got that because they were family.

Also, they respected the dollar amount she offered to pay them for their help.

The field glasses had been mailed to them from the internet. That's why they had to improvise. They had to get their own surveillance equipment. That was a bummer, but they needed the money, and they agreed to do the job. They liked the dollar amount of how much they could expect in compensation. It was all good.

The watchers' client had given them strict instructions not to interact with anyone or anything that they saw, no matter how unusual the situation seemed. Especially, they were warned that any violence wouldn't be tolerated, and shooting from a Marine-issued M40 sniper rifle would qualify as violence.

The M40 wasn't the only weapon that they had. Each of them was armed with sidearms: two Berettas and two Glocks. Their client hadn't mentioned to them they shouldn't be armed. But they were country boys, after all.

They took the warning of no direct action with a grain of salt because they figured she was supposed to say that. She had to say that because of her status in the government.

She had struck them as a woman who was on the verge, like she knew she was going to have to give the green light on violent action, eventually. All she needed was a little push.

And what else were they going to do to the family that lived in the house? They weren't just documenting their comings and goings for no reason.

The watchers figured it must've been for recon's sake. What they weren't sure of was if they were also the assault team or if she was merely using them to build up the intel for an assault from her SWAT guys. They hoped for the former.

However, the temptation for immediate violence had crossed over one of their minds. The oldest two watchers, in particular, had these thoughts. Going in and taking everyone out in the main house would've been easy enough. Not their first night, or the rest of that whole week, but now, today, it would be very easy. It'd be easy because yesterday the lady of the house and that wrangler in charge had fired everyone—all their cowhands. Well, all but two, but they were going to go too. No doubt.

They had sent them away. The cowhands were unemployed again, which made the watchers a little mad because for guys like them, finding work in Montana was difficult enough, and that was how it used to be. Now, finding work for roughnecks and cattle wranglers and ranch hands in the state was very hard, damn near impossible.

Yesterday, there were ten cowhands on staff, but they had been sent packing.

The four watchers couldn't hear the conversations. They didn't have audio surveillance equipment. But they were positive that the conversations were all one-sided, and it went like no money left and times were tough and so on and so forth.

A conversation that cattle ranchers had countless times with countless workers over countless years in the region.

The watchers had heard these same conversations themselves.

They recognized some of the cowhands that were let go. They had seen them around town. One of them they knew on a first-name basis. And the rest, they didn't. Some of the ones they recognized seemed upset, and a couple of them seemed doubly so.

The one that they knew fell into this category, which was good.

The watchers thought that when the time came, they could approach some of them, persuade them, and add them to their cause.

The first watcher suspected that there was no SWAT assault team waiting in the wings. He was pretty sure that their client was going to have them kill the occupants of the house. Maybe not right away, but soon. That may not have been her original intent, but she would come around. He was pretty sure.

They reckoned she would call for an assault on the property because of the way she had talked about the husband, in particular. It was something that her agency wasn't supposed to take part in, not without courts and legal warrants and judges' signatures, or without directors' approvals and endless red tape.

They were told that the husband was a part of a massive injustice. He was an American traitor of sorts. They assumed, from what she had said, that his crimes were so bad that she didn't even care about what happened to the children. They assumed that if the children died in the crossfire, that'd be acceptable, that'd be something she would overlook, like a casualty of war.

At least, that's what they assumed. She said none of that.

Besides the husband, the wife of the family was some kind of foreigner, and to them, that was part of the problem. They cared little for foreigners.

This one was a real looker, though, the type that no man could resist. She was Eastern European, maybe Russian, maybe Ukrainian, or maybe one of those Slovak women. They weren't really sure. They knew little about her. Not that it mattered.

Then there were the children. As far as they were concerned, the children of a traitor and a foreigner were expendable. There was a bullet for each one of them. Not a problem.

A WORD FROM SCOTT

Thank you for reading Without Measure. You got this far—I'm guessing that you enjoyed Widow.

The story continues in a fast-paced series that takes Widow (and you) all around the world, solving crimes, righting wrongs.

ONCE QUIET, the next thriller in the Jack Widow series, Widow gets stranded because his bank account is empty, a banking error (or is it). He finds temporary work/housing on an isolated cattle ranch where a seductive wife maybe be hiding secrets more deadly than anything Widow's faced before.

On vacation in NAME NOT GIVEN, wanting to surf the waves on Cocoa Beach, Widow finds a pair of Army dog tags discarded and abandoned. If that's not strange enough, someone has filed the name completely off. Before he knows it, a serial killer is on the loose, killing woman who have gone AWOL from their posts and suspect number 1 is Jack Widow.

If you love Tom Clancy, then THE MIDNIGHT CALLER must be your next read. This one has Jack Widow in a NYC hotel, when the phone rings from an internal line at midnight. A woman with a Russian accent pleads for his help. Saving her will propel Widow into an international conspiracy with Russian spies, American conspirators, and a missing nuclear submarine.

What are you waiting for? The fun is just starting—once you start Widow, you won't be able to stop...

THE NOMADVELIST

NOMAD + NOVELIST = NOMADVELIST

Scott Blade is a Nomadvelist, a drifter and author of the breakout Jack Widow series. Scott travels the world, hitchhiking, drinking coffee, and writing.

Jack Widow has sold over a million copies.

Visit @: ScottBlade.com

Contact @: scott@scottblade.com

Follow @:

Facebook.com / ScottBladeAuthor

Bookbub.com / profile / scott-blade

Amazon.com / Scott-Blade / e / B00AU7ZRS8

ALSO BY SCOTT BLADE

Printed in Great Britain
by Amazon